CANDLELIGHT
Ecstasy Supreme™

"YOUR SEX DOESN'T INTEREST ME," KELLY REPLIED COOLLY.

Wicked lights danced in Cole's eyes as he drawled, "It doesn't?"

Conversation with sexual innuendos wasn't new to her, but there was something about this man that gave it all new meaning. "I think you know exactly what I mean."

Cole stood up. "You forgot to ask all the important questions. Why I want a domestic job," he said smoothly. "Oh, and if you're worried, I'm not in the least effeminate."

"I'll say," she muttered under her breath. "My secretary will be in touch when I make my decision. Thank you for coming." She also stood and offered her hand, but she never expected the shock of his touch to travel up her arm. The slight narrowing of his eyes told her she wasn't the only one affected.

"Well then, Mrs. Connors, I'll be waiting for your call. . . ."

CANDLELIGHT ECSTASY SUPREMES

CAUTION: MAN AT WORK

Linda Randall Wisdom

A CANDLELIGHT ECSTASY SUPREME

For Lydia Paglio. You not only encouraged me when I needed the boost, but you showed me a much broader range for my work and that reaching for the stars just meant going that little bit further. For that I thank you from the bottom of my heart.

To Our Readers:

Candlelight Ecstasy is delighted to announce the start of a brand-new series—Ecstasy Supremes! Now you can enjoy a romance series unlike all the others—longer and more exciting, filled with more passion, adventure, and intrigue—the stories you've been waiting for.

In months to come we look forward to presenting books by many of your favorite authors and the very finest work from new authors of romantic fiction as well. As always, we are striving to present the unique, absorbing love stories that you enjoy most—the very best love has to offer.

Breathtaking and unforgettable, Ecstasy Supremes will follow in the great romantic tradition you've come to expect *only* from Candlelight Ecstasy.

Your suggestions and comments are always welcome. Please let us hear from you.

Sincerely,

The Editors
Candlelight Romances
1 Dag Hammarskjold Plaza
New York, New York 10017

CHAPTER ONE

"Talk about a harebrained scheme, Cole!" The gravelly male voice bounced off the office walls. "Do you really think you can get out a decent story pulling a stunt like that?"

"This is no stunt, Harry." Cole leaned back in his chair, resting an ankle on his knee. His well-worn jeans weren't the designer kind and the cream-colored cotton knit shirt with dark blue piping had seen better days, but there was no denying his aura of quiet assurance. "I believe this could be the beginning of a whole series of articles on the changing role of the male in today's society."

Harry Scranton, features editor for the San Francisco–based magazine *Bay View,* studied the man seated opposite him. Cole Bishop had been with the magazine for almost five years and carried the reputation of getting stories other writers shunned—not only getting them, but bringing them across with a no-holds-barred style that made him so popular with the magazine's readers. National magazines had been courting Cole for the past three years. So far he seemed to be happy working where he was.

Harry could only wonder when Cole would decide to move on to greener pastures. This particular story could be the beginning of that move.

"You honestly believe there's more to write about this subject than we've already written?" He appeared properly skeptical. "I should think that angle had been covered enough."

"Not if you had overheard the conversation between two house husbands the way I had." Cole grinned at the memory, his teeth flashing white against a deeply tanned face, thanks to a recent two-week vacation in Tahiti. "Hell, Harry, they stood there in the middle of the grocery store discussing which detergent was the best for the money, the problems with their kids' schools, and who did what to whom on the morning soap opera! I want to go out there and find out what makes them so damn happy with this type of so-called work."

"Don't tell me. You're going to marry some avid women's libber and keep house for her, right?" Harry lit up a smelly cigar and puffed deeply. "Just tell me something—who goes through the pregnancy?" For once he didn't see Cole's idea as the brilliant flash that he had all the other stories in the past.

Cole grimaced. "No, thanks, one marriage was more than enough," he replied grimly. He reached down and pulled a sheaf of newspapers out of his briefcase. "You'd be surprised how many advertisements for domestics there are. I figure on answering some of them."

"*Domestics!* Come on, man, do you honestly think any reasonably sane husband would allow his wife to hire a good-looking guy like you to keep house? He'd be more worried about whether you were making his wife's bed or occupying it! Not to mention how do you propose keeping a low profile while doing your research? I can't imagine any of your ladyfriends appreciating your new line of work."

Cole's lean fingers ruffled his dark brown hair that had grown shaggy recently. "I thought I'd look for something down in the southern part of the state. Maybe even Arizona or Nevada."

Harry shook his head, still unable to accept this new idea. "I can't see it working," he mumbled. "Maybe you do have a good idea here, Cole, but what makes you think you can get hired as some kind of housekeeper? What are you going to use as references? That you're great at plain cooking and do simple housework?"

Cole's dark blue eyes twinkled. "Leave that up to me," he replied with his usual unerring confidence. "Believe me, within six months I'll be able to find out what's making more and more men turn to the fascination of domestic bliss with the emphasis on domestic." He placed his fingertips together in the shape of a steeple. "I'll have a story for you. Oh, yes, will I ever have a story," he repeated quietly. "I'm sure some sweet grandmotherly type widow wouldn't mind having a bit of extra protection around her house."

The glass-enclosed office was spacious and modernistic, with the decor in shades of pearl gray and pale blue. Vivid green hanging plants proved an excellent foil for the soft colors. Seated behind a pine-colored desk was an equally vivid woman, her honey-blond hair hanging down her back in relaxed waves. Her slender figure was clothed casually yet expensively in designer jeans and a sapphire-blue silk shirt. Her long nails painted a bright red waved around in the air as she spoke into the phone.

"Listen, Darren, I know that you feel Marla would be great for this campaign, but look at my side." She spoke urgently, as if pressed for time. "Marla isn't happy unless

13

we use her choice of photographer, generally whomever she's sleeping with at the time. Not to mention that we always have to work around her idea of hours. The budget just can't handle her games." Her conversation was interrupted by the buzzing of the intercom. "Can you hang on a minute, Darren?" She pressed the hold button, then the intercom. "Yes, Rachel?"

"Mrs. Peyser is on line four, Kelly," the disembodied voice informed her. "She insists on talking to you right now."

Kelly sighed. Her housekeeper called only if there was a problem with the boys. "Okay, thanks." She looked up at the ceiling, her eyes closed as if in prayer. "Please, God, let this be a call saying she broke a leg or something. I swear, if one of her relatives died ... I can't afford to allow her to leave!" She punched another button. "Good afternoon, Mrs. Peyser." Her voice was falsely bright. The equally artificial smile disappeared as she listened to the voice on the other end. "I'll be home in twenty minutes." She quickly switched back to the other line. "Darren, I'm sorry, I have an emergency at home. Why don't you stop by tomorrow morning around ten and we can go over the arrangements. Fine, I'll see you then."

She pushed herself back from the desk and stood up. The owner of the disembodied voice on the intercom opened the door. A serious-looking woman in her forties peered at Kelly over a pair half glasses perched precariously on the bridge of her nose.

"Did this one break her leg too?" she asked in a gritty voice that still hadn't lost its New York accent even after having lived in southern California for the past twenty years.

"I doubt it. She sounded much too healthy." Kelly grabbed her black leather satchel that doubled as a briefcase and purse and swept past her secretary. "I'm not sure

14

if I'll be back today or not. Darren is coming in tomorrow around ten."

"You mean I'll have to lie for you again if anyone, especially Mr. Baxter, wants to know where you are?" Rachel called after her, mentioning their boss's name.

"No, tell him the truth—that I went home to kill my kids!" Kelly shouted back, running for the elevator.

A few minutes later she was in her pale green Cutlass on the freeway, a grim expression on her lips. It was still there twenty minutes later as she turned into a driveway of a two-story Spanish-style house.

Kelly got out of the car, cocking her head to one side as she became aware of how quiet her surroundings were. "The calm before the storm," she muttered, slamming the car door shut.

She found the front door unlocked. She was still conscious of the unusual silence in the air. The living room looked all right. The walls had been painted in a warm, cream color; the couch and love seat were covered in an antique gold print. Everything looked the same as when she had left that morning.

"Mrs. Peyser." Kelly raised her voice. "Kyle, Kevin."

"Hi, Mom."

Kelly spun around, facing one of her sons, his jeans and cotton T-shirt decidedly grubby. "Where's Mrs. Peyser?" she demanded. "And which one are you anyway?" It was disconcerting even *she* couldn't tell her boys apart at times.

He couldn't look up at her face. He stared down, studying his tennis shoes that had seen better days. Oh, Lord, she had only bought those shoes a couple months ago and he already needed new ones.

"I'm Kevin, Mom," he muttered. "Mrs. Peyser's in her room."

"Did she hurt herself?"

15

Kevin shook his head silently, still refusing to look up. "She's packing." His mumble was barely audible.

"What!" Kelly dropped her satchel on a polished wood chest near the front door and pressed her hand to her forehead. "Please, God," she sighed, "let this be some horrible dream that I can wake up from. Let me be taking a nap at the office. I don't want to hear what I think I'm going to hear."

"Hi, Mom." Another small voice piped up, sounding very cautious, as if unsure of his welcome. A carbon copy of Kevin, wearing a Winnie-the-Pooh T-shirt and grubby tan shorts, appeared in the doorway. His liquid brown eyes watched her warily.

"I want the two of you to go into the den." After taking a deep breath to control her temper, she spoke slowly and distinctly. "And you sit there quietly until I have finished speaking with Mrs. Peyser. Then we're having a war council." She walked down the hallway to the back bedroom with the full bath that was designated for the housekeeper's use. Kelly knew only too well the boys would obey her . . . or else.

The twins watched their mother storm down the hall, then faced each other with wary expressions on their face.

"Think Mom's really mad, Kyle?" Kevin chewed his lower lip.

"Mom's not mad." Kyle grimaced. "She's *mad*."

"I bet she'll tell us we won't be gettin' anything from Santa Claus this year." Kevin turned, walking slowly toward the rear of the house. "Again."

Kelly slowed as she approached an open door off to one side.

"Mrs. Peyser." Her voice was again falsely bright.

A gray-haired woman in her early fifties straightened up from her task of packing a large suitcase and turned a grim face to Kelly. "I realize I'm not giving you any notice,

16

Mrs. Connors," she said stiffly. "But I'm sure you can understand why."

"Mrs. Peyser, can't we sit down and discuss any of the problems the boys are giving you." Kelly stepped forward, her hand outstretched in entreaty. "After all, they're just small boys."

The older woman's features turned frosty. "Those *small boys* are disruptive, completely disobedient, and have no regard for their elders," she snapped. "They're obnoxious, noisy, and—"

"Now, wait a moment, Mrs. Peyser," Kelly calmly cut through the woman's tirade. "My boys may sometimes act a little thoughtlessly, but they're still just typical boys."

"Mrs. Connors." Her voice was now as cold as an arctic wind. "I found a dead frog in my bath this morning and to my way of thinking, that isn't the act of typical boys."

Kelly had a hard time restraining herself from smiling. This sounded like one of Kevin's tricks. Then, remembering that his joke was costing her an excellent housekeeper, her lovely face sobered.

"I'd like to think that you might reconsider." Her voice was coolly polite, silently letting the older woman know she wouldn't beg. "Naturally, they'll be punished for their actions. And of course, if you don't care to stay, I'll have your check ready for you when you leave."

Ten minutes later, after her housekeeper left, Kelly was pacing the carpeted floor in the den. The two boys sat silently on the couch awaiting their sentence.

"What am I supposed to do now?" Kelly demanded of her sons, continuing her pacing. "I've had enough problems in finding a suitable housekeeper without this. Why did you do this?"

"Mrs. Corman stayed more than a year," Kyle piped up with a helpful air. "She really liked us too. *You* got rid of her."

17

"Mrs. Corman drank like a fish," she pointed out, raking agitated fingers through the blond waves. "I couldn't keep her away from the Scotch." Crouching down on her heels, she gazed at them with angry eyes. "To say I am angry with you two is an understatement." Her low voice burned with a throbbing intensity. "By all rights I should give you both the spanking of your lives, but I don't dare touch you right now. I want you two to go upstairs and stay in your room until I can bear to look at you again."

Deciding obedience was safer, the two small boys slid off the couch and scurried out of the den. Their hurried footsteps could be heard running up the stairs, followed by the closing of their bedroom door.

Kelly remained in her crouched position, resting her forehead against the edge of the couch. She suddenly felt very tired. What would happen now? The last thing she expected was to be engulfed by something very large and furry.

"Alfie!" She pushed the overly affectionate English sheepdog off her shoulders. His large pink tongue lolling, the dog sat on his haunches and studied Kelly with warm eyes.

Alfie, short for Sir Alphonse, had been Kelly's idea of a watchdog. What she didn't expect was that the small cuddly puppy she had bought three years ago would grow up into a people-loving dog who would probably lick a burglar to death instead of taking a chunk out of his hide.

The alarm shook Kelly from a deep sleep and as she turned over to shut it off her eyes popped open in horror. Nine thirty! The boys had been playing with her clock again. They had come up with the idea that if they turned her alarm off, she wouldn't have to go into work.

"Damn!" She threw the covers back and jumped out of bed, screaming at the top of her lungs. "I'm going to kill

18

you two! Kevin, Kyle, get up!" she ordered as she ran down the hall to their room, only to find it empty. On her way out she yelled over her shoulder. "Alfie, get off the bed!"

The large sheepdog opened one eye and watched the wild woman run from the room. He yawned and went back to sleep.

Kelly flew down the stairs on the verge of panic. "Kevin, Kyle, where are you?"

"Here, Mom."

Kelly raced to the back of the house. Entering the kitchen, she looked around in shocked disbelief as the smell of burned toast reached her nose. Every cabinet door and drawer was open and Kyle was standing on a stepstool getting ready to insert a knife into the toaster.

"Kyle, no!" she shrieked, as her child stopped his action in midair. "What do you think you're doing?"

"Cookin' breakfast," he replied, surprised that she'd be angry.

"Why are you putting the knife in the toaster?" she asked in a low voice.

"To get the egg out," Kyle answered matter-of-factly. "It stuck."

Feeling as if she were in the twilight zone, but desperate to hold on to her sanity, Kelly asked calmly, "What egg?"

"The egg we cooked in the toaster," Kevin piped up. "You told us never to turn on the stove. You never said nothin' about the toaster. It's for your breakfast," he announced proudly.

"That's very sweet, but I'd still feel better if you'd put the knife down, Kyle," Kelly ordered as she viewed the shambles of what had once been her kitchen. "Go upstairs and get dressed in clean clothes. I'll have to see if I can find someone to watch you today."

"I'm hungry!" Kevin wailed.

19

"You're always hungry. When I find you a baby-sitter, I'll send a box of cereal with you." Kelly could feel a headache coming on and it wasn't even ten o'clock. Ten o'clock! Darren was coming to the office at ten. Obviously today wasn't going to be any better than yesterday. Maybe if she ignored the kitchen, it would go away.

Kelly ran back up the stairs to her bedroom, tore off her nightgown, had a quick shower, and dressed swiftly in a rose-colored cotton T-shirt dress and backless heels. Luckily her legs were still tanned enough so that she could dispense with panty hose. After she finished dressing she made a quick telephone call to her neighbor, Jenny, to see if she could keep an eye on the boys that day.

"Boys, are you ready yet?" she called out.

"Yeah," they replied in unison. "Why are you yelling?"

"Because Mommy likes to yell," she said breathlessly, herding them toward the stairs.

"Where are we going?" Kyle asked curiously.

"Jenny's going to watch you today."

"Mom!" they both groaned. "That means we have to play with Becky!"

"You'll live." Kelly grabbed her satchel as she pushed the boys out the front door.

Ten minutes later she drove away with the memory of two mournful faces watching her.

Keeping one eye on the rearview mirror to watch for policemen, as she certainly didn't need a speeding ticket today, Kelly made it to the office in record time.

Darren was already in the outer office waiting impatiently. Dressed in frayed cutoffs and a T-shirt that read I'M A VIRGIN, THIS IS A VERY OLD T-SHIRT, and holey tennis shoes, he looked far from the part of an executive with one of California's leading T-shirt manufacturers. His shaggy sunstreaked blond hair and thick, unkempt beard finished the picture.

"You're late," Rachel informed her sourly.

"Ugh!" Kelly moaned, then turned to the young man with her polished ad-executive smile and greeted him sweetly. "Good morning, Darren. I hope I haven't kept you waiting. Come on back." She led him into her office, closing the door behind her.

"I still say that beard's hiding a weak chin," Rachel called after him.

"Can't you get a real secretary instead of Attila the Hun?" Darren demanded, flopping down in the chair opposite Kelly's desk.

"Rachel is perfect for me. She keeps out the riffraff," Kelly retorted. "Now, if you'll shut up and listen, I'll tell you why you can't have Marla in your ad campaign."

A half hour later a slightly mollified Darren left.

"Are you sure he gets paid a salary?" Rachel asked Kelly. "Or just his choice in T-shirt rejects."

Ignoring her comment, Kelly informed her that she was looking for another housekeeper.

"Again?" Rachel opened her mouth to say more, but Kelly cut in.

"Don't ask. Please, just call a couple of domestic agencies. I need a housekeeper fast."

"So what else is new." Rachel turned to the phone.

"Don't you need to look up the phone numbers?" Kelly asked her.

"Hardly." Rachel shot her a dry glance. "I don't think anyone has ever had the bad luck with housekeepers that you've had. If this keeps up, you're going to gain the reputation of being a jinx."

Kelly trudged back into her office, wincing at the pile of papers on her desk. Eyeing the trash can, she decided against pitching everything and got back to work instead. Twenty minutes had barely passed when Rachel walked into the office.

21

"Would you like to hear the results of my telephone calls to the various domestic agencies?"

"I have a strange idea that I'm going to hear it whether I want to or not." Kelly leaned back in her chair, bracing herself for the worst. "You're quite efficient, Rachel, it didn't take you long."

"Yes, I am, and no, it didn't," Rachel informed her. "Seems you're not too popular—out of the ten calls I made I got five definite nos, four hung up, and one said yes until she found out whom I was calling for."

"I have to have a housekeeper!" Kelly wailed. "The others leaving weren't my fault!"

"May I make a suggestion?" Rachel asked calmly.

"What?" She was feeling very desperate.

"Run ads in the newspaper."

Kelly chewed on a fingernail. She admitted silently that she liked the idea of the agencies doing the prescreening for her, but it looked like this time she would have to do everything on her own. Why did she have to be the one to end up with housekeepers who either left due to an illness in the family or because of the woman's own ill health? Maybe Kelly was a jinx after all.

"Would you be able to word an ad so it would keep out the flakes?" she asked her secretary.

Rachel smiled triumphantly. "I already did. With luck, you'll get calls by the end of the week."

"As long as one of them pans out," Kelly prayed out loud. She dug her satchel out of her desk drawer. "I really have to get out of here." She looked up as her office door opened. Her exasperated voice turned cheerful as she came face to face with Sheldon Baxter III, president of Creative Concepts and her boss. "Mr. Baxter, how nice to see you," Kelly lied, inwardly wondering what brought Old Stoneface, as his employees affectionately called him, down from the mountain known as the executive suite.

"Going to lunch, Mrs. Connors?" He pulled out an old-fashioned pocket watch from his vest pocket and flipped it open. "It isn't noon yet. A business lunch, or are you having trouble at home?"

"Trouble? I don't know what you mean, Mr. Baxter." Kelly gazed at him with wide-eyed innocence.

"What I mean is that you left early yesterday due to a family emergency. When I first hired you you were told that this position wasn't your regular nine-to-five position, but it doesn't mean you can leave early either," the tall, pompous man informed her. "Perhaps the pressures from home don't enable you to perform your duties here efficiently."

"I have no problems at home," she assured her boss, all the while knowing there could be problems at Jenny's house. The boys may not enjoy playing with little Becky, but that didn't stop them from getting into mischief. "I have very capable household help," she fibbed cheerfully.

"I certainly hope so, Mrs. Connors." He turned to leave, muttering something about women's lib under his breath.

"He doesn't believe you," Rachel told Kelly once they had been left alone. "But, then, he wouldn't believe our mother if she swore on a stack of Bibles. It's a good thing he didn't insist that you take a lie detector test."

"Are you sure the two of you are related?" Kelly turned to her secretary.

"I had once asked my mother if there was any chance that he might be adopted." Rachel grinned. "No such luck."

Kelly shook her head in amusement. It was difficult to believe the dour-looking yet extremely successful advertising executive could be the brother of this woman with her sharp, dry wit. There were times when Kelly could cheerfully strangle Rachel, but there were also times when she

23

wouldn't have known what to do without her. She had once asked Rachel why she didn't have a higher position in the company and the older woman had told her she was very happy where she was since it meant she didn't have all that much contact with her brother. She may overstep the normal boundaries of the everyday secretary, but she certainly kept Kelly's office life in perfect order. In the three years they had worked together there were days when Kelly threatened to fire her, but it was only an empty threat. Besides, how do you fire the boss's sister?

Later that evening, after assuring herself that the boys were asleep, Kelly sat down with a glass of wine and stared numbly at the stack of papers she had pulled from her satchel.

Sipping her wine, she gazed reflectively at the fire burning in the large stone fireplace that separated the den from the living room. How different her life would have been if she and Dave had stayed together. Her lips twisted bitterly as she lifted her wineglass in a mock salute.

"To you, David Connors, and your overactive libido," she intoned solemnly.

Her thoughts were interrupted by the unexpected ring of the telephone. Debating whether to answer it or not, Kelly's curiosity finally won out. Pushing herself to her feet, she crossed the room to pick up the old-fashioned black candlestick telephone.

"Hello."

"Hi, babe." The man's voice was low and sexy.

"Hello," Kelly repeated, a little less sure of herself.

"Miss me?" asked the now familiar, arrogant voice.

"No," she said curtly, leaning against the table. Anticipating his next sentence, she said simultaneously with her ex-husband, "I'm so lonely without you, babe."

Dave stopped short, hearing the sarcasm in Kelly's voice. "Aw, come on, Kelly, it's been a long time."

"What happened this time, Dave?" she sighed. "Did Daddy ground your little girlfriend for staying out too late?"

"That's not funny," he retorted, anger now replacing his thin veneer of charm.

"It wasn't meant to be." She was already bored with the conversation. "What do you want?" She was anxious to get this over with.

"You, babe," Dave said in a suggestive voice.

"I thought your age limit for bed partners was eighteen. Of course, there was that one exception. Sara was nineteen, wasn't she?" Kelly clipped. "Get to the point, why are you calling?"

"I was hoping to talk to *our* sons." He could sound like the wronged party when it suited him, and this was one of those times.

"Now?" Kelly was clearly irritated. "Do you have any idea what time it is? Five-year-old boys generally go to bed long before ten o'clock."

"Can't you wake them up?" he demanded impatiently.

Kelly finally had had it. "Let me make this perfectly clear. I have no intention of waking *my* boys up at this hour just to talk to a father they barely know exists. A phone call every three or four months or whenever it fits into your schedule won't get you the Father of the Year award. If you really want to talk to them, try calling during the day!" She slammed the phone down, grabbed her glass of wine, and marched back to the couch.

After taking a few sips of the amber liquid Kelly replayed in her mind Dave's phone call, which painfully reminded her of her celibate state while he went to bed with a majority of the women in southern California. Having two young sons could put a crimp in any woman's social life, although she had never resented them. Yet, there were times when it felt good to go out to dinner with a nice-looking man and carry on an adult conversation. She certainly had her share of admirers, but they seemed to drop out of sight after a while, fearing that she was looking for another husband, which was the furthest thing from her mind.

"Dave may have been a good lover, but he certainly wasn't worth waiting in line for," she muttered to herself as she angrily tackled her paperwork. The trouble was, that last big confrontation of four years ago decided to intrude into her thoughts. There had been no warning that day.

Kelly had pulled her station wagon into the wide driveway and stopped. A small smile curved her lips when she saw the dark brown Corvette already parked to one side. Dave must have decided to come home early. Well, that was fine with her. She wondered if Sara, the babysitter, had put the boys down for their nap.

Leaving the grocery bags in the back of the car, she entered the house with a feeling of anticipation. Dave hadn't come home for an afternoon lovemaking session in a long time.

The house was quiet when Kelly walked in. A glance toward the glass patio doors showed the boys weren't by the pool.

Good, they must be sleeping, she thought.

"I hope Dave remembered to pay Sara," she murmured as she climbed the stairs, one hand resting on the wrought iron railing.

Well, she could play at surprises, too, she decided as she began unbuttoning her blouse while walking quietly down the hallway to the master bedroom.

Two minutes later Kelly's scream of outrage rent the air.

"You dirty, stinking bastard!" She was standing at the

top of the stairs and scooped up the bundle of clothing lying at her feet. Then she descended swiftly, heading for the kitchen.

"Kelly, baby." A dark-haired man appeared at the head of the stairs, fumbling with the zipper of his jeans while following her down the stairs. "You've got it all wrong."

"Wrong!" she shrieked, spinning around to face the man she had been married to for close to four years. "Tell me, Dave, what exactly did I get wrong? The fact that Sara happens to be stark naked in *our* bed? Let's see, did she faint and you decided to take her up there to loosen her clothing to help her recover, is that it?" She halted next to the trash compactor, opened it, threw the clothing inside, slammed the door shut, and turned it on before Dave could stop her. "Well, let's see how your little playmate is going to explain to her parents why she's coming home without a stitch of clothing on, shall we? As for you, I suggest you get up there, get that tramp out of our bed, and pack your things. You've got exactly five minutes to get out of this house."

"Kelly, you're being unreasonable." Dave attempted to placate her, but she merely jerked away from his touch.

"Unreasonable, hell, I'm being very calm." She faced him with deadly eyes. "Just don't take too long, or I may change my mind and put your clothes in with Sara's."

Without success Dave spent another ten minutes trying to reason with an outraged Kelly. They were so engrossed in their argument, neither saw a guilty-looking Sara, wearing one of Dave's shirts, sneak out of the house.

Dave finally gave up and retreated upstairs to finish dressing. Maybe if he gave Kelly some time to herself, she'd come to her senses and realize how crazy this was. Damn! If only Sara hadn't been so well-built and receptive, he wouldn't have been tempted.

"After this, anything you have to say to me you can say

27

through Jerry," Kelly screamed after him as Dave left the house.

"Jerry!" He spun around, recognizing the name of their lawyer. "Now, look, Kelly, you're letting this get out of hand. Don't do anything you'll be sorry for later, because if I leave now, I won't come back," he bluffed.

"On the contrary, I think I'm finally realizing what you've been doing all those nights you claimed you had to work late. I'm finally smartening up," she replied in an even voice, crossing her arms in front of her. No amount of threats or cajoling were going to move her. Deep down she was beginning to question how many times this had happened before she had finally found out. For some reason she didn't believe this had been the first and she didn't want to hear any lies.

"And what do you think you're going to do in the meantime?" Dave sneered, shaking his fist at her. "You've barely worked a day in your life. That liberal arts degree you have isn't even worth the paper it's written on. You wouldn't know what to do without me," he finished arrogantly.

"I'll do just fine." Kelly's voice dripped icicles. "Goodbye, Dave."

She waited until the Corvette could be heard roaring out of the driveway, Dave's jeering words still ringing in her ears. True, what could she do? They had married right out of college and Dave had preferred to have his wife at home. Now she had a pretty good idea why. With a faint feeling of dismay Kelly thought of her little boys upstairs. As far as she was concerned, they were all hers and her responsibility. Well, that was now *her* problem, not Dave's, as he smugly reminded her so many times in the past. Even though the boys were a planned pregnancy, he soon discovered that fatherhood was a long-term commitment, one that he hadn't cared for.

Kelly had walked back upstairs and into the bedroom. The first thing she did was strip the sheets off the bed and stuff them into a bag intending to throw them out. Sitting on the floor, she picked up the telephone directory and leafed through until she found the number she wanted.

"Hello, Salvation Army?" Her voice was neutral as she spoke. "I'd like to arrange for the pickup of a bedroom set please."

Kelly sighed deeply. Why did she have to remember that now? Dave's infrequent and very intrusive telephone call did that to her. She glanced up at the clock. It was now going on eleven and she should think about getting some sleep. It would be a busy day tomorrow. She only hoped she'd receive some responses to the newspaper advertisement.

Two days later Cole sat in a back booth of the coffee shop adjoining his motel. With a feeling of despondency he studied the newspaper ads laid out in front of him.

It had been a little over a month since he had first spoken to Harry and so far his search had been fruitless. Harry was already having a good laugh when Cole called in the day before. He suggested Cole come back home and work on something else. The younger man refused. He'd get this story one way or another.

Cole couldn't help but notice the waitress looking his way with an interested glance. He'd better find a new coffee shop soon, since he certainly didn't need any complications. Besides, she looked a little young for him. At the ripe age of thirty-seven, he had discovered that he definitely preferred his women a good deal over the age of consent.

Of the seven interviews he had embarked on so far, only one had resulted in a job offer. As the offer had come from

a very effeminate man in his fifties, Cole had promptly
declined.

Ah, here was one! He studied the small advertisement.

WANTED—LIVE-IN DOMESTIC.
Must like children, willing to
take on all household duties.
Apply to 555–9623.

"Bingo!" he breathed. Somehow his senses told him this
was the one. "Now it's my turn to laugh, Harry, old boy."
He used his pen to circle the ad. He dug into his pocket
for a dime. He had a call to make.

CHAPTER TWO

The following week was quiet until Wednesday, when all hell broke loose.

It all started when Kelly was rudely awakened by Alfie's ear-splitting howls. Running to the bedroom window, all she could see were soapsuds spilling over from the spa into the swimming pool and an irate Alfie trying to scramble out of the spa.

"Grab his collar so we can get the soap off him!" As Kyle reached for the dog's collar, Alfie lumbered out of the spa and made a wet beeline for the open patio door.

The two boys stared at each other as Kevin said, "Boy, Kyle, are you gonna get it."

Just as Kelly leaned over to open the window she turned, having heard a noise on the stairs. In two leaps Alfie managed to jump across the pastel ombré-striped silk comforter on Kelly's bed and knocked her to the floor.

"Alfie!" Kelly screamed, pushing at the wet dog. "Get off me!"

The soaked sheepdog whimpered his distress, pressing himself closer to her for protection.

"Get off!" she ordered through clenched teeth, and gathering all her strength finally managed to push him away. As she rose to her knees she caught a glimpse of two sets of eyes, their expression so much like their father's, watching her warily.

"Mom—" Kevin began.

"I don't want to hear it, Kevin," she said in a deadly tone.

"But Mom—" Kyle pleaded.

"I have just had it with you two," she declared shrilly, advancing toward them. She grabbed each boy by the arm and none too gently propelled them toward the bed. Sitting down, she released Kyle while at the same time pulled Kevin over her knee. While paddling a howling Kevin she grimly assured him it was *not* hurting her more than it was him. Before Kyle could make his escape, she gave him the same treatment, then commanded the two sniffing boys to dry the dog, change their clothes, and *sit* until she told them otherwise. They scurried out of the room without a backward glance.

Kelly felt a cold, wet nose at the back of her neck. While she had been reprimanding the boys Alfie had cautiously climbed up on the bed behind her. She shot him a deadly glare.

"Well?"

He slithered off the bed with his tail between his legs, his eyes on her the entire time as he crept out of the room.

Then Kelly finally viewed the wet, muddy splotches on the silk comforter. It was undeniably ruined. Her eyes filled with angry tears. Refusing to give in to the temptation to cry, she slowly rose to her feet and headed for the shower.

An hour later Kelly left two very quiet little boys at Jenny's house before driving on to work.

"You have one interview today and two tomorrow,"

Rachel announced when Kelly entered the office. "Judging by the scarcity of replies to the ad, you better hire one of them."

Kelly wrinkled her nose. "I know. I can't depend on Jenny's goodwill indefinitely," she sighed.

Knowing time was limited before the first applicant would arrive, Kelly began her work with a vengeance.

"Miss Hudgins is here," Rachel announced over the intercom. There was just the slightest bit of hesitation in her voice. Oh, no, what was wrong with this one?

"Send her in."

The door opened and a primly dressed gray-haired woman timidly entered Kelly's office. For one crazy moment Kelly thought of a story about a meek rabbit she had read to the boys once.

"Miss Hudgins?" Kelly's voice came out a little higher pitched than expected.

"Yes." The woman's voice was barely audible. She stood uncertainly in the doorway, clutching her purse between her fingers.

"Won't you come in and have a seat." Kelly tried to smile but failed miserably.

"Thank you," Miss Hudgins whispered in a nervous voice. She perched on the edge of the chair as if ready to bolt at the slightest movement.

"So-o-o," Kelly began uncertainly. "Ah, do you have a resume with you?"

"Oh, yes," replied the soft-spoken woman, withdrawing a folded sheet of paper from her purse and offering it to Kelly, adding, "I also have my references, if you'd care to see them."

Oh, God, Kelly prayed silently to herself as she accepted the sheet of paper. Naturally Miss Hudgins's work references were glowing. Everyone had loved Miss Hudgins and had been sorry to see her go. "May I ask why you left your last position, Mrs. Hudgins?"

"Oh, yes."

Kelly waited, but no response came. "Then, why did you leave?" she prompted, desperately wanting to break the silence.

"Well." Miss Hudgins's fingers played nervously with the clasp of her purse. "Mr. and Mrs. Phillips were transferred to the East Coast and while they wanted me to accompany them I preferred to stay in a warmer climate."

"That's understandable," Kelly answered politely, ill at ease with this woman. Eager to discourage her, she began: "I have two boys, a very large house, and an equally large dog. I work extremely long hours and can't be bothered with any petty household details."

Before she could continue, Miss Hudgins spoke up. "It's always better to have too much to do than not enough," she said piously. "I love children and animals and I just love taking care of a house. I've always felt that there's nothing better than a good coating of wax on furniture to give it a healthy and loving glow."

"Y-yes," Kelly stammered. This woman wouldn't work out at all!

"Boys and dogs go together. I'm sure they're no trouble."

Kelly couldn't believe her ears. "Trouble?" she repeated.

"Small boys are expected to get into a little mischief now and then." Miss Hudgins smiled serenely.

Kelly took a deep breath. There was only way to get across to this woman. "Miss Hudgins, my mischievous little boys have washed our dog in the spa, tried to cook an egg in the toaster, and emptied a five-pound bag of dry dog food in the toilet just to watch it swell up in water the way it did in the TV commercials. Actually I'm sure that

34

if my boys were of age, they would both be in the county jail," she concluded ruthlessly, knowing there was some exaggeration in her words, but they were desperately needed.

During Kelly's discourse Miss Hudgins turned so pale that Kelly thought the woman would faint from shock. "Now, if you'd like the job, and after seeing your excellent references, I'm sure we could come to some agreement. Can you start tomorrow?" Kelly asked politely.

The older woman rose unsteadily to her feet. "Thank you for your time, Mrs. Connors, but I really don't think this job is for me."

Kelly breathed a silent sigh of relief. "I'm sorry to hear that, Miss Hudgins," she said aloud, walking the older woman to the door. "Thank you for coming by."

Kelly returned to her office, carefully closing the door behind her. She turned and leaned against the door panels, collapsing in uncontrollable laughter until the tears rolled down her cheeks. She shifted her position when she felt the door move.

"What did you do to her?" Rachel demanded with mirth in her voice.

"I don't think she wanted the job that badly." Kelly continued to laugh.

"I had an idea she might have been a little too high-powered for you," the secretary commented dryly.

Kelly continued laughing so hard, tears came to her eyes. "Are you kidding? That poor woman wouldn't have lasted five minutes with my boys. Actually I think she would have had trouble with Little Lord Fauntleroy!"

Rachel shook her head in amusement. "Cheer up. After her, how can it get any worse?"

"I don't know, but the way my luck has been running lately, she may end up my best bet," Kelly sighed. "I guess

I better get the layouts finished on the Elliot account or your dear brother will have my head."

"Don't worry, I'll protect you," she declared confidently. "Just remember I'll be standing right *behind* you."

"That's what I thought."

That evening Kelly picked up a pair of subdued little boys at Jenny's house. They quietly obeyed her instructions for them to watch television while she fixed dinner, which was then eaten in silence. Kelly was surprised that both boys ate everything on their plates and even went to bed without being told.

The thought of spending her evening washing the dinner dishes and cleaning the kitchen, not to mention the laundry that had been rapidly piling up, was depressing. She had also noticed a more than light coating of dust on the furniture and knew some housecleaning would have to be done over the weekend.

After she poured herself a Coke Kelly began her cleaning chores fervently, praying a housekeeper would appear in her life just as the good fairy had in Cinderella's.

"How had I gotten all of this done before?" she asked herself as she tossed the dirty clothes into the washer. The answer was easy—she hadn't been working in an office eight to twelve hours a day and bringing paperwork home on top of that. She could only hope that a new housekeeper would be found soon before she lost what was left of her sanity.

The next morning Kelly had to leave early for a breakfast meeting with a new client. She apologized to the accommodating Jenny for leaving the boys with her again and promised to make alternate arrangements for the following week.

"Don't forget you have two more appointments today,"

Rachel informed Kelly when she walked in and handed her a sheet of paper with telephone messages written on it. As Kelly entered her office, Rachel commented, "I'm sure you'll especially like Mrs. Butterworth. She should be here in about twenty minutes."

Turning her head, Kelly started to feel a little uneasy seeing the mischievous gleam in Rachel's eye. "Mrs. Butterworth?" Kelly asked in disbelief. "Oh, Lord!"

Kelly sat at her desk giggling to herself. "Mrs. Butterworth! I don't know how Rachel does it." She tried to mentally put a face with the name and could only see the rounded glass figure filled with syrup that she always put on the table when she made waffles. "Oh, no, she's probably another Miss Hudgins!" she groaned. The buzzer blared in the room, startling her from her daydream. "Yes, Rachel?"

"Mrs. Butterworth," Rachel announced sweetly. Why did Kelly get the impression that Rachel had something up her sleeve? She sounded much too pleased with herself.

"Thank you. Show her in please."

"Okay." Rachel clicked off.

The door opened and a blank-faced Rachel ushered in a sweet-faced silver-haired woman in her sixties.

Kelly sat back in her chair, hoping her facial expression didn't reflect the shock she felt inside. She stared at the gentle-looking woman who was now seated across from her. She couldn't find fault with the slightly old-fashioned floral print dress or the hair combed into a neat bun under a dark-colored hat. Kelly knew her boys would walk all over this woman in two days, maximum.

As Rachel was closing the door she said quietly, "I'll hold your calls."

"Well, Mrs. Butterworth, tell me about yourself," Kelly said serenely.

37

"Exactly how large is your house?" the older woman rapped out in a harsh voice.

"Well, ah—"

"Is it one story or two?"

"Two, but—"

"How many children do you have?"

"Twin boys."

"How old?"

"Five, but they're—"

"You mean they're not school age?"

"Well, they don't start school until next fall, but they stay out of the way playing with the dog."

"Dog?" Mrs. Butterworth was highly indignant. "I'm very allergic to dogs."

"Well, he stays outside most of the time," Kelly argued, wondering who was interviewing whom.

"You bet he will. My health won't allow me to climb stairs. I don't approve of smoking or drinking, and I won't clean up after large parties. My weekends are my own. If I'm to run errands, I expect to be paid mileage. Of course, I'll need to see the house before I make my final decision." Mrs. Butterworth sat back and looked at Kelly expectantly.

By this time Kelly was sitting up straight and gripping the sides of her chair, the smile now gone.

"*My* house?" she groaned.

"Of course, your house." Mrs. Butterworth rose to her feet, indicating the interview was over. "I'll get your address from your secretary and be by sometime this weekend. Naturally, I realize you'll be interviewing other applicants. Good afternoon, Mrs. Connors." She turned abruptly and marched out of the office.

Kelly sat glued to her chair, staring in disbelief at the empty spot that Mrs. Butterworth had occupied.

Rachel opened the door far enough to stick her head in,

grinning wickedly. Seeing Kelly's stunned expression. "How'd you do?"

"I think she's considering me." Kelly managed to find her voice. "Would you please cancel the next appointment."

"Can't, too late."

"You have to," Kelly pleaded. "I can't handle another Miss Hudgins or Mrs. Butterworth or worse." She cringed at the thought.

"All right, all right, I'll try," Rachel conceded, returning to her desk. Five minutes later she looked in. "Too bad, no answer. I guess you get to see Mrs. Bishop at three."

Kelly finally collapsed in her chair, wishing the jack-hammer behind her eyes would go away.

"Rachel, do you have any aspirin?" she moaned. "If I have to face another person like the one who just left, I'm going to need some help!"

Except the two white tablets didn't help. Kelly didn't care to interview any more prospective housekeepers after the first two disasters. At the same time she was getting angry that the last applicant was running late.

An hour later she punched the intercom button, waiting for Rachel to answer her.

"I thought you wanted these letters to go out today?" the secretary's voice sighed in her ear. "Again, as I've told you for the past twenty minutes, I will let you know when she arrives."

"I just want to get this over with!" Kelly wailed.

"You and me both." Then Rachel's swiftly indrawn breath could be heard. "Oh my God."

"Don't tell me!" she moaned, covering her face with her free hand. "She just came in, right? And she looks like a witch, doesn't she? It's bad enough the kids have the Wicked Witch of the West for a mother. They don't have to have one for a housekeeper too. Is that what she looks like? If so, just tell her the job is filled. I couldn't stand looking at another broom-flying candidate if my life depended on it." She could barely hear the mumble of words from Rachel's end as the visitor announced themself to her.

"Kelly, C. Bishop is here," Rachel muttered.

"Send her in." She wrinkled her nose, then quickly straightened up the pile of papers on her desk before the door opened.

Kelly's cool, polite smile froze on her face as the next candidate for the position as her housekeeper walked in.

"Oh my God," she breathed, unable to believe her eyes, because before her stood the most gorgeous man she had ever seen.

She judged him to be just six feet tall, probably in his late thirties, with dark brown hair and midnight blue eyes framed by dark, thick lashes. His jeans hugged lean hips and taut thighs while a white long-sleeved cotton shirt was left open at the throat and a tan corduroy jacket covered his broad shoulders. Kelly couldn't keep her eyes off the rugged features of the man's face. It took her a moment to realize that he had been speaking to her.

"I-I'm sorry?" Kelly stammered, flushing furiously and hating herself for her adolescent reaction.

He extended his hand. "Cole Bishop, Mrs. Connors. I'm sorry I was late, but I got hung up in traffic."

Kelly stared dumbly at his outstretched hand for a moment before cautiously giving him hers.

"I'm pleased to meet you, Mr. Bishop. Is your mother in the outer office?" Surely *he* can't be the one applying for the housekeeper position!

Cole looked confused for a moment, then grinned as the meaning of her question sunk in. "I didn't realize my mother had to come with me."

Kelly could feel the color rise in her cheeks under the tall man's assessing gaze. "I'm sorry, Mr. Bishop, I'm afraid that I don't understand why you're here."

"I'm here about your advertisement," he said slowly, as if explaining to a small child.

"You can't, you're a man," she protested.

"What does that have to do with it?" he asked lazily. "Do you mind if I take a seat?"

Kelly laughed nervously. "Oh, forgive me, please, sit down." As he seated himself, she continued, "There must be some misunderstanding. I advertised for a housekeeper, not a handyman."

While she had been looking him over, Cole had been doing a little studying of his own. The last thing he had expected was to walk in and find a woman who belonged in a fashion magazine. When he had first called about the interview he had been cautious, implying the interview was for his mother. The secretary had only said that the position entailed household duties and taking care of two small boys. For some reason Cole had expected a woman with the harsh features that went with the advertising game. He had done a little checking on Kelly Connors, but could find out only that she was thirty-two, divorced, and by hard work had made herself quite a name as an account executive with Creative Concepts.

What he found before him was a gentle-looking woman with rich honey-blond hair that he'd bet his last dollar on that it was her natural color. From what he could see above the desk she had a good-looking body and any man would love to hear her husky voice late at night under the covers. Oh, yes, this was the job he wanted!

Careful, Bishop, he silently warned himself. There was also a wariness in this lady's eyes that told him she wasn't too happy with the male sex. How long had she been divorced? No matter. Either way, the separation hadn't

41

been an amiable one. He was going to have to play this very carefully so that he wouldn't blow the whole scheme.

"I'm aware of what you need," Cole said coolly, not betraying by a flick of an eyelid the double entendre. "Your ad didn't specify what sex."

"Sex is understood." She was rapidly losing control of the conversation. Whatever happened to the interviews where the one doing the hiring was in charge?

"Not where I come from," he replied, thoroughly enjoying her discomfort.

"I don't know who put you up to this, Mr. Bishop, but this joke has gone far enough. I just don't have time for these adolescent games," Kelly informed him tersely, fighting to regain control of their talk.

"I don't know what your problem is, lady, but I'm here about your housekeeper position." Leaning forward in his chair, he rested his arms on his knees. "Now, are you going to interview me or not?"

"Fine!" she snapped. "I have a large two-story house with a pool and spa, twin boys aged five, whom even I can't tell apart at times, and a huge English sheepdog. Of course, there are all the normal duties—cooking, cleaning, washing, ironing, not to mention the yard work and pool upkeep. Do you think you can handle all that?"

"Sure," he replied blandly.

"What makes you so sure?" she challenged him.

"My sister became quite ill after her husband died and I helped her out by taking over the household. She has four kids, ranging in the age from six to twelve, one very large house, two cats, a great Dane, and a boa constrictor named Fred," he added sarcastically. "The kids seemed to survive from my cooking and there were no complaints about my housekeeping," His sister had promised to cover for him if anyone wanted to call her, although she laughed during the entire conversation. There was no denying that

Cole was a decent enough cook and even kept his apartment neat and tidy, but that was quite different from the day-to-day household chores that cropped up.

"Why would someone like you want to do domestic work?" Kelly asked.

Cole arched an eyebrow. "I didn't realize there were physical requirements for housekeeping." Inwardly he was still cautioning himself about his overly big mouth, but she seemed to thrive on the snappy comebacks.

"I'll need to see some references." By all rights she should have thrown him out of her office, but there was something compelling about him—a faint light of challenge in his eyes that she just couldn't ignore. Just as she couldn't ignore the interest those same eyes showed when he entered the office. She was playing with fire here, but she couldn't back away. Not just yet.

Cole reached into his shirt pocket and withdrew a sheet of paper. He handed it to Kelly, knowing she wasn't going to call his sister or even Harry, who had said he would vouch that Cole had worked for him and his wife for the past year. Harry hadn't stopped laughing either. He still thought this story was idiotic.

Kelly studied the names written on the paper. "I do have other people to interview," she explained formally.

Cole didn't like this turn of events. She was withdrawing from him and that wasn't what he wanted. For a few moments he had forgotten that he was here for an assignment. Wouldn't it have been great if he could have met her at a party? Talked to her, taken her dancing. He bet she was a great dancer. Then back to either his place or hers. Maybe this was a mistake. How could he work for someone who looked like her and concentrate not only on getting his story but keep his sanity at the same time?

"Meaning I won't be considered," he commented in a low voice.

"How do you figure that, Mr. Bishop?" she asked icily.

"You won't consider me because of my sex, right?" Cole asked bluntly.

"Your sex doesn't interest me," Kelly replied coolly.

Wicked lights danced in Cole's eyes as he drawled. "It doesn't?"

She grew flustered. This kind of conversation with its sexual innuendos was nothing new to her, but there was something about this man that gave it a new meaning. "I think you know exactly what I mean."

Cole stood up. "You forgot the all-important question, Mrs. Connors. Why I want a domestic job," he said smoothly. "I was in the navy for fifteen years and after bumming around the world and later trying a variety of jobs found that this line of work suited me just fine. Oh, and if you're worried, I'm not the least bit effeminate," he tacked on.

"I'll say," she muttered under her breath, then cringed, afraid he had heard her. "My secretary will be in touch when I make my decision. Thank you for coming." She also stood up and offered her hand.

When Cole's hand warmly enclosed hers, she hadn't expected a shock to travel up her arm. The slight narrowing of his eyes told her she wasn't the only one affected.

"I'll be waiting for your call, Mrs. Connors." His low voice danced up her spine the way his touch traveled along her arm. Each was equally unsettling. He released her hand and left the office.

"Whew!" Rachel entered the office as soon as Cole left. "If you don't want to hire him, I'll be only too happy to let him clean my house."

"You have a one-bedroom apartment," Kelly pointed out.

"It just means he won't have as much to clean."

"Rachel, you're a dirty old lady," she accused.

44

"No matter what, of the three he's your best bet," Rachel told her.

Kelly shook her head, not wanting to remember his dark blue eyes studying her or the way one corner of his mouth turned up crookedly when he smiled. "Whatever happened to the motherly housekeepers like the ones on TV?" she groaned. "One was afraid of her own shadow, the other could probably take on the world, and the last belongs more on an football field than in a kitchen."

"Which one are you going to hire?" Rachel asked her. "You don't dare take too much more time trying to find someone, you know."

Kelly shook her head. "I'll have to think it over tonight and call the lucky person tomorrow."

"Do you want me to call his references?"

She shook her head again. "For some reason I have an idea we'd get nothing but glowing praise. This is one time I'm going to have to play it by instinct and hope it all works out. I just can't go through all of this again!"

"Neither can I," Rachel dryly inserted her own opinion.

That evening after dinner Kelly called the boys in for a conference.

"I think you know I've been trying to find a new housekeeper," she began. "And I think I found someone."

"This one won't get sick or have to go take care of someone else, will she?" Kevin asked.

"I hope to make sure that won't happen," Kelly replied.

"What's she look like, Mom?" Kyle asked curiously. "Is she old like you?"

"Kyle, questions like that tell me you might not make it to your sixth birthday," Kelly said sweetly. "I'll have you know that I'm not ready for the old folks' home yet. And the housekeeper I have in mind is a man." Why didn't she just hire Mrs. Butterworth and get it over with?

45

Correction, wait until the woman informed her she would make a suitable employer.

"A man?" the boys spoke in unison. Then the questions came flying.

"Will he be a daddy to us?"

"Do we have to listen to him?"

"If we're bad, will he spank us?"

"What's he gonna do?"

"Just what Mrs. Peyser and the others did," Kelly explained. "He'll clean the house, watch after you two, and cook the meals."

"Does he play baseball?" Kyle asked hesitantly.

For the first time, Kelly saw the true lack of a male role model in the family. How could she forget the Saturdays when the boys would be out in the front yard and see their friends playing with their fathers? Damn Dave for never paying attention to them these past four years!

"I'm sure he would if you asked him nicely," she said huskily. There was no doubt about it; if Cole Bishop wanted the job, he had it.

"Mom, Mommy."

Kelly groaned, rolling over to pull the pillow over her head. Was it morning already?

"Mom." The little voice persisted as a small body jumped on her legs. "You awake, Mom?"

"No." Her voice was muffled by her pillow.

Kyle picked up a corner of the pillow and laid his head down next to Kelly's. She stared into his brown eyes.

"Hi, Mom," he whispered loudly.

Unable to keep a straight face, Kelly burst out laughing. She grabbed Kyle before he could escape and started tickling him unmercifully. Hearing his brother shriek with laughter, Kevin jumped on the bed to join in the game by tickling his mother. Hearing her screams, Alfie came to

46

her rescue by standing in the doorway and barking loudly, as if to ward off any intruders.

"I give up!" Kelly shouted, vainly attempting to fight off the two small boys and the large dog. "You win, I'm too old for this. Okay, you two, run in and get dressed. With luck this will be the last day you'll be at Jenny's." She shooed them off the bed.

"Will he fix us our favorite breakfast when he comes?" Kyle asked her.

"Anything you want, pet." She smiled fondly at her older son by five minutes.

The joyful sounds of "pancakes!" and "pizza!" came out in unison.

"Pancakes, yes; pizza, no," she informed them. "Now, get going! I have to get dressed so I can call Mr. Bishop up and offer him the job."

Kevin stopped in the doorway and looked around. "Will you ask him if he can teach us football?" he asked quietly.

Tears sprang into Kelly's eyes. There was so much that the boys wanted to learn that she couldn't teach them. It was times like this that she realized how badly they were going to need a male influence as they grew older. "Sure," she murmured.

She didn't have to make a mental note to call Cole the moment she got into the office and offer him the job. The looks on the boys' faces were reminder enough. She only hoped this would work out for all of them.

CHAPTER THREE

"Use one and three quarters cup for large-capacity top-loading machines," Cole muttered to himself, studying the back of the large orange and yellow detergent box. "Hot wash for white and color-fast, warm for permanent press, and cold wash for dark and bright colors."

"Whatcha doin'?"

Cole turned to find Kevin, or was it Kyle, standing in the open doorway of the laundry room. "I'm doing the laundry," he mumbled, pushing wads of dirty clothes, without regard to color or fabric, into an almond-colored washing machine.

"Then why are ya readin' the box?" the small boy asked curiously. "Mom and Mrs. Peyser just poured the soap in."

"Because I like to be accurate." Cole closed the lid and switched on the machine. "I sure hope this is a large-capacity washer," he prayed under his breath. "Which one are you?" he said, turning back to his inquisitor.

"Kyle." He grinned broadly. "Kevin's wearin' a blue

48

shirt," he went on to explain. "Are you gonna read somethin' for the dryer too?"

Cole groaned silently. This wasn't going to be as easy as he thought it would be.

"Why don't you boys go into the living room to say good-bye to your mother before she leaves for work," he suggested smoothly. "Then after I finish washing the breakfast dishes and clean up the kitchen, we'll see about going for a swim."

Kyle's eyes lit up and he ran off shouting his brother's name at the top of his lungs.

"They sure were right when they said a woman's work was never done," Cole muttered to himself, remembering he still hoped to vacuum the living room carpet and finish the laundry before lunchtime. How could he think of lunch when they had just finished breakfast? With two perpetually hungry boys it was very easy. He smiled as he heard the thunder of two pairs of feet running. It had barely been a week and he was already growing fond of Kevin and Kyle. They were good kids and really didn't give him any trouble. Not after they had found out that frogs didn't frighten him.

Cole walked out of the laundry room and through the kitchen when he heard the boys talking to their mother. He walked in on a scene that he was hardly prepared for.

Kelly hugged and kissed the boys good-bye only to have Kyle tug on her skirt.

"Aren't you going to kiss Cole 'bye too?" he asked innocently.

Kelly's mouth fell open. The amusement lurking in Cole's eyes didn't help much.

"Sounds fine to me," he murmured, much to her irritation.

"There's no reason to kiss him, Kyle," she explained through clenched teeth.

"But he lives here now," Kevin piped up. "Becky's mom kisses her dad good-bye. Why can't you kiss Cole?"

"Because he isn't your father." She silently damned Dave for being the cause of all this. If she hadn't caught him in bed with Sara, this never would have happened. At least not as soon as it had.

"I bet he'd like you to kiss him," Kyle told her.

"Did you put them up to this?" she hissed at the tall man who stood to one side, his arms folded across his chest.

"Hey, they do well enough on their own." He grinned wickedly, enjoying her obvious discomfort.

Kelly's eyes flashed fire as she stalked up to Cole and prepared to plant a quick kiss on his cheek, only to have him turn his face at the last moment so that her lips landed lightly on his. For a brief second Kelly faltered, not understanding the electric shock waves shooting through her body. She hurriedly stepped back and stared at him with eyes that blinked rapidly, as if unable to comprehend what had just happened. Kelly was so stunned that she hadn't noticed that her look of surprise was mirrored in Cole's eyes.

"Have a good day, Kelly," he said quietly. That was also a first, because he usually called her Mrs. Connors.

She picked up her satchel and fled the house. It wasn't until she reached the office that her breathing returned to normal.

"Things still working out all right at home?" Rachel greeted Kelly when she entered her office.

"Just great," she informed her with a wry smile. "The boys clean up their rooms without protest, eat their vegetables without complaining, and pick up their toys before they go to bed in the evenings."

"Sounds too good to be true," the secretary commented. "How long do you think it will last?"

"It's already lasted longer than I thought it would," Kelly admitted, remembering how easily Cole fitted into the household.

Kelly could see that Cole found Kyle's and Kevin's soft spots and worked on them. After all, what red-blooded boy is going to turn down a man's help in learning the rudiments of football and how to properly pitch a baseball? He had them as slaves for life.

Yes, Kelly couldn't complain about Cole's housekeeping at all. The house always looked neat and clean, the kids were now on a reasonably sane schedule, and while Cole's cooking might not be gourmet, it was delicious and filling. She had a vague suspicion that her vast collection of cookbooks had been gone over a great deal lately. There was just one niggling problem though. While the boys obeyed Cole and he was good with them, she couldn't help but be bothered by having a man doing the household chores. The first time she realized this uneasy feeling was the afternoon she had come home from work, only to discover all the laundry had been done and put away. That was fine; it was just the thought of someone as ruggedly masculine as Cole handling Kelly's silky lingerie, folding and putting it away. On a whim last year, she had gone out and bought the most expensive and sexiest underwear she could find in a nearby boutique. A perverse part of her wondered if he thought of her wearing those lacy pieces of next-to-nothing. She preferred to forget about the day she had no towels in the bathroom and after calling for one of the boys to bring her a towel, Cole was the one to answer her plea.

Her face still burned at the memory. Deep down she had an idea that what had bothered her was that Cole hadn't really looked at her. Yet, if he had, she probably would have fired him on the spot. It was incidents like that that made her wonder if she made the right choice in hiring him.

"You're off in left field again," Rachel informed Kelly, snapping her fingers in front of the younger woman's face. "It couldn't have something to do with that sexy hunk at your house, could it? After all, you were the one who told me that the house is kept neat and the boys enjoy him being around. So what complaints can you have?"

"It's not that," Kelly began helplessly, not really sure what she was going to say. "Oh, I don't know. There are times it seems too complicated. My neighbors have been giving me strange looks since I've always been the stubborn single on the block. I mean, I didn't even really bring any men home to meet the boys so I wouldn't confuse them. Do you know that when I arrived home yesterday I found Cole mowing the front lawn!"

"That sounds really serious," Rachel replied in a dry tone.

"You should have seen some of my neighbors!" She shook her head in hopes of banishing the memory. "Cole was out there wearing nothing more than a pair of cutoffs and tennis shoes that probably were left over from World War One."

"Since it was a pretty hot day yesterday, I can understand why he left his dress shirt inside. Or was it because of his tennis shoes?"

"Be serious." Kelly chided. "There were three women out in their own front lawns doing yard work wearing the tiniest bikinis allowed in public."

A trace of a smile crossed Rachel's lips. "I guess they felt it was only fair to show off their own attributes."

Kelly groaned. "I can't let him stay, Rachel," she continued to moan. "It isn't fair. It won't be long before he'll be bored with the boys pestering him to play ball with them or to go swimming."

"That kind of job a man would dislike?"

Kelly glared, silently declaring silence. "You know very well what I mean. I can't afford to let the boys become too attached to him only to have him walk out on them one day."

"That could have just as easily happened with one of your other housekeepers," Rachel pointed out.

"It's not the same," she argued. "The boys are getting to the age where a father figure is very important in their lives and I can already see some of the influence he's had on them."

"Is it a bad one?" Rachel asked her.

"No," Kelly admitted quietly.

"Then relax and be glad that the boys are well taken care of and that they have someone who enjoys being with them," she advised. "That's what counts."

Kelly knew Rachel was right, but it was still hard to take well-meaning advice when *she* was the one who was bothered by the addition of Cole Bishop to her household.

Kelly's nerves were on edge for the balance of the day, which didn't improve her work performance any.

"May I make a suggestion?" Rachel stuck her head around the open door preparing to tell Kelly she was leaving for the day.

"What?" Kelly said through clenched teeth, resenting the intrusion into her thoughts after an agonizing telephone call to Darren. Why was he giving her all these problems *now?* She had arranged three models for him to interview, but he still insisted on using Marla for the ad campaign. Men!

"Go home, have a glass of wine, put your feet up, and relax," she advised. "If you think this through logically, you'll feel so much better tomorrow."

"Will I?" Kelly's voice dripped acid. "Didn't you hear what happened when I went out for lunch? Carl Weatherby stopped me and asked how it felt to have a resident stud who could even clean house!" Her voice rose with every word. "Before I could entertain the notion of knocking his teeth out, he wisely walked away."

Rachel shrugged. "I guess it had to happen. Look at it this way, they're all jealous. The men, because you've turned down dates with all the single ones and several of the married ones; the women, because a few of them remember seeing Cole when he came into the office and they know that you now have him all to yourself in the privacy of your home. They'll prefer dreaming up their own idea of sleeping arrangements rather than ask for the real details."

"I'll finish proofing this layout for Darren, then I'll try your prescription, doctor," Kelly promised.

Rachel shook her head, knowing that Kelly would be at her desk until the late hours of the evening. "I'll bring you back some dinner then." She held up a hand to forestall any protest. "See it from my point of view. I have to keep you healthy. I can't afford to break in a new boss."

Kelly called home and told Cole she would be working late. Even the sound of his deep-timbred voice in her ear was enough to send shock waves through her body. She hadn't realized that in hiring a male housekeeper she had taken on much more than she expected. She talked to the boys for a few moments, told them to go to bed without any arguments, then returned to her work. When Rachel returned with a steak sandwich and French fries, Kelly ate without an appetite.

By the time Kelly had finished her work and headed for home it was close to midnight. The house was dark as she walked in.

Feeling too wired to go upstairs to bed, she went into

the kitchen to pour herself a glass of wine. Taking the glass and walking into the darkened den, she paused to kick off her high heels. Knowing her way in the dark, she strolled over to where she knew the couch to be. Before Kelly sat down she reached out to place her glass on the nearby table. Instead of the glass coming in contact with wood, it dropped to the polished parquet floor with a loud splinter.

"Damn!" she screamed.

"What in—" A light flipped on in the room and a disheveled Cole stood in the doorway.

Kelly spun around, noticing the couch was against the wall instead of facing the fireplace. The table that should have been to her right was now over near a chair. "What happened to the room?" she demanded.

"I rearranged the furniture." He walked over to the broken glass and squatted down to pick up the shards. "The boys had a lot of fun helping me."

"*What!*" Her voice rose to a shriek more from shock at the sight of his silky textured dark hair so close to her thigh. "I think I should inform you, Mr. Bishop, that I hired *you* to do the housework around here, not for you to turn my boys into slaves! Also, I don't recall ever saying that I didn't like the arrangement of this room."

Cole straightened up and watched her with puzzled eyes. "Did you have a hard day at work?" he asked solicitously.

"Yes!" she hissed, her hands clenched at her sides. "And the last thing I needed was to come home and find my furniture all moved around. I suppose that if I had gone upstairs and tried to go to bed in the dark I'd probably end up on my—"

"Wait a minute there, lady!" he rapped out, leaning over her taut figure. "I don't take that from anyone, especially a loud-mouthed broad like you! For your informa-

55

tion, all the boys did was have the fun of telling me where to place the furniture. The heavy work was left to me. Does that satisfy you?"

"You're fired!" Her eyes narrowed in rage. "I want you out of here by morning."

"Fine with me," Cole snarled, moving away from her and stalking out of the room. A moment later she could hear the slam of his bedroom door.

"Men!" She headed for the recently moved table and picked up the mail. One particular envelope with its pink slip of paper showing through the windowed envelope piqued her curiosity. The contents brought back her temper. "*What!*" She crushed the paper in her hand and headed for the back of the house. Without bothering to knock she threw open the door to Cole's room. She began to falter when she realized he was wearing nothing more than white briefs, but she certainly wasn't going to back down now. "What is the meaning of this?" she shrilled, waving the crumpled paper still in her fist.

"You tell me." He turned to her, showing no signs of embarrassment at his state of undress.

"This is a late notice from the electric company saying that I haven't paid the bill yet, although I distinctly recall giving you the bill to pay over a week ago." Kelly's breathing was rapidly becoming more and more agitated.

"Then it just sounds as if they crossed in the mail." Cole was unperturbed by her fit of temper. "You know how computers are. They probably have those late notices ready for mailing the day the bill is due. Happens all the time."

"Not with me it doesn't," she gritted. Right now she'd use any excuse to keep her anger directed at him. Not because she felt he had been negligent in his duties, but because the masculinity he wore as easily as he wore his clothes was beginning to wear on her nerves.

56

"You've already fired me; what do you expect to do next? Hang me by my toes?" His own dark blue eyes were now narrowed in temper. "Since you see me as such a horrible monster, the least I can do is make the accusation true." Before Kelly could say a word Cole had strode across the room and hauled her into his arms. His mouth had fastened on hers now, stilling any form of protest.

Kelly's arms lifted, intending to flay Cole's back with her fists but they seemed to have a mind of their own. Instead, they slowly wound their way around his neck and allowed her fingers to inject themselves into his hair. His tongue coaxed her lips to part and then there seemed no turning back. Their brief kiss that morning was only an appetizer for the meal to follow. There was a tart taste to his tongue, as if he had drunk a Coke not too long ago, and there was a very masculine taste that slithered over the sides and roof of her mouth, taking up her feminine taste to complement it.

Kelly had been kissed by men in the past four years but nothing had prepared her for the total onslaught Cole brought about. He took his time by tracing her moist, parted lips, teasing each corner and sliding over the smooth surface of her teeth before returning to the dark depths. She wasn't even aware of her own tongue participating in the sensual byplay as it curled around his tongue, pausing to tentatively dart into his mouth. Cole's groan and the growing male hardness against her thigh told Kelly of his arousal, as did her own swollen breasts aching for his touch.

"Damn!" Cole swore as he abruptly pushed Kelly away. "This was not what I had planned on." He stood back a short distance and raked his fingers through hair, already tousled from Kelly's touch.

She stood watching him, willing her respiration to return to normal. "I'm sure it wasn't." She spoke in a ragged

57

tone unlike her own. "I would just appreciate it if you were gone in the morning before the boys got up." She turned to leave the room.

"What are you going to tell them?" His quiet question followed her.

She stopped and turned her head. "Just that things didn't work out."

"You aren't mad because I rearranged the furniture or because your electric bill might have been a little late." Cole's hypnotic voice was doing strange things to her senses. "You're mad because I happen to affect you in a very elemental way and you don't know how to handle it. You're a coward, Kelly Connors."

Kelly spun around. Her head was held high and she regained the poise that had been holding her together for the past four years.

"I'll leave your check on the kitchen counter."

He smiled, shaking his head in silent wonder. "You can't keep running forever," he argued mildly. "Have it your way. I guess you always do." He turned away.

Kelly closed the door after her and walked back to the den on shaky legs. She quickly wrote out the check and left it on the kitchen counter. A few more minutes was taken to clean up the broken wineglass, then she went upstairs to bed, but not to sleep.

The boys were vocal when they heard of Cole's leave-taking. What Kelly didn't like was that they blamed her. Naturally she hadn't mentioned that he had been fired, only that things hadn't worked out. It was still bothering her that he hadn't even taken the check she had left him. Kelly had found it torn neatly in two and laying on the counter.

"Everything was fine. We liked him a lot." Kyle pouted.

58

"It was cause you didn't like him, Mom," he accused with a much too adult insight.

Kelly reddened under this unexpected attack. "I'll find someone else you'll like just as much," she promised tensely.

Both boys shook their heads.

"Not like Cole," Kevin muttered sadly.

That day was only a taste of what was to come. Kelly had constant headaches. She had to talk once more to domestic agencies and place ads in the newspaper. She had even called Mrs. Butterworth, but the woman had already found a position to her liking. No, she didn't know of anyone looking for a live-in housekeeping position.

"What now?" Rachel asked Kelly a week later.

"Want to become a housekeeper?" She looked up with a groan.

"You had a good thing and you blew it, my girl," Rachel informed her dryly.

"Tell me about it," Kelly sighed. "The boys are unnaturally quiet, they obey my every word, and I never have to repeat myself or shout from the top of my lungs. It's positively eerie. I found someone to watch them during the day for the next couple weeks, but I'll need someone full time by then."

Thinking for a moment, Rachel's eyes glinted. "Well, there is a solution to your problem," she said slowly.

"What could that be?"

"Call Cole Bishop up and tell him you made a mistake."

Kelly looked up, horrified. "I can't do that! I fired the man!"

"So unfire him. Appeal to his masculine instincts," Rachel urged, not missing the faint blush creep up Kelly's neck. "Good Lord, you're a woman. Don't you remember any of those little feminine tricks? It's not as if you look like Mrs. Butterworth, and he certainly doesn't resemble King Kong."

"Tell me about it," Kelly muttered, remembering the man in all too perfect detail. Especially what those briefs not only revealed but what they didn't hide!

Rachel left the office for a moment and returned, carrying a piece of paper. "Here's his number. It certainly couldn't hurt to try."

"Not unless he's discovered a way to strangle people over the phone," Kelly said dryly, taking the paper. Her eyes fell on Rachel, who had been ready to make herself comfortable in one of the chairs. "Would it be at all possible to keep this conversation private?"

"Sure. I can close the door."

"Fine, then you can go back to your desk and do some work while I make my call," Kelly suggested sweetly.

Rachel sighed as she rose to her feet. "I just wanted to make sure you didn't blow it."

Kelly picked up the phone and punched out the number, nervously waiting as she heard the ringing on the other end. What she hadn't expected was to hear a man's voice reciting the name of a motel. She asked for Cole Bishop and waited a moment as the connection was made. Why was he living in a motel?

"Bishop." His deep voice filled her ear.

"Ah, this is Kelly Connors." Why was it so difficult to keep her voice sounding normal around this man?

"Did you call to fire me again?" he asked derisively.

Kelly's face flamed. "Actually, I called to apologize for my unforgivable behavior that night," she said slowly.

"Before or after you fired me?"

She took a deep breath. This was going to be more difficult than she thought. Her fingers tightened on a pencil she had picked up. "I—I also called to see if you had found work yet," she said with a false brightness.

60

"Why?"

"I—ah—I thought that if you hadn't found a position yet, you might be willing to come back to work for me." She waited tensely for his reply, positive it would be a roaring no.

"I might be willing to discuss it," he said finally. "Such as over lunch tomorrow."

Kelly glanced at her calendar. "I'm afraid I have a luncheon appointment tomorrow, how about—"

"Then I guess we can't discuss it."

Kelly closed her eyes, feeling another pounding headache coming on. He certainly wasn't going to make it easy for her, but then she really couldn't blame him. "All right, tomorrow," she conceded.

Cole named an expensive restaurant not too far from Kelly's office, saying he'd meet her there at one.

"For someone who's unemployed you certainly have expensive taste," Kelly said sarcastically, intending to have the last word.

"Only when I'm not picking up the bill, Mrs. Connors. I'll warn you now that I have a hearty appetite. See you tomorrow." The click sounded loud in her ear.

She slammed the receiver down. "I can't believe this!" she exploded.

Rachel opened the office door. "Don't tell me he was foolish enough to turn you down?"

"Worse." Kelly outlined Cole's words.

"He's not going to make it very easy for you," Rachel decided. "If you're smart, you'll wear something sexy tomorrow. Show a lot of leg and cleavage, not to mention wearing an expensive perfume guaranteed to upset his libido."

"He's not worth it," she muttered.

In the end, Kelly's feminine vanity took over.

61

Her bright turquoise silk shirtdress was calculated to hug each curve of her body while the top was left unbuttoned to the cleft between her breasts. A silver pendant swung gently between the mounds of rounded flesh. After a great deal of hunting through her closet Kelly finally discovered her black high-heeled sandals and stepped into them.

"All this for some hard-nosed male," she muttered, dabbing on Joy, a Christmas gift from her parents the previous year. She brushed her hair up into a loose knot with a few stray curls hanging down. Kelly had wanted to give off the aura of a soft, delicate woman, and she felt she had accomplished her goal.

"You look real pretty, Mom," Kyle told her as she was getting ready to leave the house.

"Thanks, darling." She stooped down to hug him tightly.

"I think you look pretty too; I just didn't say so." Kevin looked peeved at being left out.

"I know you did, love." Kelly also gave him a warm hug. She hadn't told them about her lunch date with Cole in case it didn't work out. She didn't want to raise their hopes.

When Kelly walked into the office Rachel's eyes traveled over her slowly, her facial expression not betraying her thoughts.

"Now I know where the saying, deadlier than the male, came from," she said finally. "He won't stand a chance."

"That's what I'm hoping for," she said grimly.

Kelly worked herself into a frenzy that morning, determined to keep her mind off watching the clock even as the hands slowly inched their way toward one o'clock. When the time came she suddenly resembled a condemned prisoner going to her execution.

"Loosen another button," Rachel called after Kelly's departing figure.

"Oh, sure, and get arrested for indecent exposure," Kelly muttered, walking swiftly toward the elevators.

Since the restaurant wasn't far from her office, she decided to walk, needing the extra time to fortify her defenses.

Kelly's first indication of Cole's intention to be in charge of this confrontation was his showing up fifteen minutes late. She sat at her table and fidgeted with a glass of Chablis, silently wondering why she was putting up with this, when a smiling hostess directed Cole to the table.

How does he do it? Kelly thought to herself irritably, watching the hostess fawn over Cole as if he were a movie star or a famous athlete. She looked up, smiling tightly as he dropped down into the chair across from her.

"Good afternoon." He flashed her a grin, offering no apology or explanation for his tardiness. "Don't tell me you're one of those people who starts drinking at noon?" He glanced at her almost empty wineglass.

"Only when necessary. Would you care for something?" she asked with a forced politeness as the waitress approached them.

Cole shook his head, smiling up at the entranced waitress while Kelly defiantly asked for another glass of wine.

Conversation was further suspended when they gave their lunch orders, Kelly ordering crab salad and Cole settling on a steak.

What else? Kelly thought to herself as she listened to him say how he wanted his meat cooked. "I guess I should explain further as to why I called."

Cole held up his hand indicating silence. "I don't believe in ruining a good meal with business talk."

Kelly opened her mouth while her eyes glittered with

temper. "Then why couldn't we have had this meeting in my office?" She bit out the words.

"Are you kidding? And pass up a meal like this?" Cole had been surprised by Kelly's call. He had a pretty good idea that she hadn't been able to find another housekeeper and he certainly hadn't found anything. His brief stay in her house hadn't really given him enough material for his article, so he had hung around, hoping another job would come up.

Come off it, Bishop! he argued with himself. The only reason you went back to the same motel was because you were hoping she would call you. All you've been thinking of is the honey-sweet taste of her mouth under yours and the erotic thoughts of her equally sweet body writhing under you in sexual torment. Damn! Now you're sounding like a romance novel. He shifted in his chair, feeling that familiar, tightening sensation in his slacks. This was getting ridiculous! If he wasn't careful, he'd really make a fool of himself.

"Have you been working as an account executive since your divorce?" Cole asked conversationally, also wanting to know more about Kelly.

"What makes you think I'm divorced?" Kelly demanded, looking down at her salad and wondering why she had ordered it while at the same time wishing the waitress would return so that she could ask for another glass of wine. "I never said I was. I could be widowed for all you know."

He shook his head. "You forget, I've been in your house. There are no family pictures except ones of you and the boys, and you have never mentioned your husband. Kevin and Kyle once mentioned how their dad was supposed to see them at Christmas but something had come up. Luckily, he had thought quickly enough. He had al-

64

most ruined his whole set-up of the so-called caring father."

"Oh, yes, and I know exactly *what* came up," she said bitterly, remembering the sweet young thing Dave had been dating at the time. She had never cared how Dave treated her, but his attitude toward the boys was a different story. "If you don't mind, my ex-husband is a subject I prefer not to discuss." The closed expression on her face bore witness to her feelings.

Cole pushed his emptied plate to one side and brought his coffee cup forward. "Okay, now as to the real reason you brought me here." He looked at her expectantly.

"*I* brought *you?*" Kelly croaked, then hastily lowered her voice, afraid someone might overhear this ridiculous conversation.

"You can't find anyone to take the job, can you?" he asked gently, resting his clasped hands on top of the table.

There was no use in lying now. "No," she admitted softly. She took a deep breath. There was no reason in keeping anything back now. "You have to understand something. I love my boys very much, but I have to work. I'm never sure from one month to the next if Dave's child support checks will arrive, much less clear the bank. Usually they don't and it's a battle to get him to make them good."

"That's why you prefer a live-in housekeeper," he verified.

Kelly nodded. "Because of their birthdates. They can't begin kindergarten until next fall, and the waiting lists in the surrounding preschools are miles long. I've had more housekeepers these past three years than I'd care to count, and it hasn't been the boys' fault. Two left due to a death in the family, one due to ill health, and one I had to fire because she drank on the sly. Kevin and Kyle have been going through some rough times, and I feel the least I can do is give them as much of a stable home life as possible."

Cole nodded in understanding. It was evident that she had her sons' welfare in mind and he couldn't fault her for that. "Why not just remarry?" he suggested.

"I'd have to be on my deathbed to do anything that drastic, and even then I'd reconsider," she replied stiffly. "But I am asking if you'll agree to work for me again."

Cole was tempted to tease her a little bit, but he could see the white-knuckled grip she had on her wineglass. Any more pressure and the stem would surely snap.

"I can't afford the boys' lives to be in this crazy upheaval any more than necessary," Kelly went on. "All I ask is that you be willing to stay on for at least a year." Could she handle a year of his constant presence? For the boys, anything.

"As long as I promise not to rearrange the furniture?" he couldn't help asking. "Or step out of line?" He brought to mind that tumultuous kiss.

Kelly's face flushed with embarrassment. "I won't beg," she whispered tautly.

A faint smile touched Cole's lips. He wasn't going to agree to stay the year because his article certainly wouldn't take that long. As it was, his conscience was beginning to nag him about the horrible trick he was playing on this very lovely and desirable, but also very vulnerable, woman. Yet another part of him said he'd be a fool to give up a chance like this for his article. He barely glanced up when the waitress began to place the check in front of him.

"My boss is paying," he told the young woman, but his eyes remained focused on Kelly's face. Luckily he didn't need to say any more. She got the message loud and clear.

66

CHAPTER FOUR

Kelly flipped through a series of photographs of models wearing the barest of bikinis and draped in seductive poses.

"They have no bustline, no hips, and no thighs," she moaned to Rachel as she continued to sift through the photographs. "It's disgusting!"

"You have nothing to worry about," the secretary observed dryly, picking up one of the pictures and turning it over. "These measurements can't be those of a grown woman."

"A grown woman at the ancient age of fifteen," Kelly grimaced. "The old lady in this group is twenty-two."

"All this trouble for that furry young beast," Rachel snorted.

Kelly smiled at the older woman's unkind description of Darren. Poor Darren! Kelly had been handling the T's and Rags account for almost two years, and during that time Darren and Rachel snapped at each other like two scrappy cats. Yet, deep down, Kelly had a sneaking suspicion the two had an uncanny affection for each other.

Wouldn't that explain the bouquet of roses delivered to Rachel on her birthday and the familiar handwriting on the attached envelope?

"What about this Tallie?" Rachel held up a photograph of a sultry-eyed dark-haired beauty wearing a narrow crocheted bikini.

Kelly took the photo from Rachel to study it more carefully. "I'm sure she could keep Darren's mind off Marla," she decided with a nod. "I think that we should be allowed to leave early since we did this job in such a short time," she announced cheerfully.

Rachel looked up as Darren arrived with a large box in his arms. "Let's see what His Highness has to say first."

"Hi, love." He greeted Kelly with a big smile, setting the box on top of her desk. "I've got some goodies for you." He pulled the multicolored contents out onto her desk blotter.

"What on earth!" Kelly laughed with delight, seeing the many women's and boys' T-shirts.

Rachel picked up one of the shirts and held it out, reading the silk-screened front. "HUNK OF THE MONTH?" She glanced at her boss with a knowing eye. "I'd say size extra large isn't meant for one of the boys."

"Oh." Darren grinned slyly at Kelly. "Rachel told me about your new housekeeper and I thought he shouldn't be left out."

"Terrific," Kelly muttered, snatching the shirt out of Rachel's hands. "What about this one?" She picked up a delicate rose pink shirt with writing on the front. "Sorry, Darren, I don't read French."

He smirked and translated. "The more I know about men, the more I love my dog."

"Sounds appropriate," Rachel commented wryly, watching Kelly toss the shirt into the box.

"Since you're here, you might as well see the model

we've chosen for the new campaign," Kelly told Darren, searching beneath the T-shirts for the photograph.

He looked at the angular young miss and emitted a low wolf whistle. "Not too bad," he murmured with supreme male appreciation. "Yeah, she'll be just fine."

"Down boy," Kelly advised in a dry tone. "She's strictly jailbait."

Darren grimaced. "I think you do this to make me crazy," he muttered, tossing the photo onto the desk.

"Li'l ole me?" She affected a droll southern accent.

"Enjoy the shirts," Darren told her as he turned to leave. "Have that sweet young thing in my office day after tomorrow."

"I'll tell her to look for the man who resembles Smokey the Bear," Rachel cut in, earning a burning glare from Darren.

Kelly leaned over and whispered in a conspiratorial voice to her secretary. "Tell me something, are you having an affair with Darren?"

Rachel snorted. "Please. For one thing, he's too young; for another, he has no manners."

"But you adore him anyway," she teased. "Let's get out of here while we still can."

Kelly drove home, once again grateful that she hadn't received any hysterical telephone calls concerning the boys. No matter what her reservations about Cole had been in the beginning, they were gone now. The boys were well-behaved, the house was always clean, meals were ready on time, and she was able to dispense with the pool service and the gardener at Cole's suggestion. There was only one minor problem. Why was she having so much trouble sleeping at night?

Kelly refused to believe that it just might be because there was one very good-looking, sexy male sleeping downstairs and it had been a long time since a man showered his desirability on her. Two small boys tended to frighten many men off.

"We're having lamb chops for dinner," Kevin announced, throwing his arms around his mother's knees. "And Cole made a pie!"

"The kind that goes from freezer to oven," Cole explained, appearing in the kitchen doorway. Did Kelly always have to look so good! Even after a long day's work she radiated a fresh vitality that ate at a man's insides.

"What's in the box?" Kyle ran up, pulling on Kelly's arm and almost causing her to drop her package. "Is it for us?"

"In a way," she replied cheerfully, carrying the box into the den.

"T-shirts!" The boys shouted in unison as their mother revealed the contents.

Kelly turned to Cole and gestured him over. She could feel her color rising as she hurriedly explained. "One of my clients is a T-shirt manufacturer and brought in some of his new styles. Since Rachel had mentioned you to him, he brought some for you also."

"Is this one of your perks, Mrs. Connors?" His lips quirked into a smile, holding up a pale blue shirt that read STUD FOR HIRE in dark blue letters.

By then Kelly's face was a fire-engine red. "Darren has a perverted sense of humor," she muttered.

"What's perverted?" Kyle's ears pricked up at the new word.

"Your father," she gritted under her breath, turning back to the box. "I'll take these upstairs."

"Dinner will be ready in about ten minutes," Cole called after her as she walked up the stairs.

Kelly changed into white shorts and the French T-shirt, as she liked to call it. Now barefoot and her hair brushed

70

loose about her shoulders, she looked considerably more relaxed.

Cole's lips twitched when he read the saying on Kelly's T-shirt. He rapidly turned away so that he wouldn't let on to his boss that he was fluent in French.

"Can Larry and Wayne come over to go swimming with us tomorrow?" Kevin piped up while they dug into warm apple pie à la mode after dinner.

"If Cole doesn't mind and if it's all right with their mothers," Kelly replied absently. She smiled at the faintly surprised look in Cole's eyes and accurately read his thoughts. "I would never expect you to have to put up with half the neighborhood. If a few of the kids coming here wouldn't bother you, that's fine with me, but it's purely up to you." She watched the boys carefully carry the plates to the counter, then return to the table before being excused. She told them to take their baths and get into their pajamas, after which they could watch television for a little while before going to bed.

Two hours later Kelly wandered outside and settled herself in a chair near the swimming pool. She breathed in the warm night air with obvious enjoyment.

"This should make it complete."

Kelly looked up to find a wineglass held out to her. She accepted Cole's offering and watched him settle into the chair next to hers.

"I can imagine this is the first quiet moment you've had all day," she observed with faint amusement.

"Not exactly; they both fell asleep for about an hour after lunch." Cole's dark eyes twinkled.

Kelly could feel a jolt in her stomach at the look in his eyes. If she took too deep a breath, she would take in the citrus scent of Cole's aftershave, which didn't help her equilibrium at all.

For the past few weeks she and Cole hadn't spent very

71

much time alone. He usually retired to his room in the evenings, and weekends were his own unless Kelly had to work on a Saturday, and then he would stay with the boys. She wondered if it was all that safe to have him in the house. It wasn't her physical well-being she was worried about as much as her emotional!

"You really enjoy your job, don't you?" he observed, breaking the strangely silent tension surrounding them.

Kelly nodded. "It's sometimes frustrating, sometimes perplexing, occasionally mind-boggling, but never boring." She sipped the white wine, savoring the dry tart taste on her palate.

"Mind if I ask a personal question?"

"It depends on the question."

Cole rested the back of his head against the chair, his denim-clad legs thrust out in front of him, his bare feet crossed at the ankles. "Does your ex-husband live in the area?"

Kelly turned her head in his direction. "Dave lives in L.A. Yes, I guess you could say he lives in the area." The night had suddenly lost its magic.

He couldn't miss the bitterness in her voice. "Yet he never calls the boys. At least he hasn't since I've been here." He went on in a quiet voice, fully prepared for her to tell him it was none of his business.

Kelly took a deep swallow of her wine. "I'm going to tell you only because I'm sure it's something you'll learn sooner or later and I prefer you find out from me," she said slowly and distinctly. "Four years ago I came home to find Dave in bed with the baby-sitter. I put her clothes in the trash compactor and turned it on; then I threw him out of the house, gave the bed to the Salvation Army, and filed for divorce. In that order. He prefers girls, and I do mean girls, barely over the age of consent. At the rate he's going

I wouldn't be surprised if he picks up a social disease before the age of forty."

Cole's chuckle danced along her nerves. "You're a hard-hearted woman, Kelly Connors."

She grinned, an action that looked very much like her sons. "Damn right I am."

"You weren't even going to give the poor bastard a second chance, were you?" he asked lazily.

Her smile disappeared like the sun covered by clouds. "For all I knew, it hadn't been the first time, and I doubted it would have been the last," she said tartly.

"And Kevin and Kyle?" Cole prompted.

Kelly's lips twisted. "Dave hadn't minded boasting his virility with twin sons. He just hadn't realized that children are a long-term commitment. He'll call when I least expect it or show up on the doorstep, upsetting the boys and leaving me to gnash my teeth."

"I have an idea that if he shows up in the near future, *he'll* be the one to gnash his teeth," Cole pointed out.

"Why?"

"It sounds as if you had an overaged adolescent on your hands. He may not want you, but he still wouldn't appreciate knowing that you have a man living in your house."

Kelly laughed softly at Cole's observation. She thought of Dave's surprised face looking up at the very masculine Cole. Hmm. That would be a sight to behold! "Yes, that does sound like Dave," she admitted.

"What does he do?"

She laughed again. "He sells foreign and specialty cars. Goes along with the image, doesn't it?"

Cole joined in on the joke. He knew he had picked up useful information for his article tonight, yet he wasn't sure he wanted to use it. Underneath Kelly's cool sophisticated manner was a sensitive lady.

73

Kelly finished her wine and set her glass on the small glass-topped table next to her chair. She had forgotten what it was like to relax in a peaceful setting and have conversation with an adult male. It was very nice!

"What about you?" She decided it was only fair to turn the tables.

"What about me?"

"Any ex-wives lurking about?" Kelly wanted to know much more than what his references had told her.

"One." Why did his reply bother her so? After all, he certainly couldn't have lived all this time as a monk? "I married at eighteen and divorced at nineteen. She was in the habit of distorting the truth to suit her own means. Her first lie had been that she was pregnant." His matter-of-fact reply told Kelly there had been no love lost in that marriage.

For a moment she was very tempted to comfort him, then her inner-warning system popped into gear. She mustn't let herself get too dependent on Cole for company. She slowly pushed herself out of the chair and reached over to pick up the glass.

"Thank you for the wine," she said quietly. "It's getting late and I have an early day tomorrow. Good night." She headed for the sliding glass patio door.

"Kelly." She stopped at the rough whisper of his voice. "You can't always run away. One day you're going to be forced to face your feelings whether you want to or not."

There was no reply. Only the soft *whoosh* of the patio door opening and sliding shut.

Cole finished his own wine and looked up at the sky. He wondered if his advice was meant more for Kelly or for himself. More than likely, it was for the both of them.

It might as well have been Friday the thirteenth instead of Thursday the fifth.

Kelly had overslept that morning and had to skip breakfast. As it was, she barely made it to work in time for the weekly board meeting with Mr. Baxter.

When she arrived at the conference room the tall, pompous man flashed a look of disapproval toward her aqua minidress.

He'd probably still have us wearing hoop skirts and millions of petticoats, she thought angrily to herself, taking her seat at the oblong table.

These weekly meetings were a means by which each of the executives could update his or her associates of the accounts being handled as well as a general help session. Sheldon Baxter wanted his staff to feel free to seek advice from one another. At Creative Concepts there was no grabbing for choice accounts or the back-stabbing so prevalent in other agencies. Mr. Baxter just wouldn't allow it.

A little over an hour later Kelly escaped gratefully to her office.

"Creative Concepts is an old and established firm, Mrs. Connors," Mr. Baxter had told her in his dry voice. His eyes flicked over her minidress again with distaste. "I'm sure you will project the proper image, so our clients won't think we're an agency run by punk rockers."

"I'm surprised he even knew what punk meant," Kelly told Rachel as they reviewed that day's calendar and she told her about the meeting.

"It must have been his stint in Korea that scrambled his brains." Rachel smiled. "When Sheldon joined the army he turned into your typical wolf in a corporal's clothing."

"*Him*, a wolf?" Kelly hooted. "Tell me another fairy tale."

"You got it. I had quite a number of fawning friends

75

because of having a brother in uniform. He took great advantage of it too," the secretary continued.

Kelly sat back and tried to picture a much younger Sheldon Baxter chasing after some poor, unsuspecting woman. The picture just wouldn't click. She shook her head in disbelief.

If she had hoped the day would improve, she was wrong. Files needed for a meeting with an important client were misplaced. One of the models called Kelly, screaming that the photographer was a pervert and she ended up calming the hysterical male model and soothing the photographer's ruffled feathers.

"May I go home now?" Kelly moaned after receiving a call from Darren. It seemed that Tallie had shown up for her interview with him just a little too wound up, if dilated pupils were an indication. He wanted Marla, or else.

"Are you kidding? The fun's just beginning." Rachel shrugged, entering the office. "The telephone man is here."

"What telephone man?" she shrieked.

"The one who is putting in the new phone system," she explained patiently.

"He isn't supposed to be here today," Kelly argued. "He's supposed to come on Thursday."

Rachel shot her a droll look. "Last I looked, the calendar read that today was Thursday."

Kelly closed her eyes and took a deep breath. "Where's the aspirin?"

Rachel held out her hand with two white tablets nestled in her palm. Kelly took them and rapidly swallowed the pills. "How long will it take him?" she asked wearily.

"Most of the afternoon. From the looks of him, it could take all of tomorrow too."

Kelly groaned, holding her head in her hands. "Is there an empty office available?"

Rachel shook her head. "I already checked."

Kelly snatched up her satchel. "I don't care what Old Stoneface says, I'm going home to finish my work. If anything comes up, I can be reached there. If Darren calls again, tell him I've taken the next plane to Siberia."

"Knowing him, he'll only call you there," Rachel called after her departing figure.

Kelly's headache began to subside during the drive home. Even the noise of the boys wouldn't be half as bad as an installer constantly forcing her to move while he put in the new telephone system, a system that was supposed to save money for the company.

She changed her mind the moment she slowed and stopped the car. Even in the driveway she could hear the shrieking sounds of children from the backyard. Gritting her teeth, she pushed the button for the automatic garage door opener. For once the large door didn't lift.

"Damn!" she ground out, continually punching the button without results. Finally giving up, she turned off the ignition and stepped out of the car. After giving the stubborn door a punishing kick and calling it unladylike names, she walked toward the front door. "I wonder if the boys would consider a nap, beginning right now!"

Kelly set her satchel on the hall table and walked out toward the patio door. She hadn't expected to find about ten children of assorted ages jumping into the water and several women in various sizes of bathing suits lounging around the pool. To be more precise, they were lounging around Cole! Seeing him in the dark gold narrow swim briefs he wore reminded her of the night she had fired him and had walked into his bedroom and found him almost naked.

77

Kelly muttered another unladylike word under her breath. She pushed open the screen door and stepped outside.

"Mom!" Kyle spied his mother and ran over.

"Hello, sweetie," she laughed, accepting his damp kiss and hugging him back, unmindful of his leaving wet spots on her dress.

Cole looked up and watched the scene with hooded eyes. Somehow he had expected Kelly to reprimand Kyle for getting her wet, but she hadn't said a word. She only returned his love with her own. He felt a wrench in his midsection, wondering how it would feel just to get a bit of that warm affection.

"Kelly!" Irene, Kelly's next-door neighbor, uncoiled her lithe figure from a lounge chair. "You're such a naughty creature for keeping this delightful man to yourself," she chided, reaching up to pat her carefully styled chignon. The crocheted bikini she wore was obviously not meant for swimming.

"Well, you know me. I tend to keep to myself," she replied, although her sarcasm was lost on the woman.

Cole ducked his head to hide his smile. He hadn't missed the bite in Kelly's voice. His delightful boss was not too happy! Of course, when he agreed that Kevin and Kyle could invite some of their friends over for a swim, he hadn't known that their mothers would come along as well! Not seeing any way of getting out of it, he ended up staying outside and acting friendly to the more than curious women. He wasn't surprised by the revealing swimsuits a majority of them wore and the arch questions they threw at him, but so far he had been able to keep them at bay. He remembered an article he had done on housewife hookers about a year ago. Some of the women present today would have been prime candidates for the position!

"You're home early, Mrs. Connors," he remarked, rising lazily from his chair.

"I didn't realize that I had to keep to a timetable," she retorted. "My office is out of commission for the balance of the day and since I have some important paperwork to finish, I thought I'd come here to work." Damn! Here she had to go and explain!

Jenny looked up with a gleam of understanding in her eyes. She had an idea that there could be something going on between the two of them, but they were not willing to realize it.

"I think Becky and I'll get going." She called over to her daughter, who was playing in the shallow end of the pool. "Thank you so much for the hospitality, Cole." She smiled at Cole as she dried off Becky with a beach towel that sported a huge picture of Mickey Mouse on the front. "If you ever want some quiet time, please feel free to send the boys over." Jenny flashed a look filled with meaning toward Kelly. Luckily most of them took the hint. They had only wandered over out of curiosity, and that had now been satisfied.

One by one the women left, although Irene made sure to be the last.

"It was very nice meeting you, Cole," she purred. "If you ever want some quiet time, feel free to send yourself over." She shot a fuming Kelly an arch smile and left.

"I hope you're satisfied." Cole turned to Kelly.

"*Me? You're* the one with the harem draped around the pool," she gritted, thrusting her jaw out. "I have an important project to finish and I came home hoping to find peace and quiet. I didn't realize that I would find an orgy instead!"

"What's an orgy?" Kevin spoke up.

Kelly turned to him. "Why don't you and Kyle go up

79

to your rooms, put on dry clothes, and go over to Jenny's to play," she suggested.

"Mom." There was pleading in Kevin's voice as he looked up. "You're not going to spank Cole, are you?"

Kelly took several deep breaths. She looked up to encounter the humor lurking in the midnight blue depths of Cole's eyes and it didn't help her temper any.

"That could prove interesting," he murmured suggestively.

"Go!" Kelly ordered her sons, looking down at them with angry eyes.

The boys scurried into the house, surprised that she hadn't told them to dry off thoroughly first.

"Did you get any lunch?"

Cole's unexpected question threw Kelly off balance.

"No, and I don't think I care for any," she snapped, spinning around to march into the house. She grabbed her satchel and headed for the stairs.

"Wait a minute." Cole followed her but wasn't able to catch up with her until she stopped in front of her room. "Why are you so angry?"

"I—am—not—angry." Kelly bit out each word with great precision.

Cole found himself reaching out to run his fingertips lightly along her arm under the short bell sleeve. "Your eyes are sparkling like rare gemstones, and your color is a little higher than usual," he informed her in a low, caressing voice. "Not to mention that your respiration is probably going a mile a minute." His eyes flickered over her heaving breasts.

"Don't." Her quiet order was easily ignored.

"Don't what?" He raised his eyes now, fastening them on the entrancing shape of her lips.

"Look at me like that," Kelly whispered roughly, jerking away from his touch.

"How am I looking at you, Kelly?" His words drifted over her softly.

"As if you knew what I look like without any clothes on."

Cole smiled. "Well, I do know what you wear under that dress, which is designed to show off your very shapely legs. Legs that I wouldn't mind having wrapped around my hips."

Kelly gasped at his word picture, only because it was too easy to see in her mind. She opened her mouth to deliver a scathing lecture, but the boys leaving their room and mumbling their good-byes halted her heated words. She waited until she heard the sound of the front door closing.

"You going to fire me again?" Cole baited her.

"Do you see any reason why I shouldn't?" she rasped, opening and closing her fists at her sides.

"One." As before, there was no warning as he pulled her into his arms. Kelly lifted one arm as if to hit him, but Cole easily twisted it behind her back with one gentle hand. The other grasped her jaw and kept it immobile as his lips feathered over her face, making sure not to touch her lips.

"Damn you," she breathed roughly, only aware of the warm half nude body against hers and the faint chlorine scent of his skin.

"No, damn *you*," he muttered, drawing circles around her ear with his tongue and laughing when she shivered under the caress. "Damn you for your delectable body and big brown eyes and hair the color of fresh honey. For the perfume you wear that I can still smell when I go to bed and the smile you give the boys. Damn you for being the most desirable woman I've seen in years," he groaned, now capturing her mouth in a soul-searing kiss that jolted

81

Kelly down to her toes and back up to the center of her being.

Kelly's mouth parted automatically to Cole's thrusting tongue, allowing him to explore every crevice of its dark warmth. There was no thought of rejection when his hand released her arm and slid around to cup her breast and run his thumb over the peaking nipple. She linked her arms around his neck and pressed her body closer to his, feeling the swell of his arousal nestling against her middle.

"Oh, Kelly, so sweet," Cole murmured huskily, now cupping her buttocks to draw her up against him even closer. "Yes, move against me. Let me feel your hips against mine. Your breasts are so soft. Is the hard tip as honey sweet as the rest of you? I bet your skin feels like velvet. Your tongue is just slightly rough and exciting."

Kelly could feel her body melting under Cole's love talk. Her hips mimicked the thrusting motions of his and her fingers combed through the silk of his hair.

"I bet it's the first time you've had the urge to make love with your housekeeper," he chuckled in her ear.

His words proved to be the much-needed cold shower. Kelly jerked out of Cole's embrace and stepped back a few paces. Now her anger was taking over. She couldn't speak one word without giving away her feelings. Instead, she whirled around and entered her room. She slammed her door with an alarming finality.

Cole smiled at the explosive behavior. This was one time when actions definitely spoke louder than words!

CHAPTER FIVE

Kelly could feel another headache coming on as the next day passed slowly. She couldn't blame herself for her moodiness. She had remained in her room until dinnertime, knowing the boys would be back by then. She had no compunctions about using them for a shield and Cole knew it.

The dark lights in his eyes, the curve of his lips, even the husky sound of his voice, told her he knew what was racing through her mind. She was more than vitally aware of him and wanted to fight it, but couldn't.

Saturday afternoon Kelly enjoyed a lazy hour lying in the sun while Cole had the boys by the side of the pool, intent on teaching them how to dive.

"You have to keep your arms straight out in front of you," he instructed them, demonstrating the motion while his eyes kept drifting in Kelly's direction.

She reminded him of a sleek golden cat in narrow strips of black cloth as a concession to civilization. He knew that participation in a dancersize class three times a week kept her body in more than good shape. He cursed silently at the tightening of his midsection and abruptly dove into the water, deciding his best bet was a quick cooling off!

Kelly stretched drowsily and turned over onto her stomach. She sleepily wondered why Cole chose to spend today at the house. Most Saturdays he took off and on a couple weekends he didn't return until Sunday. She figured he probably had a ladyfriend or two or three stashed away somewhere even if he had never mentioned anyone special. She could just make out the sound of the doorbell pealing through the house.

"Doorbell," she mumbled, barely raising her head.

"It's my day off, remember?" Cole teased.

"Sadist," Kelly grumbled, raising herself up unaware of Cole's appreciative gaze on her black bikini and the flesh it left uncovered. Her hair had been swept up into a tousled topknot in deference to the hot day. "All right, all right," she muttered crossly as the doorbell sounded two more times in rapid succession.

Kelly was filled with further displeasure when she opened the front door to find her ex-husband standing on the doorstep and a young woman with long dark hair and wearing brief white shorts and a red tube top standing behind him.

"What do you want?" Kelly demanded ungraciously, interrupting Dave's hungry gaze over her bare curves.

His lips twisted in a mocking smile, ruining his good-looking features. "To see my sons, of course." He shrugged, stepping inside. "Oh, this is Ellie," he said carelessly.

"Hi," the young woman offered shyly. She couldn't have been more than eighteen to Dave's thirty-four.

Alfie appeared at the door belatedly. Kelly supposed that the dog had been upstairs sleeping on one of the boys' beds. Seeing what he considered a stranger, the normally docile sheepdog lowered his head and emitted a low warning growl. Kelly almost burst out laughing. Funny how even dogs didn't like Dave! Why couldn't she have known better seven years ago?

"Where's the boys?" Dave turned to Kelly, ignoring the dog standing protectively at her side.

"Swimming." For a moment she hesitated. Cole was out there also. In those dark gold briefs that almost matched his skin and that left very little to the imagination, he created quite an impressive comparison to the small-boned Dave. Why should she worry if he got the wrong impression? After all, Dave was the one who had been actively bedhopping these past three years.

"Come on, Ellie." He walked toward the back of the house.

Kelly hurried after them. She wanted to be there to see it all!

"Hi, boys!" Dave's hearty greeting was cut off as he stooped and stared at the man standing beside them. He spun around and faced Kelly. "Who the hell is that?" he demanded.

"Your dad?" Cole asked Kyle under his breath.

"Yeah." The small boy sidled closer to Cole and reached up for his hand. Kevin did likewise on the other side.

"Cole, this is my ex-husband, David Connors and his-ah-friend, Ellie." Kelly's introduction was worthy of royalty. "Cole Bishop, my housekeeper." She couldn't resist her smile of triumph as she dropped the verbal bomb.

Ellie's eyes swung over Cole's impressive figure. "Wow!" she breathed, earning a dark glare from Dave.

"Sure," he sneered, unaware of Cole approaching them. "Tell me something, where does the household help sleep? Upstairs with the mistress?"

"I should think you would know Mrs. Connors better

85

than that." Cole's voice was all cold steel. "I respect her as my employer and as a lady."

Dave turned back to Kelly. "You really don't expect me to believe *that*, do you?"

Kelly's eyes flashed with icy meaning over Ellie, then back to Dave. "I don't care what you think, Dave," she said in a low voice, not wanting to alarm the boys any more than necessary. "You're not one to preach and, to be quite honest, what I do in my own house is none of your business."

His face flushed with anger. "It's my business who *my* boys are involved with. For all you know, the guy could be gay," he sneered.

Kelly almost emphatically denied that statement but prudently kept quiet.

"Now I can see why Mrs. Connors threw you out," Cole spoke up. Inside, he was a volcano of seething rage. It was only for Kelly's sake that he didn't throttle Dave Connors right where he stood. "She's a lady with a lot of class, while you, well"—he hesitated—"there're children present, so I won't go into an accurate description."

By now Dave's face was purple. Nevertheless, he was smart enough to know that in a physical battle, Cole would definitely be the winner. Instead, he focused his anger on Kelly.

"I want to take the boys for two weeks," he bit out.

Kelly's throat closed. "Why? You've never bothered with them before," she challenged.

"They were too young before," Dave argued. "You can't stop me, Kelly. The court order reads that I get them two weeks each year," he concluded smugly.

"And what do you intend to do with them for two weeks?"

"I'm driving up north to see my father and Inez and

they want to see the boys," he explained, choosing not to face her directly.

Now she understood. Dave really didn't want the boys. His parents wanted to see Kevin and Kyle, and Dave had probably counted on getting a loan from his father, who doted on his only grandsons and would do anything for them. A bitter taste rose in her throat.

"When do you want them?" Her low voice didn't reveal any emotion.

"*Mom!*" Kyle cried out at her words.

"I don't want to go with him!" Kevin put in his own opinion.

Dave's eyes narrowed. "It seems that you've done a good job of turning my kids against me."

"I didn't have to. You did that all by yourself," Kelly said woodenly.

Cole frowned darkly during this interchange. He still had a strong urge to tear Dave Connors apart with his bare hands. No wonder Kelly threw the man out. He also didn't like the way Connors's pubescent girlfriend was looking him over so intently. Whatever happened to shy young girls? Now eighteen-year-olds had the experience to shock a forty-year-old woman. He ground his teeth in agitation.

"I'll show you to the door." Kelly's eyes bored into Dave's. By now she'd had more than enough. She knew he had the legal right to take the boys for two weeks each year. But that didn't mean she had to like it.

Having accomplished his goal, Dave walked back into the house with Ellie on his heels.

"I'll be by Monday morning at eight," he told Kelly as he walked out the front door.

"Fine," she replied tonelessly, resisting the urge to slam the door after his departing figure.

"Damn." Kelly's voice broke as she rested her forehead against the cool wood of the door.

She stiffened when a pair of hands settled on her bare shoulders, even though they only massaged the tense muscles until they relaxed. She didn't pull away when those same hands gently turned her around and drew her against a warm body.

"Go ahead and cry." His whisper urged her.

"He's such a bastard," she choked. "He's not even worth crying over."

"You're not crying about him. You're crying to ease the anger you're feeling inside," he told her.

"Don't be so nice!" Kelly moaned as her tears fell on Cole's bare skin and skimmed down his chest.

"Did Mom hurt somethin'?" Kevin asked, he and his brother now standing nearby.

"Something like that," Cole replied with a faint smile as Kelly's low wail hit his ears.

"Maybe Cole can kiss it better," Kevin suggested naively.

"Um, sounds good to me," Cole murmured, raising his hands to frame Kelly's tear-stained face. Her soft, appalled "no!" was breathed into his mouth as his lips caressed and teased hers. There was no aggression in this kiss, only a sweet, pervasive warmth that stole through each moist inner corner of her mouth and down through her body when his tongue outlined her lips.

"Do you feel better now, Mom?" Kyle's innocent question was more than effective in separating them.

Kelly stepped back, keeping her eyes trained on Cole's mouth, gleaming from the moisture of their kiss.

Cole studied the almost haunted expression in her eyes and cursed silently. He instinctively knew that the reason for her emotions wasn't fear of him, but fear of herself. The worst kind of fear there was.

Kelly cleared her throat before trying to force words past her lips. "Why don't you boys get dressed and we'll go to the movies and to McDonald's for dinner," she suggested just a shade too brightly.

"Cole too?" they asked in unison.

She looked up at the man in question. "If he wants to."

"Yes, I do."

Late that night Cole lay in bed, his hands linked behind his head as he looked up at the moonlit ceiling.

Admittedly, his idea of a good time wasn't sitting in a theater with almost one hundred children of varied ages to watch *Snow White* and *The Shaggy Dog*. Kelly had ensured remaining apart from him by maneuvering the two boys between them. She did the same when they went out for hamburgers after the movie by sitting on one side of the table with Kevin next to her. Of course, what she hadn't counted on was Cole sitting across from her and it was only too apparent that she had been shaken up more by that soft kiss than by the passionate one they had shared before.

His smile was touched with humor. It had been many years since a woman had fascinated him as much as Kelly Connors had. Hell, come to think of it, he couldn't remember a woman *ever* tugging at his brain the way she did. Or maybe it was his body that was reacting so strongly.

Cole thought back to the kiss that afternoon. He had purposely kept it light and gentle, knowing that was what Kelly had needed at the time. But the time before, well, that was an entirely different story. He grimaced, feeling that familiar quickening in his lower body. Even thinking about her brought on an erotic ache. Maybe he should fly up to San Francisco in the morning and give Carolyn a call. If anyone could take his mind off a blond-haired witch, the statuesque brunette could! He only hoped that Kelly would have as miserable a night as he. Little did he know that she would sleep peacefully all night.

Cole was gone the next morning when Kelly arose. She knew what lay before her wasn't going to be the easiest of tasks. While they loved their grandparents dearly, their father was a virtual stranger to them. Josh and Inez, Dave's stepmother, drove down from Carmel twice a year to see the boys and spend time with them so they wouldn't be strangers. Josh had never shown any hostility toward Kelly for divorcing Dave, only a sadness toward his son for making such a shambles of his marriage.

"Why do we have to go with him?" Kyle cried out after Kelly had sat them down and told them about their trip. She had purposely worked hard to make it sound like an adventure, except that they weren't buying her story.

"Because he's your father," she explained quietly.

"If he's our dad, he would come to see us more. He doesn't like us," Kevin announced flatly.

Kelly took a deep breath. There were times when children were too smart for their own good. "I don't want to hear either one of you say that again," she told them in a low but firm voice. "He is your father and that is that." She almost added that they should respect him as such but she couldn't bring herself to say it. As much as she hated giving the boys to Dave even for only two weeks, she was glad Josh and Inez would be there. They would give Kyle and Kevin the love and comfort they would need for the new situation. She gathered her sons in her arms and held them tightly. "Oh, I love you two so much," she whispered fiercely, closing her eyes to keep back the tears.

Monday morning, Kelly finished packing two duffel bags for Kyle and Kevin and made sure their clothes were

90

still clean after they had eaten breakfast. She had called Rachel the night before to let her know she'd be in late.

The morning meal was unnaturally quiet. For once Kyle and Kevin didn't finish their pancakes and Kelly didn't urge them to eat.

Dave showed up at eight thirty. Punctuality had never been one of his strong points.

"Well, kids, ready to go?" His jovial voice sounded false even to their young ears.

Kevin ran up to Cole and when the man hunkered down, the small boy threw his arms around his neck.

"I love you," Kevin whispered in his ear.

Cole felt a choking sensation. "You'll be fine, tiger," he reassured him.

Dave watched the scene with angry eyes.

"I want to hear from the boys every night, Dave," Kelly hissed, her narrowed eyes backing up her words. "I don't give a damn if they call me collect, I want to hear from them."

He glanced over to Cole with cold insolence. "Aren't you afraid I might interrupt something?"

Kelly turned to the two boys. "Kevin, Kyle, did you remember to go outside and say good-bye to Alfie?" she asked brightly. She watched them leave the room and as soon as they were gone she turned back to Dave. Her hand connected with his cheek with a resounding snap. She didn't want the boys to witness this scene and had gotten them out of the room. She simply wasn't going to put up with Dave's nasty insinuations. For a moment he started toward her as if in retaliation but a look at Cole's threatening features changed his mind.

"Mom." Kyle ran up to Kelly a few moments later. "Don't worry, we'll be good." He flashed her a reassuring smile.

Their good-byes were a little tearful, but Kelly knew

Kevin and Kyle would be on their best behavior and they loved their grandparents. Dave couldn't resist one last sneer as he left, but Kelly merely ignored him.

Not wanting to see the pity she knew she would find in Cole's eyes, Kelly muttered that she was late for work and fled the house.

"It was that bad?" Rachel asked, setting a cup of coffee in front of a despondent Kelly an hour later.

"We've never been apart before," she mourned.

"Hmm, two weeks alone with a housekeeper who could put Robert Redford to shame . . ." the secretary mused, walking out of the office. "If it were me, I'd take my vacation time right now." The door closed after her.

"Cole!" Kelly groaned, buying her face in her hands. She had forgotten about him. She hadn't thought of what it meant when the boys left. Two weeks in the house alone with Cole. She had an idea she'd be better off sharing quarters with a jungle cat!

When Kelly entered the house that evening the smoky scent of a charcoal grill teased her nostrils.

"Hi." Cole ducked his head out of the kitchen. "Do you want some extra time before I put the steaks on?"

"Ah." She looked down at her khaki green walking shorts and matching striped oversize shirt. "No."

"Baked potatoes all right with you?" He turned back into the kitchen.

"As long as mine has lots of sour cream on it." Kelly looked around with a wry smile. "It's awfully quiet around here, isn't it?"

"Yeah," Cole mumbled, turning back to the green salad he had just finished preparing as Kelly arrived. He couldn't tell her that he had spent part of the afternoon at his typewriter trying to come up with a catchy lead for his story and ending up looking at blank paper instead.

92

This story wasn't turning out to be as easy to write as he thought it would. Strange, but he felt reluctant to share any of the experiences he had encountered in the Connors household so far. It would be like invading his own privacy. Something he had never worried about before with previous assignments, because the subject matter had never gotten to him any of those other times.

"You didn't have to go to all this trouble," Kelly murmured when Cole later seated her at the large glass-topped table on the patio complete with a small bouquet of flowers for the centerpiece. The steaks had been grilled perfectly, the baked potatoes filled to bursting with sour cream, and the salad tossed with her favorite dressing. A rich Burgundy was poured into the glass in front of her.

"I thought you might need some special pampering tonight," he said softly.

Her lips twisted sadly. "I look that obvious, do I?"

"It's understandable," Cole assured her.

"They've never been away from me before," Kelly explained. "This is something new for them and for me."

"What about their grandparents?" he asked her while cutting up his steak and trying a piece of the juicy pink meat.

"They come down a couple times a year to see the boys. In fact, Josh and Inez will probably spoil them rotten while they're up there," she laughed softly.

"What about your own parents?" Cole asked curiously.

"They live in Florida in one of those retirement communities geared for the avid golfer." Kelly tried a bite of salad. "My father participates in quite a few Pro-Am tournaments. Kevin, Kyle, and I flew out there last Christmas. My father was quite upset that neither boy showed an aptitude for golf."

"I know what you mean. My dad's love is tennis. If he

93

isn't on the courts by eight in the morning, it has to mean he's on his deathbed." Cole grinned.

Kelly sipped her wine and found it a perfect complement for the steak. "Do you play?" She then silently cursed herself for thinking of her question with a double meaning.

Luckily, Cole chose to ignore it. "I prefer running myself."

The conversation during dinner remained casual as each delicately probed to find out about the other. It was amazing how similar some of their tastes were.

Both enjoyed obscure foreign films that would sneak into town and later become the hit of the year, light rock music, and *any* antique store. Art shows were addicting, as were carnivals.

Cole told Kelly a few anecdotes from his travels, careful not to reveal his reasons for so much traveling.

Kelly leaned back in her chair and laughed and talked as she hadn't in a long time. She had almost forgotten what it was like to share a harmonious meal with a handsome man.

"Come on, I'll help you with the dishes," she offered, pushing back her chair and standing up.

"No, you won't, lady," he protested, beginning to pick up the plates.

"Look, since the boys aren't here, there's no reason for you to stay around for the next two weeks," she began hesitantly. "Consider it a vacation, with pay, of course," she concluded on a bright note.

What a temptation! Cole could go home, work on his article, and, perhaps, not even return. He could just make a clean break of it. After all, he probably had more than enough material for his story on house husbands. He'd never have to wash another dish or do laundry again! First

94

of all, he was going to give his cleaning lady one big raise when he got back!

"If it's all right with you, I'll just stick around here," he surprised himself by responding.

Kelly merely murmured "all right" and helped clear the table. The dishes were washed up and put away with a minimum of conversation.

"I have some reading to do for a prospective client, so I think I'll just go upstairs," she told Cole without really looking at him. When the phone rang she jumped and ran into the den.

"Hello? Kyle? Kevin? How are you, darlings? How is Grandma and Grandpa? Are you being good boys?" Cole could hear the excitement in her voice. "Where's your father? He what?" Now there was an angry tension in those soft tones. "You're going to the beach tomorrow? And a picnic too? You just be good boys. Now let me talk to Grandma or Grandpa. I love you too." There was that evident softening again. Was that how she would say those words to a man? All soft and breathless, as if from love-making?

"Hello, Inez, I hope they're not too much trouble for you. I can see that Dave's good intentions at playing father didn't last long. If he's going to be out partying all night, I can't see how he'll be able to take the boys to the beach tomorrow. It isn't right that he'll expect you to handle his obligations just because he'll probably have a hangover." Cole couldn't miss the bitter derision. "Oh, I know you'll take good care of Kevin and Kyle. That's the only reason I didn't fight him on taking them up there. Just don't let the boys run all over you. Uh-huh, I'm sure they'll be spoiled beyond repair when they get back here!" she laughed. "All right, I'll talk to you tomorrow. Good night."

95

"I gather the boys are all right." Cole stood in the den doorway as Kelly hung up the receiver.

Kelly spun around, a smile on her lips. "Considering they had pizza and chocolate cake for dinner and are staying up hours past their bedtime and going to the beach tomorrow, I'd say they're having the time of their lives," she replied.

"Since I'm not too good at baking chocolate cake, they better live it up while they can." He grinned.

Entranced, Kelly suddenly couldn't keep her eyes off Cole's mouth. This was proving all too dangerous. "Yes, well," she mumbled, turning away. "Good night." She hurried out of the room, aware that Cole watched her every step of the way.

Kelly prepared for bed as slowly as possible. She put her dirty clothes in the laundry hamper and slipped on a pale blue semi-sheer nightgown. Afterward, she cleansed and moisturized her face and brushed her teeth.

She pulled the silk comforter down to the end of the bed and folded it neatly. The pillows were propped up against the headboard and the sheet turned back carefully. Ten minutes later the bed looked as if an army had slept there.

Kelly flopped down on her stomach first, burying her face in the pillow. Then she turned onto her side. She tried lying on her back next, and when that didn't work she curled up onto her other side. The curse that left her lips indicated the depth of her frustration.

Kelly's insomnia problem was linked with the strong realization that she and Cole were alone in the house. His bedroom may be downstairs, but it was still only a short walk from her own room.

She knew only too well that Cole was physically attracted to her. And that if he thought about making love to her, she probably wouldn't put up too much of an argument.

This from the woman who nearly broke a very nice attorney's capped teeth because he got a little heavy-handed during a passionate kiss on their third date!

"So why doesn't he do something about it?" Kelly demanded of the ceiling. Unfortunately, an answer wasn't forthcoming.

Cole was wondering the very same thing as he lay in his own bed.

He kept reminding himself that Kelly was his boss, that she was part of his story, and that she was a lady to be respected. Not one to be tumbled into his bed the first chance he got. But these next two weeks certainly looked like a gift from heaven.

"Oh, God, how I want to respect her!" he moaned, punching his pillow with a strong fist. "All right, Bishop, listen up," he ordered himself. "During the next two weeks, you will think of Kelly Connors in the same context as your grandmother. That means no undressing her with your mind, no picturing her in those frilly bits of nothing she calls underwear, and no watching her mouth and remembering how it tasted." Now Cole's groan was even louder. Every muscle in his body was pulsing in reaction to the erotic turn his thoughts were taking.

"Just like my grandmother," he muttered stonily.

Five minutes later Cole was out of bed and headed for the bathroom for a much-needed cold shower.

"Why does Babcock Jewelers have to persist in remaining so ultraconservative?" Kelly grumbled, throwing her pencil on her desk. Wads of crumpled paper were scattered about on the plush carpet. She had been working on an idea all day and still hadn't come up with anything concrete.

"Because they've been around for almost a hundred

97

years and rumor has it that the chairman of the board doesn't enjoy working with ad agencies," Rachel pointed out, placing what was probably the twentieth cup of coffee on Kelly's desk.

"That's why I'm surprised that Michael Babcock is thinking of changing agencies," Kelly commented, remembering Sheldon Baxter's request for her to come to his office and giving her this new assignment. All he had told her was that the chairman of the board of Babcock Jewelers had called him that morning and was thinking of changing agencies when the contract with their current one was up. Michael Babcock had heard glowing praises about Creative Concepts and especially a Ms. Connors. He would be interested in seeing anything new the agency could come up with to boost their business. Kelly had been stunned to be given such a chance but she certainly wasn't going to throw it away, hence, the long hours at her desk the past few days and, so far, nothing she felt she could show the mysterious Mr. Babcock.

"Why don't you go on home?" the secretary suggested. "You're too tired to be creative tonight."

Kelly leaned back in her chair and stretched her arms over her head, yawning deeply. "What time is it?"

"Ten thirty."

Kelly groaned even louder. "I know why I'm still here. What's your excuse?"

"I'm proving how indispensable I am," Rachel quipped. "Is it working?"

Kelly's stomach rumbled, reminding her she hadn't had anything to eat since lunchtime. "It must be. Come on, I'll take you out to dinner. In fact, let's find some place wickedly expensive and put it on the expense account," she suggested on a mischievous note.

"I can go for that," the secretary agreed readily.

After a meal the two women enjoyed immensely, along

with a bottle of wine, Kelly didn't arrive home until almost one in the morning. Now pleasantly drowsy, she quietly let herself into the darkened house. She crept up the stairs but had barely made the second step when a growl from behind her brought a shriek to her lips.

"Where the hell have you been?"

Kelly spun around and groped for the light switch. "You—" She took several deep breaths to slow her racing heartbeat. "How could you sneak up on someone like that?" She took the offense position in this attack. "You scared me!"

"Scared *you!*" Cole rasped, standing at the foot of the stairs. He wore only a pair of jeans, his hands braced on his hips and his legs thrust apart in a threatening stance. "I know you said that you were going to be working late tonight, but when it got to be ten thirty, I got worried and called your office. When no one answered, I figured you were on your way home. I didn't realize it took two and a half hours to drive from Newport Beach to Laguna," he concluded sarcastically.

Ordinarily Kelly would have responded with a scathing retort, but with the wine she had drunk and the late hour, the humor of the situation struck her instead. When she burst out laughing Cole shot her a murderous look, not seeing the joke.

"You're drunk," he accused her.

Kelly promptly howled with fresh laughter, much to Cole's added displeasure. She sat down on the step before she lost her balance and fell.

"Mind letting me in on the joke?" he asked coldly.

"You . . . this." She waved her arms about. "You—you sound like the aggrieved housewife waiting up for her errant husband. All that's left is the line about the wonderful meal that's been ruined." She began laughing again.

Cole scowled, thinking about the pot roast he had

cooked, thanks to Betty Crocker, but said nothing. He had worried about Kelly, afraid that she met with an accident on her way home. Instead, she came home slightly tipsy and laughing, as if this were all some big joke!

"I suggest you go to bed," he growled. "My only wish is that you have a healthy hangover when you get up."

"Oh, I never get hangovers," she assured him brightly as she rose to her feet. "I guess it has something to do with my metabolism or whatever. Good night, Cole." She moved upstairs with an unconscious sway to her hips.

Fully refreshed the next morning, Kelly ate a large breakfast under a scowling Cole's eyes.

"I think there's something we should discuss before too much time elapses," he told her in a hesitant voice.

"Yes?" She looked up from her French toast.

Cole drew a deep breath, as if finding it difficult to speak. "We're going to be alone in this house for a while and I just want you to know that I'll act the perfect gentleman. I don't want you to worry that I'll get out of hand or make a pass at you," he said heavily, inwardly cursing himself for every word. "Your—ah—your virtue, or whatever you want to call it, will be perfectly safe."

Kelly couldn't stop her mouth from falling open in shock. Somehow this wasn't at all what she had imagined! Somewhere in the recesses of her mind she had seen this as the perfect opportunity to see if Cole was the kind of man she had only dreamed or read about. And now he was acting so proper that he may as well be back in the Victorian age!

"I—ah—I want to thank you for your assurance," she finally managed to reply. "Of course, I wasn't at all worried. After all, we are two adults and so entitled to do what we please." Talk about a heavy-handed hint!

Cole ignored Kelly's not so subtle remark. He didn't

want to, but he knew he'd better before everything got out of hand. "At least we have that taken care of," he muttered, turning away and standing up to walk over to the coffeepot. If Kelly hadn't been sitting there, he probably would have added a healthy measure of whiskey to the steaming coffee. That or drunk the liquor straight!

Kelly looked down at the remaining slice of French toast and decided she had had enough. "I better get going," she murmured, rising from her chair. "I don't know what time I'll be home." She hurried out of the kitchen and upstairs to retrieve her briefcase.

Kelly drove to work, preferring to concentrate on her new assignment instead of the turn of events at home. Cole couldn't mean it! He couldn't think that they could keep things platonic during these two weeks. If so, he either had to be gay or dead. And she knew for a fact he was neither. Shaking her head to rid her mind of Cole and to turn back to Babcock Jewelers, the birth of an idea came to her. Full of new brainstorms, she literally ran into her office and dumped her belongings on her desk.

"Get me Al Ramsey on the phone, please." She scribbled something rapidly on her legal-sized tablet.

"Does this mean lightning struck at some time?" Rachel asked, punching out the proper extension for the agency's art director. "Hi, Jean, is Al in? Thanks." She handed the receiver to Kelly.

"Kelly, sweetheart, what can I do for you?" The low voice rumbled in her ear.

"Can you let me have the loan of one of your artists for this morning?" she asked while still writing furiously on her pad.

"For Babcock Jewelers?"

"That's the one."

"Why don't I send up Lori Matthews to talk to you,"

101

he suggested. "She's fairly new to us and a damn fine artist. I know that she's free this morning."

"Fine, could you have her come up here at ten then. I'd appreciate it. Thanks."

Rachel looked over at the notes Kelly had made. "Um, looks good," she mused. "Do you want these typed up?"

Kelly nodded. "I'll give them to you as soon as I get them in some kind of order," she muttered, still writing.

Kelly spent several satisfying hours working with Lori. A bright, energetic redhead, she caught on to Kelly's ideas immediately.

"Are you going to rant and rave because I'm going to need these sketches by Friday?" Kelly asked as the other woman prepared to leave.

Lori smiled brightly. "No. Hopefully, my sketches will be liked so much by your new client that I'll be offered a raise!"

"If you have any other questions, just give me a call," Kelly urged, walking to the door with her.

Kelly spent the balance of the day and part of the evening working feverishly on her presentation.

The next evening was the same as she polished her work and proofread Rachel's typing. She only hoped it would go over well when Friday arrived and it was time to present her ideas to Mr. Babcock.

Friday morning Cole was in for a surprise when Kelly appeared downstairs in an Aztec-striped dress of rust, beige, black, and turquoise with a rust linen jacket cut on simple lines to best show the softly tied bow at her throat. Her hair had been skillfully twisted on top of her head with a few stray curls at her nape and her cheeks.

"Very fancy," he commented, setting a plate of sausage and eggs in front of her. "You're really going all out for this client, aren't you?"

Kelly sighed, barely nibbling on her food. "Rumor has

it that Michael Babcock is very opinionated regarding ad agencies. To be honest, I can't understand how he happened to call us specifically. He also keeps a fairly low profile personally, so it's difficult to find out too much about the man himself. I'm going by the current advertising standards he's used before and I can only hope that I can convince him that my ideas are much better." She sighed, finally pushing her plate away. "I can't eat any more."

"You'll do fine," he reassured her with a smile which she returned with a much weaker one.

At two o'clock sharp Rachel announced that Mr. Babcock was here to see Kelly.

"Give me two minutes to calm my nerves, then send him in," Kelly instructed.

"Right."

Kelly took those badly needed one hundred and twenty seconds to smooth her clothing, check her hair and lipstick, and quickly add a touch of perfume. She stood up, pasted a bright smile on her face, and walked to the door. She opened it, ready to greet her visitor, but the man who now stood before her took her by surprise.

"Mr. Babcock?" she asked faintly.

"Ms. Connors." The elderly Mr. Babcock that she had envisioned was actually in his early forties, just under six feet, with a sprinkling of silver in his dark auburn hair. He looked to be a man in excellent physical condition and he certainly wasn't too hard on the eyes!

At the same time Michael Babcock was doing a bit of his own appraising. It was obvious from the admiration lighting up his hazel eyes that he liked what he saw.

"Now I can understand why Darren Gates enjoys working with you so much," Michael murmured, taking her hand in his and holding it a bit longer than necessary.

That explains why she was asked for personally, she thought. "So you know Darren?" It was difficult to keep the surprise out of her voice. It was hard to imagine Michael Babcock in his conservative three-piece suit and Darren in faded jeans and tattered T-shirt as friends.

Michael laughed as he entered Kelly's office and took the chair she ushered him to. "Yes, I can imagine what you're thinking. Darren is the complete nonconformist while I'm strictly establishment. That's probably why we get along so well. When I spoke to him about changing advertising agencies, he suggested Creative Concepts and you." His eyes leisurely slid over her slim figure. "I'm certainly glad he did. I'm sure we'll get along just fine."

"You haven't seen my ideas yet," she reminded him lightly.

"I've seen Darren's sales reports," he informed her. "Those told me more than enough. I'm sure we can come to an amicable agreement, say over dinner this evening?"

He certainly doesn't waste any time, Kelly thought to herself with amusement. "Why don't we discuss a few of my ideas first," she suggested with a smile. "Would you care for some coffee?"

"Thank you, but no." He could see she was all business and now put on his own professional mask. "You're right, I should see your ideas and then we can move on to other things."

Kelly was only too sure what those other things were. He was a good-looking man and she was positive women considered him sexy, but frankly he didn't do all that much to her. Not with Cole lingering in her thoughts. She walked over to the easel set up at one end of her office and turned around to face Michael.

"I'm sure you realize that this is somewhat of a rough presentation since you had asked to see something on fairly short notice," she began.

"Darren said that you're always at your best when pushed for time," he replied.

"I can give results, yes, but quality for a man of your caliber takes a bit longer," Kelly replied gently. "Nevertheless, I believe I brought you that quality. Research has shown that although your jewelry price range is varied, your customers are basically in the upper income bracket. Middle income people don't bother to go into your stores because they feel they can't afford your jewelry. Therefore, we want to appeal to that broad market out there."

"Just as long as that broad market can pay my prices," he pointed out. "I don't want just anyone coming into my stores expecting to find bargain prices."

"You won't have that problem," Kelly replied confidently, setting a large color sketch on the easel.

A man and woman were depicted against a pale color wash background. Although the man was wearing a business suit, the woman was dressed in jeans and casual shirt with a toddler by her side. The woman was holding a gold chain up. Underneath was written, BABCOCK'S CELEBRATES YOUR ANNIVERSARY. Kelly went on from there to show one sketch of a woman gazing over a display of earrings placed on a black velvet cloth. EVEN ON A SECRETARY'S BUDGET was this caption. There were four more sketches. Occasionally Kelly would sneak a peek at Michael's face during her speech, but he revealed nothing of his thoughts. When she finished she turned to face him.

"I thought that these advertisements could be placed in woman's magazines, also the local magazines such as ORANGE COAST and ORANGE COUNTY ILLUSTRATED. Perhaps even advertise on local cable television."

Michael sat back, his fingers pressed together in the shape of a steeple.

"Ms. Connors, you are a lady with refined taste," he said quietly. "You've appealed to a new market without making us sound like a discount jeweler. I'd like to see some of these ideas expanded."

Kelly heaved a silent sigh of relief. She only wished she could sit down before her shaking knees gave way.

"Of course, any in particular?" she asked, keeping her features carefully masked to hide the excitement she felt inside.

"Yes, but I'd still like to discuss them over dinner," Michael persisted with a broad smile, feeling very sure of himself.

Kelly walked back to her desk and sat down. "I suppose Darren told you that I'm divorced?" She lowered her voice to a seductive purr.

"Yes, he did mention that. And that there was no steady man in your life," Michael continued smiling broadly.

"Did he also happen to mention that I have five-year-old twin sons?" That huskily spoken piece of information took the smile from Michael's face. He preferred his bachelor existence and from long experience he knew that single mothers were generally looking for husbands. That was one trap he had successfully eluded all these years and not even for a lovely and sexy lady like Kelly Connors was he going to fall into it.

"Tell me something, Kelly." His innate charm surfaced easily. "How do you feel about becoming fast friends instead?"

Kelly laughed. This was definitely a man she could like. "That sounds fine to me," she agreed.

"Then will you agree to have dinner with a friend this evening?" he pressed.

She shook her head. She had already decided that she wanted to celebrate her success with Cole that evening. He had said he was going to act the perfect gentleman around her. Nothing was said, however, that she had to act the perfect lady.

"Tomorrow evening?" Michael wasn't going to give up.

"All right." Kelly accepted. Who knows, perhaps if Cole saw her going out with another man, he'd get some ideas of his own. She certainly wasn't averse to helping Cole make up his mind about her and if Michael could help, so much the better!

Cole had spent the afternoon debating what to fix for dinner that evening. He wanted a special meal for Kelly if her presentation went well. If it hadn't, well, there was a bottle of wine chilling in the refrigerator, just in case.

All of Kelly's cookbooks lay open on the counter as he searched through each one until he found something that looked easy enough for him to make. He hoped.

CHAPTER SIX

"We're in the money! We're in the money!" A sexy contralto sounded when the front door opened and closed.

Cole came out of the den and watched a jubilant Kelly dance along the entryway in her stocking feet. Each hand held a bottle of champagne.

"Don't tell me. He didn't like your presentation," he predicted dryly.

"No-o-o," Kelly sang out happily. "He loved it! In fact, Mr. Babcock was so impressed that I wouldn't be surprised if Old Stoneface doesn't give me a raise. Rachel and I did a little celebrating afterward." She grinned.

"So I gathered." He took the bottles from her. "Dom Pérignon. You're definitely anticipating that raise, aren't you?"

"Only the best," Kelly declared airily. "Do I have time to change?" She held up her tan high-heeled sandals dangling by the straps on her wrist.

"Sure." Cole couldn't help but grin at Kelly's infectious excitement. "Tell you what, I'll even put candles on the table."

"Oh." Kelly turned back around as she remembered something. "I brought home a calorie-laden amaretto cheesecake. I'm afraid it's still in the car. My arms were pretty full." She finished her walk to the stairs.

"I'll get it," he offered, heading for the front door.

Humming to herself, Kelly entered her bedroom and tossed off her clothing. A soft-shoe dance took her into the bathroom, where she patted herself with Shalimar dusting powder, then sprayed on her favorite cologne. She changed into pale pink cotton pants and a matching loose-weave cotton sweater with a lacy pink camisole underneath that was just this side of decency. She applied a bright pink lip gloss, then returned downstairs.

Cole was setting a steaming casserole dish on the table as Kelly stepped out onto the patio.

"Whatever it is, it smells heavenly." She breathed appreciatively of the mouth-watering aroma.

"Lobster Newburg," Cole replied, turning around. For a moment he stood there with his mouth dropped open. "My God, are you wearing anything under that?"

"Of course." Kelly laughed, inwardly pleased that she had so quickly gotten his attention. Hmm, this may turn out easier than she thought! She nodded toward the bottle of champagne resting in a crystal ice bucket. "Did you bring out the corkscrew?"

"Yeah." He continued to stare at her.

Kelly felt faint tremors skimming along her body from Cole's intent gaze. "The champagne," she prompted softly.

"Oh! Sure." Cole turned back to the table and inserted the corkscrew. Then all that could be heard was a loud *pop!* and a fizzing sound of liquid being poured.

Kelly accepted the proffered glass. "To Michael Babcock and his lovely, large budget." She held her glass up high, then sipped the bubbling liquid. "Mmm, good." She closed her eyes.

Cole discovered that a tipsy Kelly was an entirely different person. He had received only a preview the night she had come home late. Now he was being treated to the entire show. She was laughing, witty, and a majority of her inhibitions had been erased by the alcohol. Little did he know that she was putting on an act to end all acts. The lady was planning on the ultimate seduction and he was her victim. Cole found that there were times when it was difficult to concentrate on anything but the gentle rise and fall of Kelly's breasts faintly visible under the sheer coverings. He found himself matching her glass for glass of champagne in order to dull the lustful feelings coursing through his veins.

"Oh, I forgot." He was surprised at how hard it was to form words. "Your ex-mother-in-law called earlier. They were taking the boys out this evening to some barbecue at a neighbor's. They'll call you tomorrow night."

Kelly nodded. "Cole, do you think I'm attractive?" She propped her chin onto her fist with her elbow on the tabletop.

Cole almost choked. "What?"

She was unperturbed. "After all, you're a very good-looking man, have gentlemanly qualities, which you proved by your speech not long ago, and I'm sure you're an excellent lover. Yet, you seem to think of me lately as someone's maiden aunt." At this Cole began coughing loudly. "Are you all right?" she asked with concern.

"Not really," he muttered, watching her pour more wine into his glass.

"I only wondered because Michael Babcock certainly found me attractive," Kelly continued in a conversational tone.

Cole didn't like hearing that piece of information, but

he wasn't about to lend his opinion of what he thought of Michael Babcock's comments about Kelly's looks. Especially not after that ridiculous speech he had made about proprieties. The only time in his life he was doing something decent and he hated himself for it!

He watched Kelly cut herself a large piece of cheesecake and eat it with undisguised relish. The lady was not only beautiful, but he'd swear she could drink any man under the table. A bottle of champagne and a carafe of wine was certainly proving that!

"Let's forget about washing the dishes tonight," Kelly suggested, jumping up from her chair. "I'll help you with them in the morning."

Cole followed more slowly, but the world still circled him at an alarming rate. He closed his eyes to stop the merry-go-round, but it didn't help.

"Oh, Cole!" Kelly rushed to his side. Had he been ready to fall? She slipped her arm around his waist and suddenly giggled. "You're drunk!"

"No, I'm not." No matter how hard he tried, the words still came out slurred.

"Poor Cole," Kelly clucked, assisting him into the house. "It must have been that second bottle of champagne," she mused.

What second bottle of champagne?

Kelly steered Cole toward his bedroom, not having too easy a time handling his big frame. Inside the room she pushed him gently onto the bed and quickly divested him of shoes, socks, jeans, and shirt. She laughed softly as she pulled the sheet free and draped it over his supine body. "What a temptation you are, Cole Bishop. If I were an unscrupulous woman, I would ravish your defenseless body." She dropped a light kiss onto his lips and circled the outline of his mouth with the tip of her tongue.

"I'm more than willing," Cole muttered just before he

111

passed out cold. His last memory was the scent of Kelly's perfume filling his nostrils.

"Augh!" Cole moaned, starting to roll over, then realized his body refused to follow his brain's dictates. He groaned as white-hot spears of pain shot through his eyes. He knew it; he was going to die.

"Good morning!" The bright chirpy voice was an ax slicing through his brain.

Cole carefully opened one eye. Kelly stood before him wearing a bright green bikini, her wet hair tied back in a ponytail. In other words, she looked disgustingly healthy.

"When is my funeral being held?" he groaned, wishing his body would just die in peace. He'd feel so much better then!

"You poor baby," Kelly sympathized as she walked over to the window and pulled the drapes shut. "I brought you something that should make you feel a lot better." She came back to the bed and began to sit on the side.

"Don't sit on the bed!" Cole's head shattered into tiny pieces from his shout vibrating inside of his head.

"Sorry." She squatted down and handed him a large glass of orange juice. "Here, drink this slowly."

Cole carefully took the glass and drank carefully. When he finished the glass he looked at her suspiciously. "That wasn't just orange juice," he accused.

"No, I added some champagne to it," she explained, then heard a fresh moan of pain from Cole. "It's an excellent combination. Hair of the dog and vitamin C."

"Or an easy way to kill a man," he grumbled, carefully laying his crystal-filled head back onto the pillow.

"I'll put a glass of water on the table here. You just go back to sleep," Kelly advised. "You'll feel better later on."

"Sure, but it would be much simpler if you would just

112

put me out of my misery first," were his last words as sleep claimed him again.

The next time Cole awoke he felt more like a member of the human race. He turned over onto his side and reached for the glass of water Kelly had thoughtfully left for him.

"How are you feeling now?" The soft-spoken question came from the doorway.

He drained the glass dry before answering.

"As if I'll live." He sat up, resting his back against the headboard while feasting his eyes on the lovely sight of Kelly, now dressed in cutoffs and a powder blue tank top. He always did like a woman wearing a tank top because a bra generally couldn't be worn under it. On a scale of one to ten, he'd give Kelly an eleven. He especially enjoyed the way the soft cotton hugged her full breasts and fully outlined the thrusting nipples. He shifted his position. This kind of thinking was very dangerous to the libido! And here he had sworn to himself that he wouldn't think of her in those terms. It was much easier said than done.

Kelly in turn allowed her eyes to skim over Cole's chest, tanned a dark teak from all his hours of swimming with Kevin and Kyle. He was the first man she had ever seen who could sport a day's growth of beard and still look sexy. She could feel the desire curling up into a heated knot in the pit of her stomach. Judging from the smile lurking in the back of his eyes, she had an idea that he was recalling her not so teasing statement about seducing him.

"I have to admit that I am feeling a bit warm," Cole told her tongue-in-cheek.

Kelly straightened up, her maternal instincts now in full force. Perhaps she had read the look in his eyes wrong. Either way, she certainly wasn't going to let this opportunity pass her by.

"There is a virus going around," she murmured, walking over to the side of the bed and leaning over to place her hand on his forehead.

If Cole was feeling warm, it wasn't because of any virus but because of the sight of Kelly's breasts so close to his chest. Her tank top had gaped open, giving him a clear view of the pearly globes, with their dusky-tipped nipples. The warm, feminine scent of her skin drifted around him —another part of the aphrodisiac known as Kelly. It was more than enough to send a man over the edge into insanity.

It hadn't taken Kelly long to realize that Cole's illness had nothing to do with a virus. She controlled her feelings of triumph but made sure to carefully check his throat for swollen glands and even pressed her fingertips against his wrist. It wasn't surprising to find his pulse racing.

"Your glands don't seem to be swollen," she commented, also fingering the sensitive area behind his ears.

Cole almost suggested that she check elsewhere if she was so bound and determined to find something swollen!

"I think I just need some more sleep," he muttered, pushing her hand away.

Kelly was taken aback by the vehemence in Cole's action. "All right," she replied softly, turning away so that he couldn't see the hurt in her eyes. "If you need anything, I'll be around." She quickly left the room.

Kelly stopped in the kitchen to pull a can of Coke from the refrigerator, then headed outside.

Alfie's pleading barks led her to the kennel.

"Okay, fella." She soothed the distraught dog as she lifted the gate latch and let him out. The sheepdog ran back and forth, barking excitedly at his freedom. "Isn't it funny that if you want out badly enough, you'll get this latch open on your own. Yet, if you think someone around here will do it for you, you'll wait for us."

114

Kelly walked over to the edge of the swimming pool, lowered herself to the concrete, and dropped her legs into the cool water.

"Damn him." The words were barely audible. Kelly leaned back and braced herself with her hands, arching her body up to the sun. She closed her eyes to block out the glare and allowed her mind to replay more interesting images. Such as how Cole looked this morning with a sheet covering him. A picture guaranteed to raise her blood pressure.

She didn't move when she heard the sound of the shower running. And she didn't move when she later heard the front door slam and the jeep's engine rumbling. Then all was quiet.

"He must have suddenly recovered from his hangover," Kelly told Alfie, who had settled down next to her. What had she done so wrong that Cole couldn't even stand being around her? "I guess he hasn't heard about my stubborn streak yet." She turned her head to look down at the dog. "Or that I'm a quick study when it comes to being a *femme fatale.*"

Alfie merely whoofed and nuzzled Kelly's side. She laughed and turned to bury her face into his fur.

"Oh, Alfie, I want him so much," she whispered fiercely, not finding it unusual to talk to a dog. "Crazy, isn't it? Lusting after my housekeeper. Talk about something that belongs in a soap opera," she laughed huskily. "I can hear it now. She's divorced, a mother, and wants to jump on her housekeeper's bones. Will she succeed or won't she? Stay tuned for the next segment. At this rate, she probably won't." Kelly reached for her can of Coke and drank deeply. "Why should I sit here and sulk while I could be busy preparing myself for an evening with a charming gentleman."

Her mind now made up to forget her troubles, Kelly

115

pulled herself up and walked into the house with Alfie hard on her heels.

Kelly spent the afternoon soaking in a bathtub filled with scented hot water and a mudpack slathered on her face. She manicured and polished her nails a pale frosted rose and gave her hair a deep conditioning treatment.

Several hours later she looked at her reflection in the full-length mirror in the bedroom and felt very pleased with the results. She had pulled her hair away from the sides and held it back with jeweled combs, leaving wispy curls at her temples. She had applied her makeup with a careful hand and the shimmery blue eyeshadow added bright lights to her eyes.

Kelly's deep-rose-colored silk dress had a halter neckline that hugged her breasts and left her back bare. The A-lined skirt just skimmed her hips and floated gracefully about her nylon-covered legs.

She knew her luxurious afternoon treatment had been worth it by the deep smile of approval Michael flashed her when he arrived.

"You look beautiful," he said sincerely, stepping inside the house.

"Thank you." Kelly returned his warm smile. "Would you care for a drink?"

Michael glanced down at his watch. "Our reservation is for eight thirty, so we'd have time for one. Scotch and soda if you have it."

Kelly nodded and walked into the den to the wet bar. She fixed Michael's drink, then poured a glass of wine for herself. Michael looked around the room.

"For having two small sons, the house is awfully quiet," he commented.

"They're at their grandparents'," she explained, handing him his glass. "Otherwise this place is far from silent."

116

Michael shook his head in disbelief. "Please don't take offense, but it's difficult to see you as the little mother."

"Then come around when the boys are tearing the house apart and I'm screaming out my lungs for them to be quiet and to pick up their toys," Kelly advised with a smile.

Michael winced at the suggestion. "I'll be frank, Kelly. You're a beautiful and sexy woman, but children and I just don't get along," he stated bluntly.

Kelly took no offense at his words. "Ah, so I'm a safe bet for an evening out with no demands on my part," she guessed.

He nodded. "There are times when I would like to escort a lovely lady, and through me you can make some very worthwhile contacts."

"Sounds fair," she agreed, setting her wineglass on the bar and walking over to the couch to pick up her purse. Her head snapped up when she heard the sound of a key in the lock. "Oh, no," she moaned under her breath.

Cole, looking a little worse for wear, walked into the den. His eyes frosted over when he saw that Kelly wasn't alone.

"I hope I'm not interrupting anything," he said coolly.

Michael looked a little surprised at the unexpected intrusion. "I doubt this is one of your sons." He glanced curiously at Kelly's red face.

"Uh, Cole Bishop, Michael Babcock," Kelly said hurriedly. "Mr. Babcock is a new client of mine."

"Really?" There was a wealth of meaning in Cole's sardonic voice. He turned to Michael. "I'm Mrs. Connors's housekeeper."

Kelly had to give Michael a lot of credit for acting as if a woman engaging a male housekeeper, and a good-looking one to boot, was an everyday occurrence.

"I'm sure it's much easier for Kelly in raising two boys

to have a man around the house," he replied tactfully, glancing down at his watch then up at Kelly. "We'll have to leave now in order to make it to the restaurant in time."

"Yes." She gratefully grabbed for the excuse. She shot deadly torpedoes in Cole's direction. "Have a good evening."

"I'll certainly try." Why couldn't he sound more convincing to her ears?

Kelly left the house knowing that Cole was probably watching her from the living room window. She allowed Michael to assist her into his silver Rolls and resisted the urge to glance toward the house.

She wasn't surprised that the restaurant Michael chose was French and very expensive. It went along with his custom-tailored clothing and handmade shoes.

"I do have to admit that I'm curious about your housekeeper." Michael waited until their wine had been poured before bringing the subject up. "Most of the ones I've seen are blessed with a blue rinse on their hair and wear support stockings along with orthopedic shoes."

Kelly smiled. "Yes, I suppose most housekeepers do fit that image, but when a person is desperate to find someone to keep house and watch his or her children, he or she will grab the first suitable person who comes along."

Michael frowned. "I only hope that man is safe around your boys. I don't mean to frighten you, but there are— well, child molesters around."

Kelly swallowed her laugh. "He's wonderful with the boys and I trust him implicitly."

Michael was astute enough not to pursue the subject further. Instead, he was the stimulating and charming dinner companion a woman would enjoy being with. Yet, he didn't hold her interest as easily as Cole always had.

Michael suggested dancing after dinner and Kelly accepted, knowing a full evening out was exactly what she needed.

The club was small and intimate, and Michael made no mention about moving on to somewhere more private.

When Kelly finally arrived back home, it was two thirty in the morning.

"I enjoyed our evening, Kelly," Michael said sincerely as he walked her to the front door.

"I did too." Impulsively she reached up and kissed him lightly on the lips.

"Lunch on Tuesday?"

Kelly shook her head. "But I'll see you Friday when the preliminary sketches are ready." She unlocked and pushed open her front door. "Good night, Michael."

Kelly locked the door after herself and walked along the dark hallway to the stairs. This time a light snapped on before Cole's voice could frighten her.

"Glad to see you could make it home," he announced sarcastically, appearing in the den doorway, a whiskey-filled glass in one hand. A drink that was probably not his first. "So, is your new client suitably impressed with your many talents?" he sneered. "After all, you're certainly looking like a woman on the prowl this evening."

Kelly spun around and faced Cole with rage mirrored on her face. "*Don't say it!*" she gritted. "You with your high and mighty statements about respecting me and how safe I'll be here with you. That I won't have to worry about you giving in to your baser instincts. Would you like to know what I think about our respective places? I think it's a pile of—" Cole sliced his hand across the air, halting her tirade.

"Kelly," he warned in a dark voice, straightening up. "Don't start saying things we'll both regret."

"You're the one who made the rules," Kelly continued to rant. "Fine, then *you* can be the one who lives by them.

119

Just remember *my* rules. This is *my* house and I'll do what I want here. If I decide to bring a man here and take him upstairs into my bedroom to do unspeakable things to his body, that's my business and no one else's." She blinked rapidly to forestall the tears that threatened to fall. There was so much more she wanted to say, but the words stuck in her throat. "Damn you," she whispered brokenly, then turned and ran up the stairs. A moment later her bedroom door slammed shut.

Cole muttered a curse and moved away. "Me and my honorable ideas," he berated himself before heading for the bar and pouring himself another drink.

Kelly slept late the next morning and woke up with a blinding headache. She groaned, stumbled out of bed and into the bathroom to fumble for the aspirin bottle. She had just returned to her bed when a soft knock sounded at her door and opened. Cole walked in carrying a tray.

"I heard you moving around and thought you might like some coffee," he said quietly, setting the tray on the bedside table.

"I'm not hung over."

Cole poured the coffee, added cream, and handed the cup to Kelly. "I didn't think you were," he commented. "This is just my way of apologizing. You were right. It isn't any of my business what you do here." He looked down at Kelly, a pensive expression on his face. Her hair was sleep-tousled, her features slightly flushed, and a nightgown strap was hanging precariously on one shoulder to reveal the curve of her breast. She had never looked more beautiful. He coughed to hide his agitation. "I'll be out the rest of the day and probably won't be back until late this evening. I already fed Alfie."

"All right." She ducked her head and concentrated on

the steaming cup she held in her hands. "Thank you for the coffee."

Cole nodded and quickly left the room.

Kelly put her coffee cup back on the tray and stared at the closed door. Her mind was now made up. She had never had the occasion to seduce a man before, but she knew she certainly had all the right equipment. Now was the time to put it to good use. She spent the afternoon going through her wardrobe, discarding her less flattering clothes and selecting the outfits that would help her in her goal. This was more than a battle of the sexes. This was an all-out war.

Cole was busy fixing breakfast on Monday morning. He had driven down to San Diego the day before and spent the hours aimlessly driving around the town. To say he had been mad as hell when Kelly had come home so late would have been an understatement. In truth, his stomach had been tied up in knots all that evening waiting for her to come home, afraid that she would bring that guy inside with her. Then everything including the kitchen sink would have hit the fan.

Cole knew that Kelly was a healthy woman with normal desires. He also knew that he didn't dare cater to them. Not if he wanted to keep his self-respect. There was that dirty word again—respect. His cape of honor was weighing heavily on his shoulders right about now.

"Good morning!"

Cole turned in the direction of the chirpy voice. "Ah—" he choked, his mouth hanging open.

Kelly sauntered into the kitchen wearing a lipstick-red silk and lace chemise and black fur-trimmed high-heeled slippers.

"I hope the coffee is ready," she sang out, walking over to the counter and checking the coffeemaker. There was no concern in her voice or in her manner regarding her state of undress.

"Aren't you afraid you'll catch a chill?" Cole snapped, turning back to the bacon cooking in the frying pan which badly needed his attention.

"In this weather?" Kelly laughed merrily, pulling a chair out from the table and seating herself with her legs crossed in Cole's range of vision. "The newscaster on the radio said that it's going to be at least ninety-five degrees." She took a sip of her coffee. "In fact, if the air-conditioning in the office is acting up as much as it had last week, I'll probably be home early."

Cole groaned inwardly. There was something going on in Kelly's devious mind and he had an idea it had something to do with him.

Kelly's bright chatter continued all through breakfast, much to Cole's discomfort. Every time she moved her body, he was positive the spaghetti-thin straps on her chemise would take a nose-dive.

"Oops!" She glanced over at the wall clock. "I guess I better run." She stood up and stretched her body until the already short slip rode even higher up her shapely thighs. Cole's eyes couldn't help but fasten on the entrancing view. With a slight wiggle to her hips, Kelly left the kitchen.

He could see that she wasn't going to make it any easier when she came downstairs fifteen minutes later. The dress she wore was little more than the chemise she wore underneath and of the same cheerful color. She wore her hair up in deference to the hot day predicted, and strappy high-heeled sandals completed her outfit.

Cole's last memory of her that morning was her cheerful wave of the hand and the scent of her perfume in the air after she left the house. He cleaned the kitchen in record time and decided to clean the swimming pool even though it had been cleaned only the day before.

Kelly took her lunch break at the nearby bookstore browsing through any book that contained how-to's on seducing a man. She figured every little bit of knowledge would help. She purchased the books that looked the most interesting and took them back to the office to do some studying.

"Always thoroughly research your product," she murmured to herself after giving Rachel orders that she wasn't to be disturbed for the next hour.

Kelly did leave her office around three, taking a briefcase filled with paperwork home with her. She decided to put Plan B of her attack into operation when she got home.

Cole had spent a strenuous morning between cleaning the pool, mowing the front and back lawns, and giving the boys' bedroom a thorough cleaning. Afterward he took a quick shower and decided to do the grocery shopping.

What he hadn't expected when he returned home was to find Kelly's car in the garage.

"That hadn't been a promise she'd be home early," he gritted, reaching for the grocery bags in the back of the jeep. "That had been a threat."

The house was silent when Cole entered. There wasn't even an answer to his hello.

"Where is she?" he muttered to himself, walking into the kitchen. His reply came in the shape of a feminine squeal from the backyard. An answer Cole didn't like.

Kelly was in the middle of the back lawn washing an unhappy Alfie. That wasn't so bad except that she was wearing only a string bikini bottom and a snug-fitting T-shirt. Her hair had been pulled up into a ponytail just behind her left ear. Her T-shirt was also a very wet scrap of material revealing the absence of a bra.

123

"She's trying to drive me insane." Cole turned away from the window to noisily put away the groceries.

"Cole?" Kelly suddenly appeared at the kitchen window and tapped on the glass. "I'm all wet thanks to wonder dog out here. Would you mind bringing me a Coke please?"

"Yes, I do mind!" Cole shouted. "What do you think I am, your maid?"

Kelly's smile danced on her lips. "Actually, I do believe that is your job description, isn't it?" she asked demurely.

The refrigerator door was flung open, then slammed shut in concert with Cole's explicit curses. He carried the frosty can out to the patio door and pulled the screen door open.

"Here's your Coke," he snarled, holding out the can.

"Thank you, Cole," Kelly said politely, accepting the can. She glanced down at the top of the can and held it out. "Would you mind opening it for me? I'm afraid I might break a nail."

He jerked the can out of her hand. "You washed the damn dog and you didn't seem to worry about breaking a nail," he yelled, flipping the tab up and back and thrusting the can back at her.

"Thank you." Kelly flashed him a cheeky grin and seemed to skip over to the pool area. "Why don't you change your clothes and come out for a swim? You'd feel so much better."

"Like hell I would," Cole muttered darkly, watching her set the can on a small table and walk over to the pool. Her arms went over her head and she executed a perfect dive into the water and when she surfaced, her T-shirt was plastered against her skin and the pale-colored material outlined her nipples in perfect relief. Right then Cole knew a cold shower would be advisable although not too helpful.

Kelly lazed in the pool for about an hour, keeping her ears tuned to any sound from the house. There was no indication that Cole was going to take her up on her invitation. All she heard was the sound of the shower running from his bathroom.

"I hope it doesn't help," she murmured to herself, diving under the water and swimming to one end of the pool.

Cole was silent during dinner, his mood bordering on sullen. And Kelly's white strapless terry-cloth playsuit wasn't meant to assist him in keeping his composure. Any minute he expected her top to fall down.

"I'll be busy with some paperwork for the rest of the evening," Kelly informed Cole as she took a second helping of the chicken noodle casserole he had prepared.

"Fine." He heaved a silent sigh of relief. Now he would be spared her company.

Except that he forgot that Kelly's desk was in the den. Oh, she was quiet, with only the occasional murmur to let him know she was there. But he didn't need any sound to remind him. He didn't even need to smell her perfume and the feminine scent of her skin to recognize her presence. All Cole needed was to ask every nerve in his body. They were screaming that she was seated nearby and they were demanding relief.

It would serve her right if I went over there, pulled her out of that damn chair, and took her on the carpet. He suddenly decided that the book he was reading wasn't all that interesting. He stood up abruptly. "Good night."

Kelly looked up. "It's only nine o'clock," she commented with false innocence.

"It's been a long day," was his disgruntled reply.

Kelly knew better, but was smart enough to know that this wasn't the time to dispute Cole's words. She merely murmured her good night and returned to her work.

Kelly was awakened in the early morning hours by the

125

soft sounds of water splashing outside. Since it wasn't unusual for Alfie to get out of his kennel and decide to take a swim, she got out of bed to investigate.

What she found instead of the sheepdog frolicking in the pool was a very male figure swimming laps. With no moon or lights to illuminate his body, he was only a pale blur in the water. When he turned over to float on his back, Kelly could see that Cole was naked. She gasped softly at his sheer masculine beauty. She stood to one side of the window and watched him until he got out of the pool and dried himself off. When she heard the patio door close and lock, she quietly made her way back to her bed. It was a long time before she fell back asleep.

Cole lay in bed, not even breathing hard from the many laps he had swum. He thought he had seen the curtains moving in Kelly's bedroom window. He hoped he was wrong. The thought of her lying awake upstairs was more than enough to get him to forget all his good resolutions. He turned over on his side and tried the age-old prescription of counting sheep to fall asleep. Hours later he could truthfully state that it didn't work.

CHAPTER SEVEN

The war raged on. This wasn't your everyday war with guns blazing, bombs falling, and the cavalry riding to the rescue. It also wasn't the kind of war that could be negotiated at conference tables.

This was was fought in an affluent suburb, with silk and lace the uniform of the day.

Kelly retired early one evening and returned downstairs an hour later to retrieve a book she had "forgotten." The fact that she was wearing only an ecru silk lace teddy wasn't lost on Cole. He watched her hunt for the book for almost ten minutes before she headed directly to the chair where she had previously left it. The words whispered under his breath weren't to be repeated.

Kelly had done away with her how-to books and decided to rely on instinct. After all, women had been working hard to snare their men for centuries. Why should she have any trouble? Of course, the victim might not have been as stubborn as Cole was proving to be.

"There's only one problem," she mused to herself one day. "Just what will I do with him once I catch him?" A smile suddenly appeared. Oh, she'd know what to do all right!

The fine art of seduction was still something new for Kelly. For all the years after her divorce she had never gone after a man or tried to initiate an affair the way she had with Cole. Before she had met him no man had ever interested her enough. *Affair* was never a word she considered part of her vocabulary. Until now. After all, what else could she have with Cole once she had the chance to break down his defenses? She certainly didn't want a man permanently in her life again. One was more than enough!

By choice Kelly had been a virgin when she had married Dave. In the beginning of their marriage they had indulged in marathon lovemaking. But as the years passed it had dwindled down to once-a-week sex. She had a pretty good idea that lovemaking with Cole wouldn't be "wham-bam, thank you, ma'am." It would be long and leisurely, and giving and taking. It would be the kind of lovemaking that she would remember all her life.

"Do you have a fantasy, Cole?" Kelly asked him over breakfast Wednesday morning. "You know, a sexual fantasy."

He choked on his toast. She'd been full of surprises lately. He drank his orange juice to dislodge the piece of toast stuck in his throat.

"Actually, I've always had dreams of seducing Princess Di in the throne room at Buckingham Palace," he said sarcastically. "The idea of making it with royalty has always turned me on."

Kelly frowned at him. "I'm being serious," she chided, shaking her finger at him. "I have a fantasy."

Cole didn't like this casually spoken announcement. "A sexual fantasy?" he dared to ask.

She leaned her elbow on the table and propped her chin

128

on her hand. Her eyes had turned dreamy and looked as if she were gazing toward far-off place.

"Do you know what my fantasy is?" Kelly's voice lowered to a seductive whisper. "I'm at a party. You know, the kind that's very exclusive and filled with all the right people. And then I look across the room and this man is watching me."

"Tall, dark, and handsome, I suppose," Cole broke in sardonically.

"Mmm," she breathed, still ensconced in her pretended world. "And there he is, just watching me for a while. Somehow I sense that he doesn't belong there. Who knows, perhaps he crashed the party for reasons of his own. After a while he approaches me and asks me to dance. He's witty, charming, and filled with sensuality. Next thing I know he has escorted me from the party and out to dinner, but we're not really hungry for food. We spend the rest of the night together. A night I could never forget although I had never learned more than his first name and that is all he knows about me."

Cole tensed during Kelly's husky narration. She wanted some stranger to pick her up and make love to her!

"Don't you consider that dangerous?" he demanded tautly, leaning forward. "If such a harebrained idea came to pass, you could end up with some pervert or a psychotic rapist."

Kelly's smile was maddening. She slowly rose to her feet and walked out of the kitchen. At the doorway she halted and turned her head. "Or you," she concluded softly.

Before Cole could blink or fumble for a reply, Kelly was gone.

It was getting more and more difficult for Cole to be around Kelly each day. Michael had shown up once to take Kelly to dinner and once to dinner and a play afterward. It took every ounce of self-control for Cole not to slam his fist into Michael Babcock's carefully groomed features.

What was going on between them? Cole wondered to himself. Kelly was never out till all hours of the night and Michael was rarely invited inside. When he was, it was never for longer than a half hour. Just barely long enough for a drink. From the solitude of his room Cole could hear the sound of the front door closing and the throaty purr of the Rolls when Michael left.

Cole had never felt jealousy regarding a woman before. Not even his ex-wife had generated that emotion when she had begun playing around during the last few months of their marriage. He just plain hadn't cared. There had been times when he had wondered if he would ever care so much about a woman that he'd consider breaking a man's face if one looked at his woman the wrong way. Right now, that time was growing all too close.

It was difficult to remain objective when Kelly insisted on walking around the house in next to nothing or when she spiced up the conversation with sexual innuendos. Cole could only take so many cold showers!

Kelly sat at her desk and idly drew pictures on the piece of paper in front of her.

"Yes?" she answered the intercom buzz.

"Mr. Babcock is on line three," Rachel told her.

"Thank you." Kelly punched the button. "I gather you received that promo kit I sent you," she greeted him gaily.

"And I wholeheartedly approve," he replied. "You've done a wonderful job, Kelly. Now I'd like to give you the recognition you deserve."

"Oh?" she teased. "Do I get a mink coat or a diamond necklace?"

"How about a party filled with some very influential businessmen?" Michael dangled the bait in front of her.

"I'm talking about what could be a great deal of prospective business for the agency and, most importantly, a group of powerful contacts for you."

Kelly knew she couldn't turn down an invitation like that. New contacts were something she could always use.

"When is the party to be?" she asked.

"This Friday. You're not going to turn me down, are you?" Michael asked her.

"I wouldn't miss it for anything," Kelly said sincerely, searching her mind for just the right dress to wear to the party. "What time shall I be ready?"

"I'll pick you up at seven," he informed her, "if that's all right with you."

"Fine, I'll see you at seven then."

"How about lunch tomorrow?" Michael asked.

"I can't." Kelly glanced quickly at her calendar. "I'm afraid you'll have to wait until Friday evening," she teased.

"Then I'll just have to force tomorrow to go faster, won't I." He chuckled. "I'll see you Friday then, love. Take care." With that he rang off.

Kelly hung up, then picked the receiver up again. Cole answered on the third ring.

"I'd like to ask a favor of you," she explained softly. "I'll be attending an important party Friday evening with Mr. Babcock. Would you mind getting my black silk dress out of the guest room closet and taking it to the cleaners if you're going out today?"

"Sure," Cole rasped into the receiver. He didn't sound too pleased about her request.

"Thank you," Kelly said pertly. "Oh, I'll be home at my usual time," she informed him before she hung up.

"Wonderful," he muttered under his breath, hanging up the telephone. "Just the news I've been waiting for all day." He turned and headed for the stairs. He hadn't

131

planned on going out today, but he knew if he didn't leave at that moment to take care of Kelly's dress, he probably wouldn't at all.

Kelly picked up some correspondence she had drafted and took it out to Rachel. Her eyes widened when she found her secretary reading a thick paperback book with a brightly colored cover.

"What are you reading?" Kelly demanded.

Rachel held up her hand for silence although her eyes never left the page. "Let me finish this page first," she asked quietly. A moment later she stuck a piece of paper in the book to hold her place.

"I really hate to tell you this, Rachel, but we don't leave the office until five. Was the book so good that you were afraid the world would know the plot before you had a chance to finish it?"

Rachel shrugged. "This is guaranteed to be the hottest book of the year. I just want to see what they consider hot."

Kelly picked up the book. *"Flames of the Heart,"* she read aloud, then studied the cover in greater detail. Nothing was missed; the torn bodice showing just enough breast, the masculine body held tightly against the more pliable feminine form. She thumbed through the pages, then stopped at one particular scene. Her golden-tanned skin flushed a bright red at the vividly explicit writing. "Wow," she whispered under her breath. She hurriedly set the book down as if afraid the hot words would scorch her fingertips. "I—I think I'll go to lunch now," Kelly murmured, turning around and walking back into her office. "I have some purchases to make."

Cole was relieved to see Kelly more decently covered that evening, although her pale peach cotton floor-length caftan didn't really hide all that much. It just accented all the right places and gave the impression that she wasn't wearing any underwear.

After dinner, with a book held in one hand, Kelly settled herself in an easy chair in the den while Cole came in and turned on the television.

Kelly remained engrossed in her book for about an hour. She looked up with a warm smile.

"You just have to hear this," she invited softly. "I've never read anything so beautiful in my life."

Cole turned away from the baseball game he had been watching. "It doesn't really matter if I want to hear it or not. I'm sure you'll still read it to me," he grumbled good-naturedly.

Kelly dislodged her finger from the place in the book she had earlier decided to read from. She had already read the passage to herself and in remembering the words, her voice grew huskier.

Adam picked Lorna up in his arms and carried her into their bedchamber. He quickly dispensed with her dress and laid her on the bed before pulling off her undergarments. In no time she was blissfully naked, lying there with her pale skin luminous against the dark green silk of the comforter. "You are truly beautiful, my love," he murmured in that deep voice that sent shivers along her spine. He lightly touched one ripe breast and moved up to encircle the taut pink nipple with his thumb and forefinger. Lorna groaned at the tightening sensations coursing through her body from the intimate touch.

Cole shifted uneasily in his chair. He was right. He didn't want to hear this, but he knew Kelly wasn't going to stop now.

"Tonight, you will be mine," Adam vowed with all his heart. He gazed down at her lush, nude body his eyes burning with a dark lust. His heated lips touched one full breast with reverence, his tongue curling about the tight nipple. Lorna gasped at a man's lips touching her body where no man had ventured before.

Kelly silently gulped. This may not be as easy as she thought it would be. Cole cursed under his breath, vainly trying to concentrate on his television program.

Adam stepped back and hurriedly stripped off his own clothing. He stood over the silent Lorna, allowing her to stare at his naked form. She looked at him with natural curiosity, unable to tear her eyes from his aroused manhood.

"You are the beautiful one, Adam," she whispered, reaching out with one hand to draw him to her. He laced his fingers through hers and stretched out on the bed beside her.

"Touch me, Lorna," Adam ordered huskily, taking her hand and guiding it to him. "Show me how much you want me." He chuckled at her natural reticence. "I will not harm you, my little dove. I can only love you."

Kelly's voice faltered. Was there a way she could censor part of this passage? Funny, it hadn't seemed that torrid when she had read it to herself before.

Cole grunted, grabbed the TV remote control box, and switched channels.

Adam's hands traced each valley and curve of Lorna's satin-skinned body with fiery fingertips. The tiny waistline soon learned his touch, as did the fuller hips and on down to the moist—

"Do you mind?" Cole roared, jumping to his feet. "I'm trying to watch this program!"

Kelly's eyes flickered over to the television, where an antacid commercial played merrily. Luckily she was able to quickly regain her composure. She expelled a loud sigh and stood up.

"If you didn't want to hear it, all you had to do was say so," she told him in a haughty voice. "There was no reason for you to get huffy about it." With her head held high she swept out of the room.

Cole dropped back down into his chair. He gnashed his teeth, something he had been doing a lot of lately, as he watched the TV, but he didn't really see the screen. He was too busy trying to come up with new ways to strangle one Kelly Connors. After a great deal of thought one idea did come to him. He got up from his seat and walked over to the telephone. In no time his connection was made.

"John? Cole Bishop. Yeah, it's been a long time. Look, buddy, I'm calling in some favors. I want you to wangle me an invitation to a party this Friday hosted by a Michael Babcock, but not under my own name. What? Sure you can get me one. If anyone can do it, you can. Okay, I'll hear from you tomorrow then. Thanks."

When he finished his call he moved back over to the couch. Kelly was going to find out that she wasn't the only one who could come up with surprises. Now it was his turn to come up with a few strategies of his own. He thought about the passage she had read from that lurid book and couldn't help chuckling at the memory.

"I've got to give her credit for persistence if nothing else," he laughed softly.

Friday afternoon Kelly sneaked out of her office and

135

went home early. She greeted Cole with a breathless hello as she breezed into the kitchen and headed for the refrigerator. She opened the door and reached in for the wine bottle in order to pour herself a glass.

"Starting early, are we?" Cole scowled at the glass.

"Only getting in the party mood," she answered saucily, raising the glass in a toast. "Mr. Babcock will be here about seven to pick me up."

"I can hardly wait," Cole muttered sarcastically at Kelly's retreating back.

Kelly washed and styled her hair into a loose topknot. Her makeup was applied with a slightly heavier hand and perfume stroked on in all the appropriate areas.

When Michael arrived at seven all the proper words were spoken. Cole said nothing, although he did greet Michael with a tight-lipped smile.

Cole waited until the couple left the house before he moved off toward his bedroom. In his mind he had everything planned, down to the last second. With luck his strategy would work perfectly. If not, well, he'd just make himself out to be the prize ass of the century.

Kelly wandered around the room carrying her glass of wine. She smiled, she talked, she laughed, all the time thinking how boring the party was.

She really shouldn't complain. Michael had made it a point to introduce her to anyone who could be helpful to her and she had already made some useful contacts. She had begun to circulate after he had excused himself to speak to an attorney friend of his. Here she was, attending a party of the most influential people in Orange County and escorted by the man hosting it. So why wasn't she enjoying it more?

Kelly easily evaded the too familiar clutches of a fast-talking stockbroker and sought out a safer group of people. As she stood and listened to the talk going on around her, she was aware of a strange tingling sensation along her shoulder blades. She casually glanced around but saw nothing to warrant her feelings of unease. With a vague smile she excused herself, set her half empty wineglass on a nearby table, and continued circulating. Kelly stopped abruptly when a glass of wine held by a man's hand appeared in her line of vision.

"You look as if you could use a refill."

Kelly's nerves quivered at the low-timbred voice. She slowly raised her eyes, taking in the well-cut navy blazer and soft gray shirt with a navy and gray striped tie. The dark gray slacks were equally well cut. His firm jaw was freshly shaved and the faint masculine scent reached her nostrils, vital among the cigarette smoke in the air. His dark blue eyes, carefully masked, watched her while the briefest of smiles flickered over his lips.

Cole! Kelly's mouth opened to ask how he had crashed the party. The bland expression in his eyes stopped her question.

"You'll make a boring evening more interesting if you can tell me you're here on your own," he commented lightly. "I never was one for pistols at dawn. Although for you, I think I'd make the exception."

Kelly smiled and accepted the glass. She still wasn't sure what Cole was doing here or even how he had gotten in. Michael had stationed two men at the door with a guest list and each person's name was checked and crossed off before they were allowed to enter. Yet, somehow he had crashed the party. She also couldn't help but notice that he was wearing a jacket and slacks that looked much too expensive for a housekeeper. What was going on?

"And here I thought dueling only persisted in the Deep South," she murmured, going along with Cole's game until she could find out exactly what was going on. "I'm flattered, sir."

Cole continued smiling as he gazed down at Kelly's dress, the one bare shoulder and the curves delineated by the silky material.

"I'm Cole." Had his voice always sounded this sexy or was it just something to do with this night?

"Kelly," she replied softly. "Do you know Mr. Babcock well?" Kelly lowered her voice to a husky purr.

Cole shrugged, not really giving her an answer. "To be perfectly honest"—he lowered his own voice in a conspiratorial whisper—"I crashed this party. Are you going to turn me in?"

Kelly's lips curved in a feline smile. How many men would have the audacity Cole just displayed by strolling into a private party and pretending to be a guest? "What made you choose this party?" she asked demurely, sipping her wine.

Cole's smile broadened. "I looked in and saw this very lovely lady whom I decided I wanted to meet, so I thought that this would be the time to crash my first party."

Shivers zigzagged along Kelly's spine as she listened to Cole's intimate tones. It was as if she were meeting him for the first time. There was also that faint thrill of danger in this conversation. This was an exclusive party and he was present as an uninvited guest. If he were found out to be a party-crasher, he would definitely be asked to leave.

She lifted her eyes slowly and met his gaze head on. The pink tip of her tongue passed over rose-glossed lips and returned to the interior of her mouth. The slight tilt of her head released a new enticing wave of her perfume. Her entire body spoke a language known for centuries and Cole read the nuances fluently.

"I'm glad you're a man who gives in to impulse," she replied in a husky voice.

Cole glanced around at the crush of people and winced at the loud talk surrounding them. "Then I can only hope you're a lady who believes in impulsive measures also," he murmured.

"Meaning?" She lifted a delicately arched eyebrow. She was having fun at this!

"Meaning it would be much nicer if we could find a quiet restaurant and get to know each other better," he suggested.

Kelly hesitated. "I'm here with someone else," she declined softly. What a temptation it would be! Except that Michael had been nice enough to bring her here and introduce her around. She didn't think it would be right for her to just walk out on him.

Cole's jaw tightened. "If I had been the man to bring you here, I wouldn't have left your side for a minute," he informed her, grasping her arm. "It would serve him right if he lost you."

Kelly opened her mouth to protest, but the words couldn't find a way out. Before she knew it Cole had escorted her toward an exit and out the door.

She found herself in for a further surprise when Cole led her outside to a white Mazda. She started to ask where he got the car, then quickly retreated. Right now he didn't look like he was in the mood to answer what he might consider a frivolous question.

Cole took Kelly to a quiet restaurant with secluded booths and intimate lighting meant to give the diners the privacy they would desire. Kelly glanced at the plush surroundings and turned back to Cole.

"Very nice for a kidnaped woman," she commented.

"Anything for the right lady." Cole's smile sent a jab to Kelly's midsection.

Kelly still silently questioned Cole's motives for abducting her from the party but right now was holding off asking him out loud. This evening was turning out much more interesting than any of her dreams. She looked up and caught him watching her. She hurriedly lowered her eyes and studied her fingertip circling the rim of her wineglass.

Dinner continued along the same vein. They shared chateaubriand and wine along with light conversation. Except each time their eyes met the gaze lingered a bit longer. The sexual tension built up between them and enclosed the small booth with small electric charges.

"You're very lovely, Kelly," Cole whispered. He reached across the table and brought her hand to his lips. His tongue fondled the center of her palm and reached up to circle each finger in a moist caress.

Kelly's mouth went dry. She felt a white hot lava of desire flowing through her body. "Cole, I—"

He shook his head, indicating silence. His eyes darkened with some unknown emotion. "If you have any pity for me, you'll not want any coffee or dessert."

Kelly shook her head in mute reply. The last thing she wanted was more food.

Cole hastily took care of the bill and with a hand resting lightly against the base of Kelly's spine, guided her out of the restaurant.

Side by side they walked silently out to the car. Cole unlocked the passenger door and turned to Kelly. He slowly lifted his hands to form a frame for her face and caressed the corners of her lips with his thumbs.

"Kelly," he sang, lowering his head until their lips were a breath apart, "I want to kiss you."

"Yes," she moaned. Her arms circled his waist under the open jacket. "Please, Cole, don't make me wait any longer."

But he did make her wait. His lips first touched one corner of her mouth, then the other. "All through dinner,

140

each time you took a bite of your food or drank your wine, I imagined the taste of you on my lips," he whispered. His fingertips caressed the shape of her ears and behind to the ultrasensitive hollow. "Now I'm afraid just a taste won't be enough."

Wide-eyed, Kelly looked up at his face, seeing his features tense with the same desire she was feeling. The taut strain of the fabric of Cole's slacks resting against the thin material of her dress told her the rest of the story. To enforce the story, Cole roughly thrust his hips against hers.

"I want to make love to you, Kelly. I want to undress you slowly and take you to bed. I want your body writhing with passion under my lips and hands. I want your warmth to surround and hold me," he kept on, knowing his words were arousing her as easily as his touch would have. "I want your legs wrapped around my back and your voice crying out my name as you burst into flame."

With each word Kelly felt herself melting more under Cole's spell. She linked her arms around his neck and pressed her lips to his. Her tongue darted between his receptive lips and captured his tongue in an erotic duel. Her fierce kiss conveyed her feelings to the hilt. Cole groaned out his own need as he clasped her tightly against him. It was some time before they parted to gasp for some much-needed air.

"Does that answer your question?" she asked in a ragged voice.

Cole bundled Kelly into the car and walked around to the driver's side. Fifteen minutes later Kelly found herself inside a luxurious hotel room, not even knowing how she came to be there.

"How can any one woman be so sexy?" Cole moaned, wrapping his arms around her once the door had been closed and locked behind them.

Kelly reveled to the hunger in Cole's kiss. Her lips parted readily to his marauding tongue and answered with teasing thrusts of her own. Her body shimmied against his, delighting in his reaction.

"I sure hope this dress comes off easily," Cole rasped while his fingers hunted and found the zipper. The fabric parted, allowing cool air to bathe Kelly's overheated skin.

In turn, she pulled his tie loose and began working on his shirt buttons. Once they were unfastened, Kelly began to laugh as she realized Cole was still wearing his blazer. He quickly stepped back and dispensed with the offending articles. He dropped moist, heated kisses on Kelly's bare shoulders as he slid the dress down past her hips then dealt with the black lacy strapless bra. Kelly stepped away and hurriedly kicked off her shoes.

"You really know how to make a guy crazy, don't you?" Cole muttered roughly, eyeing the black lace garter belt and black sheer stockings.

Kelly literally purred as she unfastened the stockings. "Perhaps I had a hunch that this just might be my night."

"No." Cole placed his hand over hers. "Let me." He knelt down in front of her and unfastened each stocking, carefully rolling them down to her ankles and lifting each foot to gently pull them free. A kiss was placed just above the lace of the garter belt. Kelly sighed and closed her eyes, wondering how much she would be able to take of Cole's lovemaking before she would burst into flame as he had predicted. At that moment she doubted it would be very much. The garter belt was easily unfastened and tossed to one side.

Cole stood up and his shoes went the same route as Kelly's high heels. He drew her back into his embrace, crushing her swollen breasts against his chest. Their mouths mated as if there would be no tomorrow. Cole guided Kelly toward the bed and pulled back the pale peach silk comforter to reveal matching sheets.

"No clothes allowed here," Kelly murmured wickedly, unfastening his belt and lowering the zipper of his slacks.

"Then you know what to do," he entreated huskily.

Kelly pushed down Cole's slacks and briefs, then watched him step away from the pile of clothing and stretch out on the bed.

She knelt on the bedcovers and raised her hands to cup his face. Her lips traced the masculine eyebrows, then covered the closed eyelids in butterfly kisses. The fresh scent of his skin tormented her into pressing feathery kisses over his cheeks and along his jaw, but never close to his mouth.

"You're driving me insane, witch." Cole laughed softly. In retaliation he molded her breasts with his palms and drew circles around the tips with his thumbs until they pulsed with a life of their own. "Just don't forget that two can play at this game." He reached down to press a kiss on each nipple.

"I'm so glad that's possible," she moaned softly when she felt his hand pass lightly over her abdomen. "It makes it that much more enjoyable." Love nips were planted along his throat.

Cole's laughter was ragged. No woman had ever turned him inside out the way Kelly had and she definitely was doing that now. It seemed that she could arouse him with no more than a mere look. And when that feline smile curved her lips and lights danced in her eyes, he felt ready to explode with wanting her.

Cole gently pushed Kelly back against the pillows. She laughed softly as he reached down to take one of her feet in his hand and run his thumb along the sole, although great care was taken not to tickle the ultrasensitive skin. The same procedure was repeated on the other foot. His hands wandered upward over her ankles, calves, and thighs, but he didn't touch her where she most wanted him to. Her waistline was traced with inquiring fingers and imaginary lines were drawn up around each shoulder and down her arms to her wrists but her aching breasts were left untouched.

"I could draw you from memory now." Cole lifted her wrist and placed a kiss against the vein pulsing along the surface. His teeth gently nipped her soft skin.

Kelly's own hands wandered over Cole's broad body, finding each erotic area with unerring accuracy. His flat nipples sprang to life under her soft bites and soothing tongue. She brushed her nose against the soft crinkly hair that arrowed downward past his waist.

"If a man can have a sexy belly button, I vote for you to receive first prize," she whispered, flicking her tongue into the small cavity and eliciting a tortured groan from Cole. "You really should try to sunbathe in the nude, Cole. Think how sexy you'd look with an allover tan." Her lips found his most sensitive area and closed over him with the delicacy of a butterfly settling on a flower.

Cole found he couldn't take much more. With a low growl, he pulled Kelly up and covered her with his body, kissing her with a rough urgency equalled only by her own.

"Think how painful a sunburn in certain areas of the body could be," he rasped, sliding his hands under her buttocks and lifting her to him.

Kelly gasped when Cole opened her to him. His mouth was silken fire on her sensitive skin. He gave to her as she had to him, with his tongue and teeth, sending her spinning outward. At times the sensual ache seemed too much and she tried to arch away from his loving mouth, but he refused to release her.

"*No!*" she uttered a strangled cry, reaching down to grasp his hair and pull him up to her.

"Yes," Cole muttered roughly. "I want you to give your all to me tonight, baby. I want everything you have to give and more than you've ever given to any other man."

"Please, I can't take any more!" Kelly's head thrashed from side to side on the pillow. Her hips arched up against his teasing tongue and gentle love nips.

"Shh, I'm seducing you," he replied thickly, his breath a searing brand on her skin.

"Forget the seduction, make love to me!" she almost screamed.

Cole looked up and gave her a smile that sent lightning bolts through her system. "That's exactly what I'm doing, my love," he crooned.

Time and time again Cole brought Kelly to the edge only to stop and begin again. Kelly gulped much-needed air into her burning lungs. The torture was exquisite and there was no way she could stop him from drawing her into an sensual world never experienced before. She pleaded with Cole for release, but his reply was a soft chuckle and his teeth nipped her inner thigh. She cried, she threatened, she begged, but he wasn't ready to give her her release just yet.

It was a torture in itself for Cole as he wanted nothing more than to bury himself in Kelly's body. When he finally moved up over her and thrust himself into her welcoming softness, he could hear her sob of relief echoed by his own low groan of satisfaction as she closed tightly around him.

"Cole, no!" Kelly protested, unable to stop the steady pulsating rhythm his body was setting for them, a cadence that would send her into oblivion when he wanted her there. All she knew was that she wouldn't be able to take much more.

"Yes," he injected hoarsely as his body was becoming blind to his mind. He couldn't ignore his own need too much longer. It would take every ounce of the self-control he possessed to give her the night of sensual pleasure he wanted her to have. Soon he increased his pace and thrust her over the edge, barely giving her time to recover before beginning again.

Kelly's breathing was labored, her skin flushed and heated, and her eyes dilated from this explosive lovemaking. She buried her teeth in Cole's shoulder and heard his answering grunt before she felt as if she lost all consciousness. A moment later Cole followed her with his own flowing release.

Afterward they could only lie among the tangled sheets, barely able to move, much less breathe.

"Don't ask anything of me for at least twenty-four hours," Cole muttered, closing his eyes. His chest rose and fell with his ragged breaths.

"How about if we make it a week?" Kelly suggested sleepily, curling up on her side and snuggling next to him.

Cole's hands framed Kelly's face in a loving caress and turned it up to face him. There was something new in those dark blue eyes. A glimmer she hadn't seen before.

"What do you say to some well-earned sleep. We're too old for all these acrobatics." He yelped as Kelly pinched his thigh. "That hurt!"

"Just be happy that I didn't pick a more vulnerable spot," she threatened, now biting his earlobe.

"Damn it, Kelly!"

"Don't you pull this too-old crap with me, Cole Bishop," Kelly admonished sternly. "I doubt a man ten years younger could have done what you did tonight and remain coherent. I don't know why I'm telling you this. It will only enlarge your ego."

"Among other things." Cole grinned wickedly, running his hand over her abdomen.

"What am I going to do with you?" Her laugh ended in a wail.

"Same as before?" he asked hopefully.

Kelly turned over, placing her hand on his chest as she brushed a light kiss over his lips. "You know what?" she murmured. "You're not so bad for an old man of thirty-seven."

Cole chuckled and tucked Kelly closer to his side. "All right, you've made your point. Now, can we go to sleep?" he grumbled good-naturedly.

"What's stopping you?" Her innocent question was marred by her very audible snicker.

Even in sleep they didn't drift apart. Cole's arms were wrapped firmly around Kelly, as if feeling more secure with the feeling of her body against his.

CHAPTER EIGHT

"You're a very special lady, Kelly Connors."

Kelly rubbed her cheek against the damp hair of Cole's chest and inhaled the musky scent of his skin. "You're not so bad yourself," she murmured huskily. She had discovered that being awakened by nibbling kisses was definitely preferable to the everyday alarm clock.

Cole's low answering groan wasn't from desire. Kelly looked up to see some nameless pain cross his face.

"Cole, what's wrong?" She raised herself up on one elbow.

"God, Kelly, I'm so sorry," he sighed heavily, rubbing his eyes with his fingertips. "I never even stopped to think last night. I'm a selfish bastard."

Kelly continued to stare at him, unable to understand what he was talking about. "Are—are you trying to say that you regret our making love?" she asked in a hurt voice.

His hand dropped away. "Of course not," Cole argued quietly. "Kelly, I never even thought of taking precautions."

"So?" She still couldn't understand why he was so angry with himself if he hadn't regretted their lovemaking.

Cole sat up and looked down at her puzzled face. "So, as someone who has intimate knowledge of your medicine cabinet, I know only too well that you don't take any precautions," he muttered, shaking his head in self-disgust. "I was so muddle-headed from the thought of finally having you in my bed that I didn't stop to think of protecting you."

"Poor Cole," Kelly commiserated, stroking the hard line of his jaw with her fingertips. "It's all right."

"Oh, sure," he grumbled.

"It is," she insisted quietly. Her fingertips now moved down to lightly scratch the hair-rough surface of his chest in an indistinct pattern. She chuckled at his loud groan of sensual pain. "You can stop hating yourself." She suddenly turned serious as she looked up at him. "To make it brief, I had a difficult pregnancy with Kevin and Kyle and I came very close to losing both them and my life." She noted the swift spasm of pain contorting his face at her matter-of-fact words. "Yes, even with the marvels of modern science women can still die in childbirth. I was advised that I not have any more children, so I had my tubes tied."

Cole shook his head, wishing he could absorb the emotional pain Kelly must still experience. "I wish I could have been there with you," he murmured.

Strangely, she was beginning to wish the same. Maybe it wouldn't have seemed so traumatic to a woman suffering from postnatal shock to begin with. Dave hadn't minded her not being able to have more children, but the knowledge had always deeply hurt Kelly. She was only grateful that she had her two boys to ease the pain.

"Hey." She smiled up at him. "Think that decadent bathtub in there could accommodate the two of us?"

Cole smiled back at her. "There's only one way to find

149

out." He pushed the covers back and scooped a laughing Kelly up into his arms. "Just don't expect this special service every morning," he warned her, nipping her earlobe as he walked into the large bathroom.

After their bath together, Cole ordered a champagne breakfast to be served in their room, which they consumed with great relish.

Kelly looked around the room, thought of the car outside, which wasn't Cole's, and wondered how he could afford all this—the well-tailored clothes, the high-priced hotel, the obvious rented car, and now the special breakfast from room service. Even with all these thoughts bothering her, she didn't question him. Instead, she smiled warmly and whispered, "Thank you."

Cole looked at her quizzically. "For what?"

"For making my fantasy come true." She tore off a piece of her croissant and placed it between his lips. "At first, I wasn't sure what was going on last night, then all of a sudden it occurred to me. I was at a party, a man appeared, swept me off my feet and into bed. You lived out my fantasy perfectly." Too perfectly, as far as she was concerned. No other man could have given her what Cole had last night in the way of passion and the sharing of one body with another. She sincerely doubted that another man could ever make love to her with the same hunger and fervor that Cole had displayed all through the night. And to be honest, she wasn't sure she would ever want another man.

"I had an ulterior motive other than fulfilling your fantasy," he informed her in a grave tone. "I decided that if you wanted someone to sweep you off your feet and into bed for a wild and passionate evening, it had better be me instead of some stranger who could turn out to be the missing psychopath from the state hospital."

150

"Ulterior, that sounds awfully selfish to me," Kelly teased.

"You're damn right it's selfish," Cole snapped, pouring himself another cup of coffee. "If you're going to remember a night like that, you're damn well going to remember me along with it!"

Kelly smiled. That was fine with her too.

She was in for a further surprise when Cole brought out an overnight case packed with a change of clothes for both of them.

"You remembered my makeup but forgot my bra," she announced.

"Yeah." Cole grinned wickedly.

"I also think that you shrunk this T-shirt on purpose," Kelly further accused, holding out the rose pink material.

"Guess so." He pulled a bright red knit polo shirt over his head and tucked it into his jeans. "Besides, I have a good idea that you definitely prefer men over dogs now."

Kelly spun around, her mouth dropped open in shock. "You read French!"

"Sure do," Cole admitted matter-of-factly.

"Oh, you!" She began laughing as she advanced on him with her hairbrush in one hand.

"Hey, that could be considered a lethal weapon!" He threw his hands up in self-defense.

When they later checked out of the hotel and walked out to the car, Cole explained that the Mazda belonged to a friend of his and he'd drop Kelly home first, then go over to his friend's house, leave the car, and he would pick up his jeep.

"Somehow, I thought using the jeep or even your car would ruin the mood of the evening." He assisted her into the car. "Luckily, Brad didn't mind switching cars for the night." He grinned boyishly. "Of course, he reminded me that I'll have to replace any gas that I use and I had to sign

151

a contract in blood that I wouldn't let anything happen to his precious baby. Other than that, he showed no concern."

"Why would he be worried?" Kelly asked curiously.

"We went to high school and college together and I borrowed his car one night when I had a hot date. Unfortunately, I connected with a telephone pole when I swerved to miss a dog. Brad doesn't like dogs to this day." Cole wrapped an arm around Kelly's shoulders. "What really hurt was that the lady wasn't even worth it." He dropped his voice. "Too bad you weren't around then."

"I didn't know you went in for precocious children." She dug a playful elbow in his side. "Hmm, wouldn't we have been the talk of the town?"

"So how could you get the mumps and the measles so close together?" Kelly was stretched out on her stomach on the den carpet with her chin propped up on one closed fist.

"Easy, my sister and my best friend decided to share their diseases with me." Cole reached into the large bowl filled with popcorn and gathered up a handful. He munched contentedly. "At least I didn't have my tonsils out at the ancient age of sixteen like some people who shall remain nameless."

"Oh, please!" Kelly moaned, rolling over onto her back. "I only agreed to the operation because they said I could have all the ice cream I wanted when it was all over. As it was, I could barely swallow water!"

Their day had been spent at a local craft fair, where Kelly bought hand-tooled belts for Kevin and Kyle and a large velvet mouse dressed in a calico dress for Inez, who collected mice. After a dinner they had cooked together along with kisses and hugs thrown in for added spice, they fixed popcorn and turned on an old Humphrey Bogart

152

movie on television. While the film was excellent, Cole found more enjoyment in watching Kelly's facial expressions. For a woman who dealt with sophisticated people in her work, she was unexpectedly down-to-earth in nature. Not naive, just a woman who enjoyed the smallest pleasures with the greatest joy.

Kelly yawned deeply and threw her arms over her head, unexpectedly drawing Cole's eyes to the upthrust of her breasts visible under the soft cotton of her shift. It was a warm evening, but they had opted for keeping the windows open instead of switching on the central air-conditioning.

"Let's go swimming," she said suddenly.

Cole opened one eye and peered down at her from his own sprawled position on the couch. "Too much trouble," he drawled lazily.

"Trouble? How do you consider it trouble to walk outside and jump into the pool?"

"It is when I'd have to get up from here, go into my room, and put on my suit. I don't think I have the energy," he argued indolently. "You've worn me out, woman."

Kelly scrambled to her feet and sauntered over to the couch. She leaned over, placing a hand on either side of his shoulders. "Who said anything about wearing suits?" She brushed her lips lightly back and forth over his. "Mmm, you taste salty, like the popcorn."

She continually amazed him. "Sure, and have your neighbors call the cops on us for indecent exposure or, worse, play the peeping Tom to see what we're doing. No thanks," he laughed. Did her hand really have to play along the length of his thigh?

"We have a deserted hill behind us; the houses on either side are one-story and one of those is vacant because the Pattersons are on vacation," she pointed out on a reasonable note. "Come on, Cole, besides, it isn't as if it's the first

153

time you've gone skinny-dipping," she told him in a silky voice, now moving her hand along the waistband of his jeans and down to the zipper, hovering over the tooth-edged metal.

Cole eyed her with a suspicious gaze. "I wasn't far from wrong when I talked about peeping Toms in the neighborhood."

"You should have invited me to go with you." Kelly nuzzled his neck. "It certainly would have been more enjoyable. Then it shouldn't bother you this time, should it?" She picked up his hand and pulled him from his seat. "Come on, love."

Kelly scampered outside, all the while tearing her shift off and dropping it to the ground along with her underwear. She ran over to the edge of the pool and dove in.

"Hurry up, the water's great." Kelly rolled over onto her back.

Cole couldn't keep his eyes from the pale streak of flesh luminous in the dark night. He rapidly pushed off his jeans and underwear. He walked over to the edge of the swimming pool and dove into the water, landing near Kelly. She screeched with laughter as the water splashed over her.

"I thought you said the water was great." He tossed his head to flip the dark hair out of his eyes. "It's freezing!"

"Only because the surrounding air is so warm. You'll be fine in a minute," she assured him with a laugh.

"Sure," Cole grumbled. "What's wrong with the Jacuzzi?" He yelped when a hand circled his ankle and pulled him down under the water's surface. With surprise on her side Kelly was able to give him a good dunking.

From there, the battle was on. Kelly was barely able to swim away when Cole caught her leg and pulled her under in retaliation. After that, she wasn't surprised when he slid his arms around her waist and pulled her up hard against him. There was something erotic and unearthly sharing a kiss underwater. Kelly wrapped her body around Cole's, unwilling to be even a breath away from him. It wasn't until a severe lack of air forced their heads to break the surface that they came up.

"I won't let you drown," Cole promised, refusing to relinquish his hold on her body.

"I know," Kelly whispered, licking chlorine-tainted droplets from his shoulder.

At her soft-spoken reply he looked down at her face and read the implicit trust in her eyes.

"Kelly." His voice sounded ragged. "You're tearing me apart."

She allowed her body to continue drifting against his. "I'm not just another notch on your bedpost, am I, Cole?" she asked softly, burrowing closer to him. "If I am, please tell me now. I'd rather know now and go into this with my eyes open than find out later."

"No, baby, you'll never be that," he murmured against her sleek wet hair. "You mean a hell of a lot more to me than some one-night stand."

Keeping hold of Kelly, Cole paddled them to the edge, hoisted himself out of the pool, and pulled her out. He guided her over to the Jacuzzi and assisted her down to the built-in bench. He flipped on the power switch and climbed in just as the jets began bubbling.

"See, I told you we'd have fun," Kelly laughed throatily, when Cole reached out to pull her onto his lap.

"Honey, the fun is just beginning," he vowed, allowing his lips and hands to work that same sensual magic that climaxed in the same earth-shattering results.

"You mean here?" It didn't take her long to realize his intentions.

"Sure, you were the one who said no one would see us out here." He playfully nipped her earlobe. "Trust me."

155

Kelly gurgled at that husky vow. "Isn't it dangerous to make love in a Jacuzzi?" A part of her thrilled to something new and exciting to the senses.

"Only if you end up underwater for longer than ten minutes. Try it, you'll like it." His husky whisper promised.

Kelly certainly did, on both counts. Afterward they went back to Cole's bedroom.

"If we keep this up, we'll soon indulge in the rest of my fantasies," she declared sleepily, snuggling up closer to him.

"Rest? I thought I had taken care of the main one quite nicely," he chuckled, curling his arm around her shoulder.

"Um, true," Kelly sighed. Her much-too-busy day was catching up with her, not to mention the lack of sleep from the night before. She levered herself up and dropped a light kiss on Cole's mouth, which responded immediately.

Their kiss had barely begun when a large shape bounded onto the bed and landed between them.

"*Alfie!*" Kelly shrieked, pushing at the immovable furry object. "How did you get out of your run?"

"He probably flipped the latch and sneaked out while we were in the pool," Cole grumbled, finally able to push the whining sheepdog off the bed. "There is no way I'm sharing my bed with him too." He settled back and pulled Kelly against him. "Now, let's get some sleep, please. I'm probably going to need all my strength tomorrow," he chuckled before he realized that Kelly had already fallen asleep and hadn't even heard him.

Sunday was spent leisurely, reading the newspaper, both of them arguing good-naturedly over who got the comics first, and lying around the pool, soaking up the sun, although Cole made it difficult for Kelly to lie on her chaise longue quietly as he carefully massaged suntan oil on her body. That task ended up by their retiring to her bedroom for an "afternoon nap."

"What exactly is your image?" Cole asked curiously on Monday morning as he watched Kelly apply her makeup.

"What do you mean?" She leaned closer to the mirror as she brushed on bright aqua eyeshadow and used a bright blue eyelining pencil.

"Friday you were dressed like a well-starched schoolteacher, and today, well . . ." He eyed her bright turquoise cotton culotte dress and strappy soft leather sandals in the same color. "Today you look like someone from *Rolling Stone.*"

"That's because I'm meeting Darren from T's and Rags this morning," Kelly explained, setting her pencil down. "You remember, he's the one who gave me all the T-shirts."

Cole frowned. "What's this Darren like?" he asked a bit too casually.

"Late twenties, sort of good-looking in a scruffy way, and has three cats and two dogs." She turned around and smirked. "He also hits on every model used in his advertising campaigns. They always turn him down, but he never gives up. He's also a good six years my junior."

"Older women and younger men are in right now," he muttered darkly.

"Not with me." Kelly's brows knitted in a frown as she searched for her lipstick.

"Not yet." Cole stepped up and turned her around to face him. "I don't want to be accused of ruining your lipstick," he murmured just before capturing Kelly's lips in a lust-inspiring kiss that she could feel down to her toes. His tongue wreaked havoc with the dark caverns of her mouth, plunging so deeply she could feel the vibrations in every fiber of her body. Her breathing grew labored and

157

her breasts swelled under the thin cotton of her dress. This was the kiss a man bestowed on a woman just before sliding her into bed, not just before she has to leave for work! When Cole finally stepped back, Kelly could only look at him with widened eyes. How was she going to be able to concentrate at the office today with the memory of that kiss tingling on her lips?

"That . . . is not fair," she finally managed to get out.

Cole smiled serenely. "Does this mean you won't be working late tonight?" he asked with an innocent air that didn't fool Kelly one bit.

"Work late? I'll be lucky if I manage to stay coherent until lunchtime." She tried to find her lipstick again, although it would be a miracle if her shaky fingers would allow her to apply it.

"Oh, so you're coming home for lunch then?"

Kelly looked at Cole, glad to see that he hadn't been as calm through their kiss as he had sounded. She could see all the visible signs. "No way." She laughed shakily, holding up a hand as if to ward him off. "In fact, I better get out of here while I still can."

Cole smiled wickedly as he walked downstairs with Kelly. She was turning out to be a woman of surprises. He hadn't guessed that her open and carefree nature also hid a sensual and passionate side that had erupted when he held her in his arms.

For a while he had forgotten the reason for his being in her house. It had been easy to forget when the woman walking beside him had touched his soul so deeply. He didn't want to think of what would happen if Kelly found out about his article. He had a pretty strong idea that drawing and quartering would be only a taste of the punishment she would mete out. Strange, but now the article didn't mean half as much as it had. Not when Kelly's opinion of him counted so much more. This undercover

158

research was proving more dangerous than he thought. He was actually beginning to enjoy working around a house. He, who had never bothered with learning the workings of a dishwasher before, found that housework wasn't all that bad. This assignment was turning out to be more than dangerous; it was insanity.

"I guess I don't have to ask if you had a good weekend," Rachel asked forty-five minutes later when Kelly walked into the office.

"Oh?" Kelly averted her face as she reached her desk.

"You look much too relaxed." The secretary gazed at her suspiciously. "I thought you had a party to attend. Parties don't relax anyone unless there's something floating through the air besides room deodorizer."

"I don't think the party I had attended allowed such sordid goings-on," Kelly countered dryly, settling herself in her chair behind her desk. "I did manage to give out a lot of business cards and several people were very interested in talking to me about the agency. Thanks to Michael, we should be picking up a few new clients."

Rachel had followed her boss into the office and took the chair opposite Kelly's desk.

"Mr. Baxter would like an update on the Babcock account," she announced. "He also wants you to look into the Malcolm portfolio. I don't think he's very happy with the way Todd Lucas has been handling it."

Kelly groaned. "Oliver Malcolm has got to be the stuffiest and most opinionated man in the country. Not to mention that he's a chauvinist of the first degree. His clothing stores don't make the money they used to because he refuses to believe that clothing styles have changed since the 1890s. Perhaps I can keep myself very busy for the next six months."

"It was worded more as a command than a request,"

Rachel told her, reaching for the telephone as it rang. "Ms. Connors's office. One moment please." She put the caller on hold. "I suppose you'll speak to Mr. Babcock?"

Kelly nodded. She felt twinges of guilt at having walked out on him at the party. She raised her eyebrows at Rachel. "Am I allowed privacy for my call?"

The secretary snapped her fingers. "And here I thought I'd have a chance to see how the expert does it." She rose from her chair and left the office, closing the door behind her.

Kelly waited until she was alone before picking up the receiver. "Hello, Michael." She put more warmth than usual in her voice. "Do you hate me?"

"I should," he teased back. "You must have found quite a man to lure you away from such a perfect masculine specimen as myself."

Obviously he hadn't seen whom Kelly had left with. "I do want to apologize for running out on you like that, especially without speaking to you first. Please, believe me when I say that I normally don't do things like that," she said honestly.

"I didn't think you did," Michael paused. "Tell me, Kelly, friend to friend, was it worth it?"

If he had seen her slow smile, he would have known that she felt that her evening was more than worth it. "Now, Michael, I never kiss and tell," she chided.

He roared with laughter. "That's answer enough, love. The reason I called was to let you know that I saw the new ads in *Orange County Executive* and I was duly impressed. Hopefully, all the secretaries reading their boss's magazine will feel the same way."

"They will." Kelly was all confidence.

"Then I'll be singing your praises all the way to the bank."

"Drop a few words in Oliver Malcolm's ear while you're at it," Kelly suggested lightly.

"Sweetheart, I'm a hell of a lot tougher than he is. Believe me, just turn on that feminine charm of yours and you'll have him eating out of your hand. I have to go. If you have a day free for lunch this week, let me know. And good luck with your new conquest," he chuckled.

Kelly sighed deeply as she hung up the phone. Michael used a variation of the same theme so many other men had suggested at one time or another. Feminine charm, womanly this, feminine that. Rarely a word about her knowledge of the subject or her efficient work. It all boiled down to her sex and looks. It wasn't that she was a fervent women's libber; it was only that she wanted to be recognized for her good work, not because she was a lovely woman.

She pulled a stack of folders toward her. She still had to proofread the copy for T's and Rags's new ads and for a new client who owned several lingerie boutiques in Orange County.

Kelly groaned at the sound of the intercom.

"I don't care who wants me, Rachel," she uttered a ladylike growl to her secretary. "I'm not available. I moved to Alaska, I died of the plague, I don't care which idiotic excuse you use. Just get rid of them!"

"Mr. Baxter is here to see you," Rachel announced sweetly.

"Now I know that I died of the plague," Kelly muttered, then looked up when her office door opened. "Good morning, Mr. Baxter." She greeted him with a sugary smile. "How nice to see you."

"I thought I'd come down to personally invite you to lunch, Mrs. Connors," Mr. Baxter began formally. "That is, if you don't have any prior engagements."

Kelly's mouth would have fallen open in shock if she

161

hadn't caught herself in time. *He* was inviting *her* to lunch?

"Ah, yes, I am free today," she stammered.

"Twelve thirty then." A trace of a smile flickered over his astute-looking features. With his goal accomplished, he left the office and a stunned Kelly behind.

Rachel slipped inside. "Lunch with the big boss," she injected dryly. "Are you going to hate it!"

"Why, is he going to make me pick up the bill?"

Rachel's smile was unnerving. "My dear brother is a vegetarian and always eats his lunch at the health food restaurant across the street. You, with your fetish for red meat and junk food, will definitely feel out of place."

Kelly grimaced. "It can't be all that bad," she argued faintly.

She soon found out differently. After carefully studying the menu, Kelly ordered a tuna salad pocket sandwich.

"I want you to know how pleased I am with your handling of the Babcock account," Mr. Baxter told her in his dry monotone. "Babcock is an old and respected name in the community. His goodwill can mean a great deal for the agency."

"And for me?" Kelly prompted.

Mr. Baxter smiled, if it could be called that. "I see no reason why you shouldn't receive a nice bonus for your hard work."

It wasn't the answer she was looking for. A promotion would have been more like it to her way of thinking.

"When Stan Daniels cornered the Deckard account, he was promoted," Kelly pointed out gently.

"There were many other deciding factors in that promotion," Mr. Baxter answered in a reasonable tone.

Such as he's a man and I'm not, Kelly fumed silently, looking down at her lunch as it was placed in front of her.

Until then she had never dreamed that tuna salad could

162

be ruined. She discovered that she was wrong. The pocket bread was made from a wheat mixture that left a grainy taste in her mouth, and she guessed that yogurt and some type of seed had been mixed in with the tuna. Not appetizing at all when washed down with an iced herbal tea. Altogether, it was a lunch that she preferred not to try again.

All afternoon Kelly found herself watching the clock and counting the hours until she could leave the office. On impulse, she called Cole.

"Don't bother fixing anything for dinner," she told him. "I'll bring home a pizza and some wine. After the lunch I had today, I need all the junk food I can stuff myself with."

Cole chuckled. "That bad, huh?"

"Worse! I'll tell you about it tonight."

Kelly not only picked up a pizza and wine, but a cheese-cake for dessert. She had always considered the rich pastry her main vice. Now she felt she could safely add something else to the top of that list.

"You weren't kidding about the junk food part, were you?" Cole eyed their calorie-laden dinner with amusement.

Kelly planted a heated kiss on his lips. "Mmm, I think I like the appetizer much better," she murmured, rubbing her torso against his. "You're turning me into a wanton woman, Mr. Bishop."

He returned her kiss with a fervor that robbed her breath. "Then we're even because I'm beginning to feel very much like a sex slave," he teased, linking his hands behind her back and pulling her even closer to him, if that were possible.

"Any complaints?" Kelly purred.

Their next kiss was spiced with the pungent aroma of

pizza until another kind of hunger replaced their desire. They reluctantly drew apart but knew dinner would only whet their appetite for another kind of feast.

Cole brought plates and wineglasses out to the patio while Kelly went upstairs to change into white cotton shorts and a bright red tube top.

Their meal was interspersed with nonsensical chatter and innuendos. For the first time in many months Cole found himself enjoying the company of a woman without thinking of her in purely sexual terms.

Kelly had worked hard to get where she was in the advertising world and was able to converse on just about any subject. Her laughter was natural, as was her manner, and Cole found himself wanting just to hear her voice and he enjoyed arguing about a subject playfully with her just to hear her opinion.

"I just can't believe that Mr. Baxter is refusing to give me the promotion I more than deserve," Kelly complained to Cole while they were relaxing with a glass of wine after finishing up the large mushroom-and-sausage pizza.

"At least he's going to give you a bonus," he reminded her.

"If he hadn't, I would have thrown the tantrum Old Stoneface would have expected from li'l ol' feminine me," she muttered, sipping her wine. "He had the nerve to sit there and tell me that there were other deciding factors in Stan Daniels getting his promotion. Sure, there were deciding factors. He's a man and I'm not."

"So I've noticed," Cole injected dryly, eyeing Kelly's full breasts straining against the stretchy red material of her strapless top.

She shot him a dark glare as a reminder that she was serious with her complaint. "I worked very hard on that campaign and I'm sure Babcock Jewelers's sales reports

164

are going to show a marked upswing, thanks to *my* idea. Perhaps I'm being overly confident, but I bet if I left the agency tomorrow, I could take the Babcock account with me. I even set up three appointments today with people I met at Michael's party Friday night and they all look promising. Do you realize what this means to me?"

"Then why don't you go in to Baxter and tell him what you've just told me," Cole advised. "Lay it on the line. Tell him the hard work you've put in, the useful contacts you've made, and that you feel that many of these people would prefer working with a executive higher up in the company."

"Sure, and he'd probably hand my accounts over to one of his *male* higher executives," she sighed.

"Come on, Kelly, you're not fighting for your rights," he goaded her. "You're good at what you do. Don't forget, I've seen some of the work you've brought home and you come up with fresh approaches with each client. You take the time to research them thoroughly and to know them and their product or service. Show him what he'll lose if you decide to leave. Also casually comment that any agency in Orange or L.A. County would love to have you."

"I don't know that," Kelly said gloomily.

"A bluff works wonders."

She propped her elbow on the table, her chin resting in her hand. "You're right, there is no reason why I can't lay it on the line." A mischievous smile appeared on her lips. "Go in there and be aggressive just like the men he works with every day. Sure, why not."

"That's my girl," Cole approved jauntily, leaning forward to pour more wine into her glass.

Kelly lifted her glass in a toast. "Is Mr. Baxter in for a surprise first thing in the morning," she announced.

"Go get 'em, tiger." He grinned, clinking glasses.

CHAPTER NINE

Cole's tiger showed her claws more than once that evening. After the dinner dishes had been washed and put away, they wandered into the den. Cole selected records and switched on the record player.

"Umm, very romantic," Kelly purred as Cole stretched out on the carpet next to her. She rolled over onto her stomach and slid her hands over his chest. It didn't take her long to pull his shirt out of his jeans and unbutton the cotton fabric. "I always thought Ravel's *Bolero* had some very sexy undertones."

"And overtones and sideways tones," he teased, rolling her tube top down to her waist. "And inside out tones," he muttered roughly, reaching up to capture her lips. His kiss was possessive, wanting her to know that no one would ever have the same power over her.

"Oh, Cole," Kelly sighed, burying her face against his throat when her mouth had been released. She enjoyed the abrasive feeling of his wiry hair rubbing against her sensitive bare breasts. "Don't stop now."

He twisted his body and expertly flipped her onto her

back. "That's the last thing I intend to do." He gazed down at her with passion-darkened eyes. If Kelly expected his lips to cover hers again, she was in for a disappointment. Instead, Cole's mouth feathered over the delicate lines of her jaw and back to her ear. She shivered uncontrollably when his lips traced the shell-like contour and filled the interior with warm puffs of air. "I never knew ears could be sexy until I met you," he breathed against the sensitive hollow just behind her left ear. "Did you know that just looking at your ears turns me on?"

Kelly shook her head. She was afraid that if she opened her mouth just then, only a soft agonized moan would come out.

Cole had wanted to take this slow and easy, but he doubted there was any chance of that happening. He had been thinking of Kelly all day, of having her just this way. Now that he had, his body was working very hard to overrule his mind. He tantalized each corner of her mouth with his tongue and flicked over the smooth surface of her teeth and the silky gums.

"Open your mouth all the way, Kelly," he ordered her hoarsely against her lips. "I need to taste you."

With a soft moan her lips parted and her arms circled his neck as her body arched up against his. She couldn't remember ever feeling on fire from a man's touch as she did from Cole's.

He reached up and pulled her top off over her head. For a long moment he stared intently at the rounded pearly globes of her breasts. He merely cupped the underside of the sensitive skin and allowed his thumbs to circle the throbbing nipples into hardened pebbles.

"Make love with me, Kelly." Cole buried his lips against the side of her neck and nibbled gently as his hand insinuated itself under the waistband of her shorts and beneath the silk of her bikini panties down to her feminine warmth. He gently thrust his hips against hers.

Kelly gasped as the unmistakable proof of Cole's arousal burrowed itself lovingly between her thighs. Their previous times together had been heated, passionate, and mind-spiraling. Tonight would be different. She could feel it in the very center of her being. She knew this would be special. So very special.

By now, Kelly had to touch Cole in return. Her hands roamed over his muscular back and on down to the indentation marking the end of his spine. She found a narrow ridged section of flesh, obviously a scar. She silently wondered how she had missed it during their other times of lovemaking and mourned for the pain he had encountered at one time. The elastic waistband of his briefs under his jeans proved no problem to her questing hands even as they moved around to his pulsing flesh.

"God, Kelly!" Cole lifted his head and gulped for air as Kelly's adventurous fingertips stroked and teased him.

"I'm glad to see that you've risen to the occasion," she purred throatily, reaching up to press a love nip on Cole's chin, scratchy on her lips from his day's growth of beard.

His laugh was raspy with arousal. "You little witch, you're really enjoying yourself, aren't you?"

Kelly now reached up to nip Cole's earlobe, then drew back to look at him more fully. "Yes," she replied in a low voice, amazed by this new feeling, a feeling of wanting so much more from this man and knowing she would receive this sharing of souls.

Cole smiled, rubbing his finger over Kelly's lower lip, then her upper one, and nudging his finger inside to gather the moisture from her mouth. "Me, too." His lips took over where his fingers left off. His tongue persuaded her lips to part and allow him to gather her taste from every corner. He was drunk on her, as if she were a fine wine.

Kelly's fingers dug into Cole's buttocks which tensed at her touch. He rolled away for a second, only long enough to pull down her shorts and panties and to dispense with his jeans and briefs.

She lay on her side and gazed at his body that shone bronze in the lamplight. Only a narrow strip was white from lack of exposure to the sun. Her eyes lingered on that vulnerable area.

Cole came back to Kelly and laid his palms against the dark blond hair. He rubbed lightly, feeling her rise up to greet his touch. Her hips arched up and rotated in countermovements with his hand, silently demanding release.

"I know, love," Cole murmured, continuing to stroke and probe with an erotic delicacy that sent Kelly's nerves quivering.

"Please, Cole," she entreated, arching up against his hand. She desperately wanted the passionate invasion of his body. Afraid he wouldn't readily answer her silent invitation, she reached out to tease him in turn. Cole's low groan couldn't be smothered as she caressed him. Kelly wanted him and she wasn't about to be denied.

"Yes, my love." He looked down at her and laughed softly. His tongue plunged deeply between her receptive lips. He inwardly marveled at her instant response to his touch. He wondered if any other man had found easy capitulation with this woman and prayed that he was the only one.

Kelly's soft whimpers told Cole how badly she wanted him, but he wasn't ready to give her total satisfaction just yet. No, there had to be a stronger build-up. If he could last that long! The writhing body beneath him was more than enough guarantee to make him lose his control in a split-second.

"I want this to be very good between us, Kelly," he whispered hoarsely. "I want this to be something neither

169

of us had captured during our other times together. No one will ever have experienced what we will this night." He gently parted her thighs with his knees and positioned his body over her. He slid his hands under her buttocks and raised her hips.

Kelly drew in a sharp breath when Cole's masculine force blended with her heated feminine softness.

"That's right, lovely Kelly," he urged in a low voice. "Close around me, hold me. Move with me. Take me with you. Oh, love, you move so beautifully. That's it, give me all of you."

It hadn't taken them long to establish a rhythm designed to send them into a color-filled oblivion. Kelly's head tossed from side to side at the explosions threatening to erupt inside of her body. It was a build-up that only became a forecast of a passionate detonation.

She rose up to meet Cole's deep thrusts with an aggression she didn't know she had. She could see that a thin film of perspiration covered his features and could feel the moisture coating his back and shoulders. Ecstasy came much too soon as Cole's thrusts increased until he groaned in fulfillment and collapsed on top of Kelly, burrowing his face against her throat. He rolled off to one side to relieve her of his weight. Before she could even feel rejected, he reached out and pulled her up against him.

"Were there really fireworks?" he mumbled, idly stroking her bare shoulder and her arm to the underside of her swollen breast. Tremors of aftershocks still moved through their bodies.

"Uh-huh." She nestled closer, her arm circling his throat.

"I love you." The words were almost inaudible, but it didn't matter. Kelly's mind knew what Cole spoke. His lips brushed over hers, once, twice.

"Oh, Cole," Kelly choked out, her eyes reflecting the

same glimmer she had seen in them the first time they had made love. Now she knew what it was. Tears of awareness.

Cole crooned soothing sounds. "Hey, don't go all weepy on me. I just wanted to let you know." His hand rushed damp strands of hair away from her cheek and lingered to stroke her soft skin.

She shook her head, unable to believe this was happening. She enjoyed hearing the words, but just couldn't handle the reality of what they meant. Not now.

Cole remained silent. He could read the conflicting thoughts running through Kelly's brain and understood them. This was all new to him too. He knew he had to bring them back to where they were before he scared her off.

"Tell me something. Just exactly who seduced whom here?" he teased lightly, hoping to break their somber mood. He tucked a stray curl of honey-colored hair behind her ear.

Kelly smiled, grateful for his discretion. "I think it was a joint venture." She kissed the edge of his chin in silent thanks. There was so much to this man she wished she knew about.

Cole kept his arms around Kelly in a loose embrace. Pangs of guilt were beginning to attack him. Except he knew that now wasn't exactly the time to tell her about his actual occupation. Not if he didn't want to be murdered in the nude.

Kelly felt relaxed even after her more than hectic day. This was crazy! She should feel guilty for making love on the den carpet with her housekeeper, and instead, she was more than ready to hear the fireworks again.

Tuesday morning Kelly dressed carefully for her meeting with Sheldon Baxter. Cole smiled his approval of her aqua suit and pale cream blouse with ruffled collar.

"I hope you realize that if you get that promotion, I'm going to be expecting a raise," he teased her, sliding a lingering kiss over her lips and cheek.

Kelly's eyes darkened with something akin to pain. She pushed herself out of his arms and walked a few steps away from Cole's powerful presence.

"I wonder if those old women who slip money to the young penniless men feel this way," she mused in an aching whisper, wrapping her arms around her body.

Cole cursed under his breath. He racked his brain to come up with a light reply that would take the tension-filled edge off the conversation.

"If age is the case, then I should be the one slipping the money to you," he observed. He wasn't really all that surprised that guilt had finally penetrated Kelly's conscience. She was a woman of honor and he was well aware that a lighthearted affair with no strings attached wasn't part of her nature. "I never saw it that way, Kelly. We're two human beings who happen to be physically attracted to each other and there was only one suitable ending. There's more to it, but it's going to take time for both of us to accept it." *And for you to learn about my true occupation and begin to accept me all over again,* he acknowledged to himself.

She turned to him and favored him with a faint smile. "You're not going to allow me to feel guilty, are you?"

"No way, lady," he replied forcefully. "If you want to release some of that inner frustration, do it on your boss, not on yourself."

At that Kelly laughed. "Wouldn't I give him a shock." She returned to press a light kiss on Cole's lips. "Okay, you've made your point. Just don't expect that raise right away!" She waved a warning forefinger at him. "I'll see you tonight."

172

Cole cleaned up the kitchen after Kelly had left the house, then walked into his bedroom. Lately he had been sleeping upstairs and had no occasion to use his own room, where he had hidden in the back of his closet his typewriter and box of typing paper. There was also a box of the incriminating notes he had begun during his first few weeks in the Connors household, notes he had discovered he hadn't been able to read for quite some time now. Not when they described the lovely divorcée and her two small children who need a regular family routine instead of the succession of housekeepers. With a deep indrawn breath he brought the box of notes out of the closet and set it on the bed. In no time he was sifting through the papers and reading what he had written. A majority of his previous writings was crossed out and nothing new was written in its place. He couldn't write about the woman who had stolen his heart, even though no one would ever know her identity, because he would certainly know who the unnamed divorcée was. His articles always gained a great deal of reader mail and this story would be no different. In fact, he expected even more reader response than usual. Could he honestly expose Kelly to that?

When Kelly arrived at her office, she found Darren trading one-liners with Rachel.

"I don't have an appointment with you this morning," Kelly accused.

"No, but I knew you wouldn't mind seeing me," Darren informed her with a smug smile. This time his T-shirt read I MAY NOT BE PERFECT, BUT PARTS OF ME ARE EXCELLENT.

"I'm sorry, Darren, but I don't think I'm in the mood for you today." Kelly accepted the pink message slips from Rachel and walked into the office.

173

"Then I'm afraid that I'm going to put you in an even worse mood," he sighed, following her and collapsing into the chair next to her desk.

"I don't want to hear it," she declared, dropping into her own chair.

"We won't be renewing our contract with Creative Concepts when it expires in two months." Darren adroitly dropped his bomb.

"What?" Kelly finally squeezed out a word. "Why?"

Darren shrugged. "We've decided we're ready for an in-house advertising department and want to get it going now."

Kelly closed her eyes. Excedrin headache Number 824. One of your best clients is leaving you flat. She drew a deep breath.

"Darren, I know we've had some rough times, but I've always thought of you as more than just my client. You're also a good friend."

"You're the best, Kelly," he complimented her sincerely. "In fact, I'm more than ready to offer you the position as advertising director for T's and Rags. Since our eastern division is doing so well, we can offer you big bucks and certainly better hours than you have here. You'd probably be even able to spend more time with your kids. Right now, there's serious talk about starting a sports and dancewear line." He leaned forward in his chair. "Your advertising ideas have increased our sales like crazy. We'd really like you to come in with us. Who knows, I could probably even wangle a percentage of the profits for you. After all, you'd only deserve it."

Kelly smiled. Darren was the perfect salesman. He could sell sand to the residents of Nevada. "You certainly can be tempting, can't you?" she laughed.

He glanced down at his watch. "I've got to run. Aerobics class starts in half an hour."

"Aerobics? Is that how you stay in shape?"

He grinned wickedly. "Nope, that's how all those lovely ladies stay in shape, and I enjoy watching them working so hard on their bodies."

Kelly shook her head in bemusement. "I should have known. You're oversexed, Darren."

He shook his head. "Just continually in lust."

She leaned back in her chair, her head resting against the back. "Tell me something. If you appreciate women so much, why didn't you ever make a pass at me?" she asked curiously.

Darren smiled faintly. He pushed himself out of the chair and looked down at her. "For two reasons. One, I knew you'd turn me down flat in no uncertain terms and we'd ruin a perfectly good business relationship; and two, you're a lady with a lot of class and you certainly deserve someone a hell of a lot better than me. And don't think I didn't hate myself many times for trying to keep my integrity because you are also one lovely woman who oozes sex appeal and doesn't know it. That's the best kind of woman a man could find. I only hope the man you end up with knows what a find he has."

Kelly was taken aback by his blunt honesty and an answer she hadn't expected. "There's much more to you than meets the eye, Darren," she said softly. "You just better hope that I never reveal your true personality or the women will swarm all over you like bees to a flower."

"I should be so lucky." He grinned cockily. "Think over the offer. I believe we could come to some very comfortable terms for all of us." With that, he left.

Kelly stared down at her desk, silently reviewing Darren's offer. She had to admit it sounded tempting, although she would want to hear the money part of it first.

175

Cole's brainstorm about having a talk with Mr. Baxter was taking a back seat to thinking over the details of Darren's visit. In slow motion she leaned over, picked up the telephone, and depressed the intercom button.

"Rachel, would you do a favor for me, please?" she asked the secretary when she came on the line. "Would you see if Mr. Baxter could see me sometime this afternoon?"

"It must be bad if you're taking the initiative to see him," Rachel said dryly. "Wouldn't you rather just take him to lunch?"

Kelly shuddered. "You've got to be kidding! I thought I had food poisoning the last time I went there. I'm still picking the seeds out of my teeth."

"Okay, I'll buzz you back when I have a time."

A few minutes later Kelly discovered that Mr. Baxter could see her at three. She wasn't able to concentrate on any of her work for the rest of the morning, and she agreed to meet a friend for lunch, downing several glasses of wine for courage.

Three o'clock couldn't come soon enough.

"When you come back, are we going to be out of a job?" Rachel asked her boss as she watched her head for the elevators.

"It depends on the mood he's in." Kelly flashed a bright smile that she didn't feel inside. "I don't see why you're worrying. He won't fire his own sister."

"Wanna bet? He'd fire our mother without a qualm."

"Terrific," Kelly muttered, stepping into the elevator. "I really needed to hear that confidence-inspiring piece of information."

Mr. Baxter's secretary, Lavinia Spencer, greeted Kelly with a thin-lipped smile. Actually it was barely more than a faint stretch of the facial muscles. Lavinia was the keeper of the house, so to speak. No one could get in to see Mr. Baxter without passing through Lavinia first. If she thought someone was unnecessarily eager to see her boss, she made sure that person didn't get past her. Kelly had a faint idea that the somber secretary would guard her boss with her skinny body if need be.

"We're glad to see that you're punctual." Lavinia glanced at the tiny clock squatting on her desk. "Mr. Baxter can give you fifteen minutes."

"Big of him," Kelly commented, waiting as the insidious secretary buzzed the inner office and announced Kelly.

"He's on a very tight schedule and you are lucky to even get in to see him," Lavinia informed her. "You may go in now."

Kelly experienced an urge, not for the first time, to ask Lavinia if she had ever played Dracula's daughter. Luckily, she wisely refrained. After all, if she made the woman angry enough, she would probably go for the throat.

Mr. Baxter's office was decorated in shades of taupe and dark brown but offered no respite with a bright accent color to relieve the monotony.

"You didn't explain to Lavinia why you needed to see me." There was reproof in his voice as he gestured for Kelly to be seated, then returned to his own chair.

"Possibly because I felt this should be discussed only between the two of us." Kelly restrained herself from wiping her suddenly clammy palms on her skirt.

"And what could that be?"

All right, just blurt out that speech you've carefully prepared, she silently ordered herself. Aloud, it didn't come out that way. "I would like to know exactly why you feel I shouldn't receive a promotion." Kelly winced. That's not at all the way she had planned to ask him.

177

Mr. Baxter's expression was forbidding. "I believe we already went over that."

Kelly shook her head. "No, *you* believed that we went over it. Actually, all you said was that there were deciding factors. You didn't mention what those factors were, and I would appreciate hearing them."

Mr. Baxter clasped his hands together. "You had mentioned that you thought that Stanley had received his promotion because he obtained the Deckard Machinery account. You forget that he has also been with me for close to fifteen years and has brought in many other lucrative accounts. A good part of those companies have remained with us over the years due to Stanley's excellent handling of his clients."

"And you're saying that I haven't done the same?"

"Not in comparison with Stanley. He also doesn't seem to have the problems at home that you have."

"I happen to employ a full-time housekeeper and don't even need to worry about staying home with my sons when they're ill," Kelly argued heatedly. "As for putting in time, I notice that Stan doesn't put in even half the overtime that I do."

"I'm sure that if you continue to work as well as you have, there will be a promotion soon enough for you," the pompous man responded, offering a promise she wasn't willing to listen to.

In twelve years or so was the unspoken part of the bribe. Kelly gnashed her teeth in frustration. "That's a comforting thought," she bit out as she rose to her feet. "It appears my fifteen minutes are almost up. Thank you for seeing me." *Thanks for nothing!* She walked jerkily to the door.

"As a reminder, Mrs. Connors"—Mr. Baxter's voice floated to her ears—"if you are entertaining the idea of leaving the agency, might I remind you that your employment contract stipulates that you cannot take any of your clients with you. Also, another agency might not be as understanding as I am about your domestic difficulties," he concluded smoothly.

"Then I guess I better triple the boys' vitamins so that they can grow up faster," Kelly shot back sweetly. "Good day, Mr. Baxter." She fought the temptation to slam the door after her.

"Oh, Mrs. Connors." Lavinia's voice was equally unpleasant on Kelly's sensitive ears. "I'm afraid you kept Mr. Baxter two minutes over your appointed time. Please ensure that you don't do it again. We do keep a tight schedule here, you know."

Kelly thought first of pulling the black bun out by its roots. "I apologize for throwing your day off. Perhaps you could have Mr. Baxter come in two minutes early tomorrow morning to make up the time." She stalked off toward the elevator.

Rachel looked up from her typing when Kelly stormed past her desk.

"Do I have to clean out my desk?"

"Only if it's dirty." Kelly spun around the middle of her office, wishing she could throw something. "I've been promised a promotion."

"Oh, is that why you're so mad?"

"I'm mad because I can have it when I've been here as long as Stan Daniels or throw the kids out of the house, whichever comes first. Just as long as thirty hours a day is committed to Creative Concepts. It's a shame that I only give them twenty-nine."

Rachel nodded. "That's Sheldon; all heart. What are you going to do? After you throw your tantrum, that is."

"Place Old Stoneface and the Dragon Queen in a compromising situation and take pictures or paint his office chartreuse or tear her hair out by the roots or break all their clocks so their precious schedule will truly be off!" Kelly ran out of ideas.

"You don't have to tear her hair out," Rachel commented. "Just dislodge a few strategically placed hair pins."

"What do you mean?" Kelly looked puzzled by her secretary's cryptic statement.

Her smiled was pure malice. She lowered her voice to deliver the deep, dark secret. "She wears a wig."

Kelly's eyes bugged out. The laughter first trickled out, then spilled all the way. She stumbled into a chair before she fell down. "A *wig?*" She gasped for air.

Rachel nodded. "I caught her in the ladies' room one day while she was rearranging that solid mass. Actually there's very little real hair under that black excuse for a wig. In other words, she's just about bald."

At this, Kelly literally howled. This was better than any torture she could imagine.

"Of course, you've never used that knowledge for your own subtle revenge." She finally caught her breath.

Rachel looked suitably wounded. "You know very well I would do no such thing. It's not my fault that she gives me strange looks when she catches me staring at her hair."

"No, of course not." Kelly began to choke. "I hope you realize that I'll never be able to look that woman in the face without laughing."

Rachel smiled serenely. "I know."

Kelly wiped the tears from her eyes. At that moment Darren's job offer was very tempting.

During dinner that evening Kelly told Cole about her day.

"The man wouldn't even listen to me," she stormed, reaching across the table to fork a piece of Cole's roast beef and placing it on her plate.

"I thought you told me you weren't very hungry," he observed dryly.

"I'm not," she admitted while trying to chew at the same time. "It's just that when I'm upset I lose my appetite yet eat like a pig. I gained fifteen pounds after I threw Dave out. Luckily I was smart enough to realize what I was doing and take the weight off before I turned into a butterball." She speared a green bean from Cole's plate this time.

"If you don't want it to happen this time, keep your hands off my plate!" He uttered his warning, menacingly.

Kelly pursed her lips and blew him a kiss. "I can think of something else I'd rather hold," she informed him in a throaty voice.

Cole shook his head in amusement. "Dishes have to be done first." He slapped her hand when she tried to steal another piece of meat. "Get your own." He picked up his plate and walked over to the sink.

Kelly shrugged. She sipped her iced tea and stared off into space.

"It's your turn to wash," Cole reminded her.

"Slavedriver," she quipped, jumping out of her chair.

The dinner dishes were washed and put away in record time and Kelly and Cole adjourned to the den, Cole to finish reading a book he had begun several evenings before and Kelly to proofread some copy. Their quiet evening was interrupted only by the boys calling their mother and eager to tell her all about their day. It also brought back a very strong realization. In less than a week the boys would be returning home. Then what?

"Come on, let's go to bed." Cole nuzzled the soft patch of skin just behind Kelly's ear. He mistook her strange quiet air for missing Kevin and Kyle instead of her silent speculation as to the changes in the household when the boys came back.

That night, after Cole had removed her blue teddy in record time, Kelly responded to Cole's lovemaking with a strong fervor that hadn't been present before. She was as much the aggressor as he was. She stroked, kissed, and probed all those areas of his body guaranteed to give pleasure. She gave her soul to him only to receive his in return.

CHAPTER TEN

Cole and Kelly stayed up most of Friday night playing strip poker. At least that was the way it started out. It only took the loss of several important items of clothing before they indulged into another, more pleasurable game.

Too impatient to climb the stairs to Kelly's bedroom, Cole carried her into his bedroom and proceeded to draw her into that sensual world that he had led her to so many times before they fell into a satiated sleep.

Kelly was awakened Saturday morning by Cole's lips gently nibbling at hers and a slow, drowsy lovemaking followed that left her feeling warm and languourous.

"As much as I hate to break up this romantic moment, I have to tell you that I'm starving." Kelly tipped her head back to look up at Cole, who had stretched out next her. "What are you going to fix us to eat?"

"Me?" He looked down with slitted eyes. "It's my day off, remember?"

"Well, then, perhaps I could talk you into cooking, say, by using some form of incentive plan?" A feline smile curved her lips as she explored the muscular planes of his chest with her fingertips.

"Such as?" Cole looked at her with amusement.

"Oh, such as you do something for me and I'll do something for you," she murmured suggestively, turning on her side and moving her hips against his.

"Fine, since I've already done something for you, you can now do something for me. I'll have steak, medium rare, eggs over easy, toast lightly buttered, hash browns, and coffee."

Kelly sat up. "That's not what I meant and you know it!" She reached for her pillow and began beating Cole with it.

"Hey, watch where you aim that thing!" He sat up, laughing even as the pillow hit him square in the face. "You're dangerous when you're hungry!" he growled.

Kelly suddenly lowered the pillow and flashed him a beguiling smile. "I have an idea," she said softly.

By now Cole was more than a little suspicious. "What?" he asked warily.

"We could fix lunch instead," she suggested brightly.

Cole laughed and shook his head. "Why do I have the feeling you're trying to outmaneuver me?"

"*Moi?*" she asked innocently, pointing at herself.

"You've been watching the Muppets with the boys too long," he mumbled, gently pushing her aside and getting out of bed. He walked over to the dresser and opened a drawer to retrieve his underwear. "I'm going to take a shower first. Care to join me?"

"Are you kidding. I want to eat first." At Cole's snicker she glared at him without success. "Food, silly!"

"Of course," he returned blandly. "What else would you have been talking about?"

A moment later the sounds of water drumming from the shower could be heard.

Kelly got up from the tumbled bedcovers and bent down to pick up her clothing. Admittedly, she was tempted to join Cole in the shower, but her rumbling stomach reminded her of another important need.

She went upstairs for a quick shower and to dress in a cotton pink-and-peach-striped culotte dress. She twisted her hair up into a loose topknot and applied a spray of cologne for a finishing touch. Makeup wasn't needed, judging from the warm glow in her cheeks.

For a moment Kelly stared at her reflection in the mirror. There was no other reason for the healthy flush in her face but the aftereffects of Cole's lovemaking. The smile on her lips was another sign of his lusty and loving care. Then her smile disappeared. The boys were to come home Monday afternoon, according to the plan they had made. Dave's sullen voice over the telephone the night before indicated that his hope of gaining a loan from his father hadn't materialized. He decided to take his bad mood out on her. She didn't care as long as he didn't vent his anger on the boys. If he did, he'd have Kelly to contend with. And wasn't there a saying regarding a mother and her cubs?

For the past three years, Kelly had had to keep a calm head about her. After all, she had Kevin and Kyle to think of. Yet, for the past two weeks she really worry about the boys. Even if Dave didn't bother with them, their grandparents would keep a close eye on them. For the first time in three years she was entirely on her own. And these two weeks had given her a new insight into herself.

If Kelly wasn't careful, she knew she could come to lean on Cole's strength and tend to depend on him too much. The last thing she wanted was a commitment with any man. Even with Cole. Now she wondered if it had been a good idea to have him promise to stay a year after all.

She practiced smiling into the mirror, straightened her shoulders, and walked out of the bedroom.

Cole was standing at the stove when Kelly entered the kitchen. Dressed only in a pair of navy blue shorts, his hair still damp from his shower, he was an impressive sight. The aroma of eggs cooking teased her nostrils.

"Umm, I guess I should have waited a little longer," Kelly said lightly, walking up behind him and slid her arms around his waist. A kiss was bestowed on his moist back. There was nothing in her manner to reveal her earlier somber thoughts.

"I have an idea it's what you planned all along," Cole grumbled good-naturedly. "We don't have any steaks, but we have bacon. Why don't you put some in the microwave?"

"Your wish is my command." She released him and walked over to the refrigerator.

Cole turned his head to watch her. "That kind of slavery I could go for." He leered at the long expanse of her bare leg.

"You wish," she gibed back.

The meal preparation was filled with laughter and teasing. Kelly found it difficult to butter toast effectively when Cole cupped his hands over her breasts and made explicit suggestions into her ear. At the same time, he found it equally hard to pour coffee into two mugs when Kelly decided to bump him and rub her buttocks against his.

"Be careful," he warned gruffly, sitting down at the table. "It's a good way to burn something important."

Kelly laughed as she sat next to him at the table. "I don't know if it's something in the water, but I certainly don't feel like myself." She picked up a slice of bacon and bit into it.

"Oh, I don't know, you feel pretty good to me." Cole raised his eyebrows comically.

"That's what I mean." She leaned back in the chair. "You make me laugh, as if this is all some kind of game." She suddenly sobered. Was that all this was to him, a game? She didn't think she wanted to know the truth.

Cole shook his head. "Not a game," he countered softly. "Just a man and woman enjoying themselves and each other. You work too hard and don't take the time out to remember you're a woman. Now you're doing just that."

She nodded. She already had.

Now that their culinary appetites had been appeased, they cleared the table and loaded the dishwasher.

"I guess we'll have to find something new to do now," Cole said, reaching over to slide his arms around her waist and pull her closer to him. He bent his head to nibble lightly along her jaw and back to her ear. "Umm, you're wearing that sexy perfume again," he murmured as his tongue discovered the sensitive area behind her ear. "Do you realize what that perfume does to me?"

"I think so," she teased, rotating her hips against him, feeling his arousal. "Although I thought that it was just lust for my body."

Cole drew back and looked down at her with the strangest expression on his face. "No, not lust," he said quietly. There was no doubting the sincerity in his voice. "This is more than just a male sexual reaction to your body. You know that, love."

Kelly reached up and placed her fingertips over his lips. She was so afraid that he was saying only what he thought she wanted to hear. "I know," she murmured, resting her cheek against his chest. She moved her face and homed in on a small brown nipple, sucking the tiny bud. The groan from the depths of Cole's being was enough to keep her arousing him with her hands and lips. She felt a delicious feminine power over this man and intended to make the most of it.

"You're doing it again," Cole whispered hoarsely, rubbing his hands up and down Kelly's back, resting them against her firm buttocks.

"What?" she murmured against his skin. "Oh, that."

"Yeah, oh, that." He barely managed to force the words past his lips.

"I guess it's just your typical everyday lusty divorcée seducing her housekeeper," she purred, sliding one hand around the waistband of Cole's shorts and beneath to feel his stomach muscles contract at her light touch. "Umm, good, you're not wearing any underwear. That makes it all the easier."

Cole laughed shakily. "What have I unleashed here?" he demanded huskily. "Lady, at the rate you're going, you'll have a dead man on your hands before the day is over. I think I'd better start fighting back." He covered her mouth with his own. His tongue demanded an entrance she was powerless to resist even if she had wanted to. When Cole fought back he did it in such a way that Kelly could only hang on for dear life. He wasn't just insisting on her surrender, he wanted her mind and soul in this sensual play. His fingertips insinuated themselves under the elastic leg of her bikini panties and crept upward. He smiled with triumph at her soft moan of compliance and the warmth his probing fingers encountered.

"Cole," she whimpered, linking her arms around his neck and arching her hips against his intrusive fingers. "You're not playing fair."

"Just as fair as you were playing a few minutes ago." He bent Kelly's body backward until she finally lay on the cool linoleum of the floor and he stretched out beside her. Her dress and panties were abruptly discarded and his own shorts pulled off and thrown to one side. He dipped his head to drop a searing kiss on her stomach. She inhaled sharply at the rough chamois of his tongue moving over her navel. "Do you like that, Kelly?" he asked thickly.

"Yes." Her voice was high-pitched with need.

"And this?" His fingers continued their sensual probe of her feminine warmth.

"Yes, yes!" Kelly cried out, reaching down to grip his shoulders. Then her voice suddenly changed to surprise and perverse delight. "Cole! Not on the kitchen floor!"

Late that afternoon, Kelly relaxed on a chaise longue and supervised Cole cleaning the pool.

"You missed a couple leaves in the deep end," she pointed out lazily, looking very comfortable in her supine position.

Cole pulled the skimmer from the water and turned around. "I could finish this a lot faster if I had some help."

"It's my day off too," Kelly declared, languidly waving a hand about.

"Lazy bum," he accused her good-naturedly, setting the skimmer down on the coping. He headed for the small shed that housed the lawn and swimming pool supplies.

"Hey, give me a little respect here!" Her so-called imperious command was answered by a loud snicker.

"I'm going to have to pick up some chlorine before the pool-supply store closes," Cole announced, closing the shed door. "Anything you want while I'm out?"

Kelly shook her head. "Tell you what, I'll start dinner while you're gone," she offered.

"Magnanimous little witch," he chuckled, bending over to drop a kiss on her lips. "I'll be back in about a half hour. Don't worry about throwing together anything too fancy. Five or six courses will be more than enough."

"After that crack I just may open a can of spaghetti. You know, that flat, tasteless kind the boys love so much?" she called after his departing figure.

"Don't forget the garlic bread," Cole reminded her.

Laughing, Kelly flopped back on the chaise. No matter what, she could never seem to one-up Cole. He always had a ready comeback. And she loved it . . . and him.

Kelly was more than ready to admit she loved Cole. She just wasn't sure that she wanted to seek any kind of relationship with him.

She thought about her boys' return home on Monday and knew some changes would have to be made in their household routine. To be honest, after these past two weeks she knew she couldn't allow Cole to remain in the house after Kevin and Kyle came home. It just wouldn't be right. Now all she had to do was find a way to tell Cole that.

"I knew there would be trouble in hiring a man," she muttered ironically, rising from the chaise. She glanced over toward the kennel where Alfie was watching her with mournful eyes. "Okay, fella, I get the message," she laughed, walking over to unlatch the gate. "You can come inside as long as you behave."

They turned out to be famous last words as Alfie ran into the house and loped toward Cole's bedroom.

"Alfie, get out of there!" Kelly ordered.

She knew that Cole's bedroom door was usually closed, but today it stood slightly ajar. She ran after the dog, who had just jumped onto the bed.

"Get off the bed." She looked around and laughed softly at the scattered clothing on the carpet. She picked it up, then saw a letter lying on the dresser. The letterhead read *Bayview Magazine*. Without thinking, Kelly read on, and with each word a chill ran through her blood.

A man named Harry was asking Cole how his research and article was going. Had he come up with any tidbits worth using yet? Also, when the hell would he be returning to San Francisco? Harry had leads for him on several new articles.

The sheet of paper was crumpled in her fist and dropped to the floor.

Numbed by this revelation, Kelly walked back outside. She had to do something, anything, before she began screaming and didn't stop. The pain was literally tearing her apart. There was only one good thing about the raw pain clawing her insides. It told her that she was still alive.

Kelly dove into the pool and swam hard, steady strokes. One lap, two. Her body soon lost count. She knew only that she had to keep on going until the pain ended.

"Kelly?" Cole called out, entering the house through the garage. "I sure don't smell anything cooking." Then he heard the splashing sounds from the pool. "Sneaky," he laughed softly, heading for his room to change into his swim briefs.

When he entered his room he knew immediately something was wrong. Then he saw the crumpled ball of paper on the carpet. The harsh word uttered was short and to the point. He spun on his heel, the paper now crushed in his hand. The screen door slid open and closed.

"Kelly."

The only sign given that she heard him was the tensing of her body. She didn't acknowledge his presence by word.

"Come out of there and talk to me." There was now an added edge to his voice. *"Now."*

Kelly swam two more laps, stopped in the shallow end, and climbed out of the pool. Cole stepped back when he saw the naked suffering evident in her features.

"You bastard," she whispered fiercely, grabbing up a towel from a nearby chair and walking past him into the house.

Cole turned around and followed Kelly inside. He

191

stopped when he found her standing in the middle of the den staring into the fireplace.

"Why, Cole?" Her anguished whisper barely reached his ears. "Have these last two weeks been part of your story? Is having sex with your boss considered part of your research?"

He rapidly crossed the room, grabbed hold of her arm, and spun her around. He hardened his heart against the agony reflected in her eyes.

"We *made love,* damn it!" Cole ground out. "It had nothing to do with my story and I'm certainly not the kind of man to write about a woman's performance in bed. Especially when it concerns *my* woman!"

Kelly's eyes were large, golden-brown orbs set in a pale face. "You betrayed me. Damn you, you invaded my life, my soul, and you left me with nothing!" In effort to make him understand, to hurt him as she was hurting, she pummeled his chest with her fists. "You're a bastard every bit as much as Dave is!" she cried out.

Cole shook her none too gently. "That's where you're very wrong," he corrected her roughly. "I'm in no way like him and if you would give it some well-earned thought, you'd know better."

"Both of you betrayed me, leaving me feel unclean!" Her sobs grew louder with each word. "Him daring to take the baby-sitter into the bed we had shared. You with your loving words and soft promises. I hate you! Hate you! Hate . . ." She choked, falling to her knees, with her head bowed. Kelly's chest heaved with the sobs overtaking her body. She was completely lost in her agony.

Cole bent down and pulled Kelly into his arms. He instinctively knew that she had gotten her rage out of her system. He picked her up and carried her upstairs to her bedroom. He sat carefully on the bed and walked into the bathroom for a dry towel and her hairbrush.

Kelly didn't protest when Cole stripped off her bathing suit and finished drying her off. He dropped a nightgown over her head, then brushed her hair free of tangles. He pushed the bedcovers back and urged her to lie down.

"I want you to rest, Kelly," he told her in a low voice, draping the sheet over her. "We'll talk later when you feel more like yourself."

Her eyes shimmered with fresh tears. "Go to hell," she whispered, turning her face away. She couldn't bear to look at him.

"It's not what you think."

Kelly's broken laugh stuck in her throat. "Funny, Dave once said something very similar."

"I meant to tell you the truth, love. I just didn't know how to begin."

"Sure." The bitter disbelief was strong in her voice.

Cole rubbed the tension lines from his forehead. He wanted nothing more than to shake some sense into this woman, but he knew now wasn't the time. She saw him as another Dave Connors, although the circumstances were very different. All he could do was urge her to rest and hopefully he would be able to talk to her in a reasonable manner later on.

"Try to sleep," he urged quietly, placing a hand on her shoulder. She shrugged it away.

While Kelly would have preferred to fight it out with Cole then and there, the tumultuous events of the day took over, forcing her mind and body to relax into slumber. Cole stood there watching her until he was positive that she was asleep, then he slowly turned away and left the room. He was going to need all his strength when he talked with her later. He only hoped it wasn't too late.

Funny, he would have sworn that when Kelly found out the true reason for his being there, she would have cut him into tiny pieces and fed him to the dog. The last reaction

193

he expected was that she would be the one looking as if she had been torn apart. Cole was hurting inside. Now he knew that he shouldn't have put off telling Kelly. As a result, he could lose the woman he loved. All of a sudden the story didn't seem important at all. Not when it meant that he could lose Kelly.

Kelly awoke a few hours later feeling drained. It turned out to be a major effort for her to get out of bed and walk into the bathroom. She grimaced at her reflection in the mirror over the sink. Her skin was flushed and her eyes red and swollen from all her crying.

"So much for glamour," she muttered, pulling a washcloth off the towel rack. She soaked it in cold water and placed it against her eyes to take down the swelling. She then took a quick hot shower and dressed in an apricot-colored cotton caftan edged in tobacco brown. For once the color did nothing for her except intensify her pasty complexion.

Cole was in the kitchen, seated at the butcher block table, a coffee mug in front of him. His brooding features were focused on the mug. Sensing Kelly's presence, he looked up.

"Want some coffee?" he asked quietly, noting the reddened eyes.

Without replying Kelly extracted a mug from the rack hanging on the wall and poured coffee from the glass pot. She took the chair across from Cole.

"Hungry?" Cole's voice was that same quiet tone.

The thought of food sent her stomach churning. "No," she replied fiercely, cupping her palms around the warm mug.

"We're going to have to talk, Kelly," he persisted. His hand reached across the table, but she jerked away before he could touch her. His eyes narrowed and his jaw clenched in agitation.

"I don't like being duped, Cole," Kelly told him in a belligerent voice, looking at him squarely. "You used me. You walked into my office and lied about your background and lied about your needing a job. No wonder you were so willing to come back after that first time. I was the only fool to hire you!"

"I didn't lie to you," he contradicted her. "My sister is a widow with children, she had all the pets, even the boa constrictor. The only difference is that she would probably tell you about the time I tried to cook dinner and almost blew up the kitchen," he concluded wryly. "Let's just say that she wouldn't allow me in that part of the house again."

"Then how did you manage edible meals here?"

"I never realized how handy cookbooks could be," he grinned.

Kelly's lips quivered. She steeled herself to keep back a smile. Why did Cole have to make her laugh when all she wanted to do was lay her head down on the table and cry?

Cole stood up and walked over to the coffeemaker to refill his cup. He braced his hip against the counter.

"It was also true about my being in the navy," he said in a conversational tone. "I lied about my age and enlisted when I was sixteen. During those years I continued with my education when I could and obtained my high school diploma and college degree. I had done some writing during my travels, which I submitted to Harry Scranton at *Bay View* magazine in San Francisco. He bought them and offered me a full-time job when I got out of the service. I've done pieces on white slavery in the bay area, drug connections, the emergence of child pornography, even an article on the popularity of health clubs for singles." He stopped long enough to take a sip of coffee. "I then decided to do a story about the abrupt change in the male role in today's society. House husbands are becoming more plentiful since Affirmative Action and the increasing number of women entering the business world."

"Why did you go to all this trouble when all you really had to do was interview some house husbands?" Kelly asked curiously.

Cole smiled at her question. Now he knew some of the barriers were down. "I wanted to find out what it felt like to be the one staying home while 'the little woman' went off to her office every day. Actually, one man wanted to hire me, but I don't think he was all that interested in my domestic abilities." He looked a little dismayed as he volunteered that bit of information. His dark eyes softened when he looked down at Kelly's face. This woman affected him as no other ever had. That was the only reason he was being so open with her about his work. Usually, if a woman questioned him about his work, he found a way to divert her attention to another, more enjoyable pastime.

"Making love with you had nothing to do with my article, Kelly. That was purely between us," Cole continued quietly, capturing her gaze with the silent command of his eyes. "When I took this job I knew I was attracted to you." His lips twisted crookedly. "Hell, a man would have to be dead not to be attracted to you, but I told myself that you were off limits."

"Then why did you finally change your mind?" she asked, only to blush when she remembered only too well who had helped him change his mind.

Cole straightened up and set his cup on the counter. He ambled over to the table and halted next to Kelly's chair. One hand rested over her nape, massaging her tension away.

"I'm sure you've got the picture loud and clear," he advised her, clearly reading her thoughts. "Lady, you did a great job of getting my mind off my virtuous thoughts and onto the delights of your body."

Kelly's head tipped back in sensual appreciation of the stroking fingertips. "The boys thought nothing of climbing all over you. I was beginning to get the same idea," she softly admitted.

Cole squatted down next to Kelly, keeping his hand on her nape. "I don't want you to hate me, babe." He pleaded silently for her understanding.

"I don't know what I want." She groaned her frustration at the conflicting thoughts running through her mind.

Cole's smile was a shade too wicked. "Look at it this way. You've gotten back at all those old stories about the master of the house seducing the young innocent housemaid," he teased gently.

Kelly's laugh began and ended with a sob. "I hate you when you make me laugh," she wailed, shaking her head to dislodge his massaging hand. "I don't want to laugh! At least allow me the privilege of being miserable!"

Relief ran through Cole's body. At least she wasn't kicking him out the door as he had been afraid she would. Or worse, shutting his words out. Until Kelly spoke again.

"What about your article?" She had to ask.

There was no hesitation. "It's my job, Kelly. But I will let you read it first. I promise there will be no mention of you or the boys by name or insinuation. It's just going to be a man's thoughts on what it was like to take on household duties."

And then what? Kelly thought to herself. Then he would return to San Francisco. Would she see him again? She wanted to, but could she handle a long-distance affair? She was having enough trouble as it was trying to handle this one in close quarters.

"There's something else. I know you're probably thinking that I'm leaving you in the lurch, and I don't want to do that." He correctly read a portion of her thoughts. "There's no reason why I can't stay on and help you with the boys until September. Perhaps with the summer over, you'll have an easier time finding a new housekeeper."

She nodded slowly, wishing he wouldn't be so damned practical. She also wished that she could tell him the hell with his kind offer and throw him out of the house then and there. But she couldn't do that. Not when the boys had come to depend on him so much. She'd just have to take things slow and easy for a while and put her mind in order before she did anything too drastic with her household routine.

"Cole?" She lifted her hand and circled his wrist.

"Yes, love?" He knew instinctively that there was more.

"I—I'd rather be alone tonight."

Cole studied Kelly's shadowed features. He could understand her reasons for not wanting him in her bed that night and because he loved her, he would respect her wishes.

"You relax. I'll start some dinner," he decided, rising to his feet.

Their shared evening was quiet, with each person immersed in their own thoughts. Shortly after ten Kelly excused herself and went upstairs. Cole's quiet "good night" followed her.

Kelly lay awake a good part of the night. She couldn't remember her bed ever feeling so large and lonely. She hadn't missed a man's arms around her in sleep after she had thrown Dave out. Yet after a week of Cole sharing her bed, she didn't want to be alone again. Her life was beginning to be nothing but a long list of contradictions.

Sunday remained subdued with Kelly occupying a chaise longue by the pool and reading a book she later couldn't remember one word of. Cole closeted himself in his room the majority of the day. The clicking sound of the typewriter carried easily through the air. Kelly thought he was working on his story, but when he later appeared outside for a swim, she didn't ask. She still had a lot of thinking to do.

Sunday night was a repeat of Saturday. By choice, Kelly again slept alone.

CHAPTER ELEVEN

Kelly purposely left the house early Monday morning. She stopped at a nearby bakery for danish and coffee, and took her meager breakfast into the office.

Kelly sat at her desk, sipping the hot coffee and nibbling on an apple danish. She knew she was a coward for not wanting to see Cole that morning, but she knew she had some heavy thinking to do first.

She still loved Cole. There were no ifs, ands, or buts about it. Yet she had also felt betrayed by his not telling her about his job before she had found out on her own. She pressed her fingertips against her temples.

"What am I going to do?" she cried to herself. If only there were a logical answer to her plea.

Kelly was working hard when Rachel arrived. The secretary noticed the tension in her boss's features and quietly filled a mug with hot coffee. She knew now wasn't the time to question Kelly as to what could be bothering her.

A few hours later Kelly glanced down at her watch and discovered that it was almost lunchtime. She then wondered why Cole hadn't called her to say that Kevin and Kyle had arrived back home. She knew Dave had planned to leave his parents' house the day before, stay over in Santa Barbara, and finish the journey this morning. So why hadn't Cole called? She had just picked up the phone to call him when her intercom buzzed.

"Yes, Rachel?"

"Inez Connors is on line one, Kelly."

"Thank you." She pushed the button. "Hello, Inez. Don't tell me—Kyle left his Star Wars collection behind, right," she joked.

"Not this time," the older woman replied. "It's just that when I didn't receive a call from you last night, I got a little worried. Everything's all right, isn't it?"

Kelly's forehead puckered in a frown. "I don't understand. Dave had told me he would be bringing the boys home today," she explained.

"You mean they're not home yet?" Inez gasped. "Kelly, Dave left with Kyle and Kevin early yesterday morning. He said he had an important appointment in L.A. this morning, so he decided to leave early."

Kelly paled. "No, they're not here," she murmured numbly. "In fact, I haven't even received a telephone call saying they'd be delayed." Was it possible for blood to grow cold so quickly?

Inez was silent for a moment. "Kelly, I'm going to call the police," she said slowly. "Of course, it may be nothing. Perhaps Dave's car broke down. He might only be stranded in one of the small towns along the coast."

"Then he should have called," Kelly insisted tersely. "He knows that I'd certainly accept a collect call." She tried to think rationally, but right now it was so hard. "Inez, let me check some things out. I'll get back to you." She hung up and turned a pale face to Rachel, who had entered the office at the sound of Kelly's cry of dismay.

"Kelly, don't think the worst," Rachel entreated, guessing the cause of her worry.

"Children of broken homes are kidnaped almost every day," she whispered, raising tortured eyes. "I wouldn't put it past Dave to try something just like that." She stood up and scrambled for her things. "I have to go home," she murmured to herself as she rubbed her forehead with her fingertips. "I just wish I knew what to do!" she sighed, then the solution came to her. "Cole. Cole will know what to do," she muttered abstractly, walking toward the door.

Kelly hurried to the elevators. Her one thought was going home and finding Cole. He would be able to help her.

Cole was in the backyard pruning the bushes when he heard the front door slam.

"Kelly?" he yelled, placing the pruning shears to one side. "I'm out back."

"Cole!" She pulled the sliding screen door open and ran outside.

He instantly noticed her look of alarm. "What's wrong?" he demanded, walking over to her.

"Did Dave call here?" Kelly was breathing hard. "Have you heard from the boys?"

Cole shook his head. "No, why?"

"Inez called me a little while ago. Dave and the boys left there early yesterday morning," she gasped, reaching out to grip his sweaty forearms. "Cole, I'm frightened. What if they've been in an accident? What if—what if . . ." Tears sprang to her eyes. "What if he's taken my babies?"

Cole's mind shot into gear. "You want to go up to Carmel?" he asked tersely.

Kelly nodded, now unable to stop her tears. "Cole, I don't know what I'll do if he's taken Kyle and Kevin. There's so many children kidnaped by parents and never seen again. What if he's done just that?" Her voice rose, just bordering hysterical.

He shook his head. "Go upstairs, change your clothes, and pack a few things," he instructed. "Then call Mrs. Connors and tell her you'll be up there sometime this afternoon."

"How can I be up there this afternoon?" she cried out. "It's almost a seven-hour drive."

"Do you trust me?"

Kelly nodded. "That's why I came to you right away," she whispered. "If anyone would know what to do, you would," she said sincerely.

Cole shaped his hand around her cheek and leaned down to drop a hard kiss on her lips. "Then go inside and do as I say. I'll take care of everything," he told her.

Kelly didn't question him as to how he would be able to arrange her arrival in Carmel in a few short hours. She knew that some way he would do just that. She went back into the house and upstairs to pack a small overnight case.

Meanwhile Cole sent his memory working for the telephone number of a friend who kept his plane housed at the John Wayne Airport. Right now speed was of the essence in order for Kelly to keep her peace of mind. He put the gardening tools away, then went inside the house. He had some packing of his own to do. There was no way he was going to allow Kelly to suffer this trauma alone. He was going to make sure to be with her every step of the way. And when he got hold of Dave Connors, he was going to take great pleasure in rearranging that bastard's face!

Once Cole set the wheels in motion, there was no turning back. Barely an hour after Kelly had burst into the house and told him her story, he had bundled her into his jeep and drove her to the airport. A two-engine airplane was waiting for them and they were soon winging their way north.

Kelly didn't speak during the flight and Cole didn't try to press her into making conversation. When her hand stole into his, he gave it a reassuring squeeze and kept it protectively in his grip.

Cole had already arranged for a rental car and with an abstracted Kelly giving directions, they headed for the Connors' beach home in Carmel.

Inez Connors had already opened the front door before Kelly could ring the bell. The older woman was tall, with short curly black hair liberally streaked with gray. A warm, welcoming smile hovered on her lips although there was a sadness lurking in the velvet-brown eyes.

"Kelly, my dear." She reached out to hug the younger woman. "I am so sorry about all of this."

Kelly shook her head, not wanting any tears to fall just yet. "You're not the one to apologize, Inez," she replied huskily. Then remembering the man standing behind her, she made the necessary introductions.

"Oh, yes, I've heard all about Cole," Inez said warmly, extending her hand toward him. "As far as the boys are concerned, you're Superman, Batman, and whoever all rolled up into one. They couldn't utter a sentence without your name in it."

"I bet Dave really enjoyed that," Kelly muttered, then paled.

"You're only thinking the worst, dear," Inez said sternly, putting her arm around Kelly's shoulders. "Come on in. I'm sure the two of you would like something to drink. Have you eaten? I fixed a casserole that should be ready in about an hour." Still chattering, she led them into the house and under a passageway dominated by a large skylight and into the living room.

Cole's breath caught in his throat as he took in the wild

204

beauty of the expansive living room. The six-piece sectional sofa was upholstered in an oatmeal-colored tweed fabric and the coffee table was a large piece of driftwood with a rectangular glass top. Dark rust velvet easy chairs lent color to what would have been a colorless room if it hadn't been for the vast oil seascape adorning one wall and the window taking the place of the wall that faced the sea. A jagged cliff led down to the water that now rolled with the evening tide.

Cole then saw the figure seated in one dim corner. A faint whirring sound reached his ears and a man came into view.

"Hello, Josh." Kelly stepped forward and bent from the waist to brush a kiss on the man's cheek. She turned to Cole. "Cole, this is Josh Connors." Her voice was warm with affection.

"Mr. Connors." Cole smiled and held out his hand. "I'm pleased to meet you."

"Josh, please." He returned the smile. He patted the arm of his electric wheelchair. "Excuse me for not getting up. I have a damn fool of a doctor who insists I use this contraption most of the day. Since I'm too lazy to push myself, I decided to go for the deluxe model."

"You know very well the doctor has a good reason for you using that," Inez retorted, entering the room.

"There is nothing wrong with my heart," Josh grumbled good-naturedly. Obviously this was a long-term argument between the couple and one conducted more with affection than anger. He turned to Cole. "How about a drink?"

"He can have whatever he wants. *You* can have tea," Inez informed her husband.

"They're all against me," he muttered grumpily, shaking his silver head.

"No, we all love you," Kelly corrected gently, dropping

205

a kiss on the top of his head. She looked up at Inez. "If you don't mind, Inez, could I freshen up before dinner?"

"Of course." She nodded. "You can take the guest room and Cole can have the couch in the den." She turned to him. "It makes out into a comfortable bed. Our guests do return, and don't seem to mind sleeping on it!"

"Look, I don't want to put anyone out," Cole protested. "I can very easily stay at a hotel."

Inex didn't miss the stricken expression in Kelly's eyes before the younger woman successfully masked it. "No, you won't," she replied firmly. "I won't have it. We certainly have the room. You're more than welcome to stay here."

A few moments later Kelly went to the guest room to freshen up and brush her hair.

When she returned to the living room she found Cole and Josh off in a corner of the room conversing in low tones.

Sensing Kelly's presence, Cole glanced up with a warm smile.

"That was fast," he teased lightly. "I figured you'd take at least an hour."

"I would have if I had needed to do my nails." she smiled, waving her crimson-tipped fingers.

"Women!" Josh shook his head in amusement. "If your hair and makeup aren't just right, you won't leave the house. I'm sure glad I have natural good looks!"

Kelly laughed and crossed the room. "Fishing for compliments?" she gibed affectionately, dropping a kiss on the top of her head.

"Not with that inflated ego of his," Inez interjected dryly, walking into the room and carrying a large silver tray filled with a pot of coffee and cups.

"What did the police say?" Kelly was finally able to

force the question out that had been plaguing her mind for the past hour.

Inez stirred sugar into her coffee and sipped the hot brew before replying. "I gave them a description of Dave and the boys and the make of Dave's car. The highway patrol is checking out all the interconnecting roads in case he had car trouble."

"If that was it, why didn't he call either you or me?" Kelly demanded on a high note. "Why this damned silence?" She picked up her coffee mug, clutching the warm cup for solace, however meager it may be.

"He may be miles from civilization and I'm sure he would know the boys couldn't keep up on a long walk." Cole's quiet voice was designed to calm an agitated Kelly. "He may have to wait until someone stops to help."

"Unless he took off with them," Kelly moaned. "Although I don't know why he would bother. He doesn't have any patience with Kevin and Kyle to begin with."

Josh grimaced. "Unless Dave thinks he's getting back at me," he muttered.

Kelly's attention was on her ex-father-in-law now. "Dave tried to get money out of you, didn't he?" she asked quietly.

Josh nodded. "He has a chance to buy in to the dealership he's with right now. He was hoping I'd advance him the financing."

"How much?" Kelly asked.

"A hundred thousand."

Kelly's mind reeled. The shock clearly showed on her face and was reflected on Cole's features.

"Naturally, he assured me I'd be repaid in a short time," Josh explained in a laconic voice that said he had heard that story before from his son. None of the previous loans had ever been repaid.

"Kelly, why don't you show Cole the garden and the path to the beach," Inez spoke up with a gentle smile.

"Sounds good to me," Cole agreed, recognizing the woman's attempt to distract Kelly. He stood up and held his hand out.

Kelly would have preferred questioning Josh further as to Dave's reaction regarding the refusal for the loan, but she could see the strain etched on the older man's face. She had to remind herself that she wasn't the only one who was suffering from this ordeal.

"All right." She took Cole's hand and allowed him to pull her to her feet.

Kelly led Cole outside and through an artfully arranged rock garden dotted with twisted bonsai trees. She found her way to the wood-planked steps that dropped down the cliff to the beach.

"This was Josh's favorite haunt before his illness wouldn't allow him to make the steep climb." Kelly hadn't spoken until they reached the sand. She pulled off her navy espadrilles and dropped them on the last step. Cole did the same with his running shoes.

"How long has he had a bad heart?" he asked, dropping an arm around her shoulders as they walked along the water's edge.

"A little over three years. Before that he was a regular dynamo on the stock market and then overwork and too little rest took over. He suffered a major heart attack and was told to retire or be dead in six months. He and Inez had used this house for weekends and vacations. They sold their home in San Francisco and decided to live here permanently. Josh paints seascapes and has become quite successful at them. A gallery in town carries his paintings." Her voice betrayed the fierce pride she held for her ex-father-in-law.

"And that's why he has the money to loan to Connors," Cole replied.

Kelly nodded. "He still plays the market off and on, but doesn't go all out the way he used to. Now he does it more for fun, a way to keep his mind active. He's also been very helpful in advising me with some minor investments. I have a pretty healthy fund built up for the boys' college expenses."

"Too bad the son can't be more like the father," he said more to himself than to Kelly.

Kelly slid her arm around Cole's waist and rested her head against his shoulder. They walked a short way in companionable silence, unaware of two pairs of eyes watching them from the large window overlooking the water.

Dinner that night was kept from being silent with Josh questioning Cole about his work. Kelly had told the other couple about Cole's true occupation and his new assignment.

Josh had been a regular subscriber to *Bay View* magazine and was well versed with the contents of Cole's articles. He barraged Cole with endless questions about his various assignments. Kelly sat there amazed at the stories she heard during the meal.

This was the man who discussed advertising campaigns with her and Bugs Bunny with the boys. This man who now talked about white slavery, the influx of drugs among the "beautiful people," government scandals, and child pornography—wasn't there a subject he didn't know about?

She asked him that very question when they later returned to the living room.

"Sure, how to get one very stubborn lady to 'ower all

209

her defenses," he whispered in her ear, although not going further to explain his mysterious statement.

Josh and Inez were determined to keep Kelly calm during the evening, although Kelly jumped each time the telephone rang. She wasn't sure she'd be much better off when bedtime came.

In her bedroom Kelly washed her face and applied a moisturizer, then undressed. The silky folds of her mint green nightgown fell to her feet and the lacy straps were carefully adjusted on her shoulders. The trouble was, she wasn't sleepy at all.

She slipped on a cotton robe and wandered out to the living room to gaze out the window. She had always enjoyed coming to this house. Here she knew she could have the peace and relaxation she needed. She curled up in chair, her head resting on the back.

After Kelly had filed for divorce the first person she had called was Josh. She had regretted telling him the reason for her and Dave's separation, but knew she hadn't wanted him to hear a very different story from Dave. She had known that her ex-husband was more than capable of coloring a tale to his own means.

Josh knew his son only too well. He had been Kelly's moral support during the trying time. He had offered her financial aid before she found a job and she had accepted, but once she could afford to do so, she had repaid every penny at the current interest rate. She also had a strong idea that it was due to Josh's intervention that she had been able to keep the house. It had been a wedding gift from Josh and Inez, and Kelly had assumed that the house would have to be sold. Instead, she had been allowed to keep it and one of the cars. Dave had also been instructed by the court to pay a certain amount of child support. That his checks had never come on time became a fact of life for her.

Kelly rested her cheek against the slightly rough fabric. With her eyes closed she could picture Kevin and Kyle as they had played tag with Cole in the swimming pool and when he had worked with them on handling a football. Their small hands on the large ball. Surely she wouldn't be left with just memories.

A small tear fell from under her closed eyelids. Then another, and more followed swiftly. Her sobs were tiny sounds from the back of her throat when a pair of warm arms circled her body and lifted her up.

"Shh, baby," Cole soothed, settling himself back into the chair and cradling the crying Kelly. "Everything will be all right. I promise you."

"Oh, Cole, they're so little," she sobbed, nuzzling her tear-stained face against his bare shoulder. "Dave has never had any patience with their never-ending questions. I swear, if he does anything to hurt them, I'll make him regret it!" she wailed softly.

Cole's hand moved over her head in the vicinity of her ear and pressed her close to him. He silently cursed himself for not knowing what to say to comfort Kelly. Here he was, a well-known writer, a man of words, and for once he didn't know what to say.

"I don't want you to worry, Kelly," he murmured close to her ear. "If he's taken the boys, I promise that I'll find them for you. And I'll make sure he never bothers you again." This was a vow from the heart, the vow of a man determined to protect his own at all costs.

"I just wish I could stop thinking the worst," Kelly whispered huskily.

Cole's fingers dug gently into her scalp and kneaded the tension from her skin. "That's your overactive imagination working overtime again, love," he scolded tenderly. He had run out of curses to rain on Dave Connors's head and was now working on some new ones. Cole was seeing a new side to Kelly's personality. Right now she wasn't the overconfident, efficient businesswoman who tackled a tough account and had the clients eating out of her hand due to her business acumen.

Tonight Kelly was a frightened young woman who, for the first time, needed a man's protection. And Cole concentrated on comforting the vulnerable woman he held in his arms. Kelly's pain was inside and he had no way of healing the raw, bleeding wounds without the help of two very small boys.

"Kelly, you have to get some rest," Cole advised in a murmur.

"No," she protested, shaking her head to reinforce her answer. "I can't bear to be alone just now." She tightened her hold on his shoulder, afraid that he would leave her.

"Okay, love." He stroked her spine with his palms. "Just lay back and close your eyes. I'm here. I'll always be here."

Under Cole's soothing caresses Kelly closed her eyes and allowed her body to relax against his chest. It wasn't long before her breathing deepened and she slipped into slumber.

Cole waited about fifteen minutes before he carefully rose to his feet with his precious bundle. He carried Kelly into the guest room and placed her on the bed, drawing the sheet over her. After satisfying himself that she would remain asleep, he left the room and quietly closed the door after him.

Cole returned to the den and shucked his jeans with impatient fingers.

If he had known as much about Kelly a few months ago as he did now, would he still have let himself into her life? Hell, yes!

Kelly was up early the next morning. A call to the

police station hadn't helped her peace of mind any. There was still no word. She set up the coffeemaker and waited for the coffee to perk. At that moment solid food was beyond her.

Five minutes later she was seated at the table starting on her second cup of coffee.

"I see I'm not the only early bird."

Kelly looked up and greeted Inez with a weak smile. "I figured a pot of caffeine would calm my frazzled nerves," she observed ironically, gesturing toward the coffeemaker. "Is Josh up?"

Inez shook her head. She poured herself a cup of coffee and sat down at the table across from Kelly.

"He didn't have a very good night," she sighed.

"I'm so sorry," Kelly breathed sadly.

The older woman hastily shook her head. "Oh, no," she reassured Kelly. "It isn't just because of all that's been going on. Josh's health has been declining steadily for the past six months, Kelly. We both knew it was coming. He's been blessed with three years the doctors didn't expect him to have. I can't ask for any more than that."

Kelly's vision blurred. Josh Connors had been her source of strength for so long. Not that her father hadn't been. It was just that Lyle Parker believed that each person had to rely on his own inner fortitude without asking for help from others. Therefore Kelly hadn't confided in him the way she had with Josh.

"What will we do, Inez?" she asked in a barely audible whisper. "What will we do when Josh isn't here?"

"You won't need to worry," Inez said confidently.

Kelly looked at her quizzically. "I don't know what you're trying to say."

"Cole is the kind of man who can be counted on in any kind of crisis. Look how he managed to bring you up here so quickly. He'll take good care of you and the boys."

"You don't understand, Inez," Kelly protested gently, ready to explain that she couldn't handle a full-time man in her life just yet.

"I like Cole," Inez announced sincerely. "Naturally, I first assumed the boys had embellished their stories about the man, but far from it; I don't think they said enough." She faced her former daughter-in-law squarely. "You're in love with him, aren't you?"

Kelly sighed deeply. "Yes, but I don't want to be." She almost wailed in her frustration to understand her emotions.

"Are you afraid to love him?" she asked perceptively.

Kelly nodded. "I don't seem to have very good luck where love is concerned. With me, it barely lasts past the warranty period," she murmured. When she realized how her bitter words sounded, she looked up, contrite. "Oh, Inez, I'm so sorry! I didn't mean it the way it sounded."

Inez shook her head. "Kelly, you don't have to apologize to me," she chided gently. "I know all of Dave's faults. He was ten when I married Josh, and he resented me from the first day. I'm just glad that Josh was never blind to his faults or I sincerely doubt that our marriage would have lasted. Actually the best thing that boy ever did was to marry you. I only regret that he didn't take his responsibilities seriously. I'm just glad that you never resented Josh because of his son's immaturity and kept the boys from him as punishment over something he had no power to correct. Spending time with them is what has kept him alive these past few years."

Kelly's voice softened at the mention of the older man. "I should be the one who's grateful. After all, if it hadn't been for Josh's and your support during the divorce, I don't know what I would have done."

"You're a strong woman. You would have survived," Inez assured her, getting up to pour herself more coffee and sitting back at the table. "Just as you'll survive now if you'll give Cole a chance. I've seen the way the two of you act around each other when you suspect no one is looking. That's more than enough proof about your feelings for the other." She chuckled. "Actually I'm surprised the house didn't go up in flames last night when the two of you looked at each other!"

Both women's heads snapped up when the telephone rang. Inez and Kelly stared at each other for a brief moment before Inez rose from her chair and walked over to the wall phone. She hesitated for a scant second before picking up the receiver.

"Hello?" Inez licked dry lips. "Yes, this is Mrs. Connors. You did?" Her voice sharpened. "Yes! *Yes!* We'll see you within the hour then." She hung the phone up and reached out to Kelly. "They found Dave and the boys! Kelly, they're all right!"

Kelly could only cling to the older woman, this time crying for the sheer joy of it. The morning suddenly looked a great deal brighter.

CHAPTER TWELVE

"Mom!"

"Mommy!"

A tearful Kelly dropped to her knees as the two boys ran to her. At that moment she ignored the scratched and dirty faces and the torn clothing. All that mattered was that her babies were all right.

As in the case of any kind of tragedy, the local news media were present. Kelly was grateful that Cole quickly dispatched the reporters without too much fuss. A sullen Dave hung back when the family entered the house so that the boys could greet their grandfather.

"Grandpa, I saw a bear!" This was from Kevin.

"It wasn't a bear," Kyle scorned. "It was probably a wolf. We slept outside cause we got lost. 'Cept we didn't have no tent."

Kelly glanced up at her ex-husband and her lovely features hardened.

"What happened?" she interrogated, advancing on him.

"The car broke down," he muttered. "Then the kids wandered off and I had to go looking for them. Some

216

mother you are!" he shouted, now taking the offensive. "Didn't you teach these brats to follow orders? I tell them to stay put and they go off wherever they want to! They should be grateful that I even bothered looking for them!"

Kelly's screech of outrage overshadowed Kevin's murmur, "But I had to go to the bathroom."

"Dave, you are so irresponsible that it isn't even funny," she yelled back, bracing her hands on her jean-clad hips. "No wonder I was always the one to handle the household matters and take care of any emergencies that occurred. I'm surprised that you can even tie your shoes!"

"Kelly." Cole's quiet voice cut through the hostility like a steel-edged knife. "You're frightening the boys."

Sanity quickly returned at his mild rebuke and Kelly took several deep, calming breaths.

"If murder wasn't a punishable offense, I would take great pleasure in taking you apart," she enunciated slowly, shooting fire-shafted darts from her eyes at her ex-husband.

"I second that," Cole chipped in.

"David." Josh's murmur was equally effective. "I'd like to see you in my study."

All that was heard was the soft whir of the wheelchair moving down the hallway.

"Mom, we're hungry," Kevin whined, pulling on her leg.

"Easily fixed," Inez said, heading for the kitchen. "Anything you boys want in particular?"

"Pizza!"

"Chocolate cake!"

The two boys ran after their grandmother in anticipation of filling their bottomless pits called stomachs.

Kelly whirled around and faced Cole. Suddenly she felt her knees give way.

"Oh, Cole," she moaned.

217

He rushed forward and took her into his arms. "You're doing fine, wildcat," he assured her, enfolding her against him. "The boys are safe and back with you."

"I can't stop shaking." Neither could her teeth stop chattering as reaction set in.

"It's perfectly normal. You've tried to be brave throughout all this and now your body is telling you it's all right to collapse," Cole explained, brushing the top of her head with his lips. "Come on, let's get some coffee and let the boys talk our ears off about their adventure."

Inez poured coffee and sliced pieces of cinnamon-rich coffee cake for Kelly and Cole while Kevin and Kyle tried to outdo each other as to who was the bravest, who saw the most dangerous animal, and who saw the police helicopter first.

"I tore my new E.T. shirt," Kyle admitted sadly.

"I'll get you a dozen E.T. shirts," Kelly promised grandly. Right now nothing was too good for her sons.

"A new bike?" Kyle asked hopefully.

Kelly smiled. She leaned over and ruffled his hair. "Settle for some new shirts, Kyle," she advised gently.

"Dad yelled at us a lot." Kevin ate his grilled cheese sandwich hungrily. "He even said words we're not supposed to say."

"An original thinker," Cole murmured, earning a warning glare from Kelly.

The three adults looked at one another in surprise when the sound of the front door vibrated through the house. A moment later Josh entered the kitchen.

"I hope there's some coffee cake left," he greeted them cheerfully.

"What happened?" Kelly asked curiously.

Josh glanced toward the boys, making sure they were engrossed in vying for Cole's and Inez's attention.

"Dave will be meeting with my attorney in a few days

and signing a paper relinquishing joint custody of the boys," he said softly so as not to be overheard.

Kelly's mouth dropped open. "Why—how?" she stammered.

Josh shook his head indicating the end of her questions. "Dave was willing, that's all that matters. I think we all know he never really cared about them anyway. All his contact with you ever accomplished was upsetting you and the boys. Now that won't happen."

Then Kelly understood. "You loaned him the money to buy into the dealership, didn't you?" she guessed.

"A small price." He waved his hand to indicate the money meant little to him as long as the people he loved were safe and happy. "I'm only sorry that Dave has given you so much trouble these past few years."

Kelly leaned over and hugged the older man. "Thank you," she whispered fiercely. "Oh, Josh, I don't know how I'll ever be able to repay you."

"Just raise those two boys right and make sure they have that strong male hand applied when necessary." Josh winked, sparing a sly glance in Cole's direction.

"Hmm, that good ol' board of education." Cole grinned, easily reading Josh's crafty thoughts.

The fears and excitement of the past two days caught up with Kevin and Kyle, and they were soon nodding off in the middle of their meal. By unspoken agreement Kelly and Cole each took a boy and carried them into the den. In no time the boys were undressed and settled under the covers of the sleeper sofa.

"I guess we'll have to wait until tomorrow to leave," Kelly said softly, smoothing a stray lock of hair from Kevin's forehead. He was so tired, he didn't stir at her touch.

Cole took Kelly's hand and drew her over to a corner of the room.

"Kelly, I don't want you to take this the wrong way." He paused. "But I think it would be best if I find a place of my own when we get back home." Kelly looked at him wide-eyed, and he rushed on thinking she was reading his words the wrong way after all. "It's really for the best, love. I just don't think I could sleep downstairs knowing you're upstairs and still maintain a reasonable state of mind," he said wryly. "After all, we both know Kevin and Kyle have gone through quite a few upheavals in their young lives and my sleeping with their mother would be just another problem they wouldn't be able to understand. I don't want that to happen to them or to you."

She stifled a tiny laugh. "And here I was, worried how to broach that very same subject with you." She sighed with relief as she rested her forehead against his chest. "I thank you for seeing the potential problem we could have had. It means a lot to me."

While the boys slept through the afternoon, Kelly and Cole again escaped down to the beach. Josh had mumbled something about finishing a painting and Inez was baking the twins' favorite—chocolate cake.

Feeling freer and more lighthearted than she had in the past few days, Kelly challenged Cole to a race along the sand. She took off with the speed of a gazelle, but his long legs quickly overtook her.

Laughing, Cole picked Kelly up and swung her around in a circle. The trouble was, he swung her so hard, he lost his balance and they both tumbled to the sand.

"That was real bright," Kelly jeered playfully, flopping backward.

"Must have been all that weight I was carrying." Cole yelped when Kelly reached up and pinched his thigh. "Wait a minute. I didn't say *whose* weight," he defended himself.

Cole rolled over, imprisoning a laughing Kelly with his

220

body. "That demands suitable punishment," he threatened with a mock leer.

"Ravishment?" She lifted her eyebrows comically. "Are you going to have your way with me, sir? Take advantage of my feminine weakness, or are you just going to get down to hot and heavy necking?"

"Aw, I love it when you talk dirty," he murmured, trailing his lips along her jawline. "Keep it up."

"That's what I'm trying to do," Kelly breathed, pulling his shirt out of the waistband of his jeans and sliding her hands over his bare back.

Cole's laughter was raw with frustration. "Where's that cool, unflappable lady I met a few months ago?" he demanded, using his tongue to find that sensitive nerve just behind Kelly's ear. Her shivered response told him he was creating the right atmosphere for instant arousal. He furthered his exploration of her when his fingers teased the taut nipple outlined by her snug-fitting T-shirt. "It's a good thing this is a private beach," he muttered thickly.

"Cole," Kelly entreated, gently digging her fingers into his scalp and rubbing her fingertips against his skin. Except he needed no guidance to cover her mouth with his own. Her husky laugh bubbled up from the depths of her throat. She nipped his bottom lip with her sharp teeth.

"Tease," Cole taunted, pressing Kelly's hips into the sand. "You would decide to play the seductress when I can't do anything about it."

"Poor baby," she crooned. There was no missing the wicked twinkle in her eyes. Her hand sauntered over his chest and down to the heavy metal zipper of his jeans, which strained under his potent arousal.

Cole groaned. His kiss this time was light, with no promise of passion. Understanding his need to cool things off, Kelly kept her caresses almost impersonal. Ten min-

221

utes later they stood up and brushed the sand from each other's clothes. They walked slowly back to the stairs.

"Cole." Kelly's hand on his arm halted his ascent. "I'd like to thank you for coming with me, and, well, for being here."

He smiled. "I had to, Kelly," he replied quietly. "You and the boys mean a great deal to me." He took hold of her hand as they climbed the stairs.

Dinner that evening was a great deal more lively with Kevin and Kyle present.

Because of their long afternoon naps, it was difficult to get them settled down later that evening. It had already been planned that Kyle was to sleep with Cole and Kevin with Kelly.

"Lucky Kevin," Cole murmured in Kelly's ear when they later retired to their respective bedrooms.

She blushed and walked quickly away, although not soon enough for Inez to see the couple and guess the subject of their conversation.

Cole suggested driving the rental car back to Orange County instead of arranging for a plane, since his friend's plane was unavailable.

"I'm glad we were able to talk." Josh offered his hand to Cole the next morning as the leavetaking preparations were finalized. "Although I'm sure we'll be seeing each other again."

Cole's eyes flickered toward Kelly, who was talking animatedly to Inez while the boys fought between themselves.

"Kelly said you enjoy playing the market," he commented off-handedly. "Is this another hunch?"

The older man grinned broadly. "Something like that."

Before Cole could reply, Kelly came up to throw her arms around Josh's neck.

"I'm sorry for being the cause of your conflicts with Dave," she whispered.

"Honey"—he hugged her tightly—"Dave created his own problems. You just take good care of yourself and the boys."

"I'll see you at Thanksgiving then." It had become a tradition to have Thanksgiving dinner at Kelly's house and spend Christmas in Carmel.

"I wouldn't miss it," he said sincerely.

Once the car headed south, Kelly leaned back in the seat and heaved a weary sigh.

"Mom, Kyle's punchin' me!"

She couldn't help but smile. Oh, yes, things were back to normal for the Connorses.

"Kyle, if you insist on hitting your brother, I'll just have to have Cole stop the car so that you and I can have a little *chat* about your behavior," Kelly spoke lightly, but with a thread of steel running through the words. "Do we understand each other?"

"Yeah," Kyle muttered, glaring at Kevin.

"All back to normal," Cole murmured, smiling at Kelly.

"Oh, yes." She laughed softly.

When they reached Santa Barbara, the boys began grumbling that they were hungry.

"Can we have hamburgers?" Kevin pleaded. "Can we go to McDonald's so we can play in the playground?"

"Let's stop there," Kelly suggested, pointing toward a large coffee shop.

"McDonald's!"

"Carl Junior's!"

When the car stopped in the parking lot Kelly turned in the seat.

"Your mother wants to eat in a *real* restaurant where

223

she can sit down and be waited on," she enunciated carefully. "Get it?"

"You can sit down at McDonald's," Kyle pointed out.

"Yeah, and we'll even get the food for ya," Kevin offered magnanimously.

"Yes, but you don't come by every five minutes to refill my water glass," Kelly explained with a straight face. Cole turned his face away and choked back a guffaw.

They were soon seated in a bright orange booth with Kelly and Cole each taking a child to sit by them.

"Can I have a hamburger?" Kevin asked his mother, afraid that a place such as this would never serve one of his favorite meals.

"Gladly," she breathed, studying the menu and finally deciding on a club sandwich and iced tea.

"Mom wants her water glass filled every five minutes," Kyle informed the waitress after she had taken their lunch orders.

"*Kyle!*" Kelly hissed, promising dire punishment when they were alone.

The waitress chuckled. "Your kids don't miss anything, do they?" She smiled at Cole.

"Nope." He grinned back.

"Cole's not our dad." Kevin sought to correct the young woman. "He's our housekeeper."

Kelly choked on her glass of water. Even Cole jerked with surprise at Kevin's revelation.

"Um-hm." The waitress nodded, although she didn't look as if she believed him. "I sure wish I had tried that with my kids. 'Uncle' is pretty old hat nowadays." She continued laughing under her breath as she moved away.

"Terrific," Kelly muttered, glaring at an amused-looking Cole. "It . . . is . . . not . . . funny."

"She's right, you know. It is much better than calling me uncle."

224

"Why would we call Cole uncle, Mom? He's not our uncle," Kyle asked curiously.

At that, Kelly fled to the sanctity of the ladies' room. She took her time brushing her hair and spraying on cologne. She timed her return with the arrival of their food.

"Coward," Cole murmured as Kelly slid into the booth.

"Out of self-defense," she retorted sweetly, tackling her sandwich rather than the smug-looking males she was surrounded by.

They finished their lunch under the jaundiced eye of the waitress. If Kelly had had her way, she wouldn't have left the young woman a penny, but Cole took charge of the bill and left a sizable tip.

The remainder of the drive was without incident, much to Kelly's relief. Cole dropped them off at the house, then drove to the airport to turn in the rental car and pick up his jeep.

Kelly unpacked the boys' suitcases and placed the dirty clothes in the laundry hamper. She was grateful that the boys were tired enough to go to bed without any argument. Once they were settled in bed, Kelly went downstairs. Cole had already returned and was seated on the couch in the den watching television.

"I thought this might help." He greeted her with a glass of wine held out in one hand.

"Perfect," she breathed, dropping down onto the cushion and snuggling up against his side.

"Kelly."

"Mmm?" She was much too comfortable to move or rouse herself to speak coherent sentences.

"If Jenny will watch the boys for a couple of hours tomorrow, I'm going to start looking for a place to live," Cole announced in a quiet voice.

She shifted her position and placed her hand on his shirt front. "All right," she conceded in a soft sigh.

They remained huddled in each other's arms until almost midnight. It hadn't mattered what the television showed. All that counted was that they were together.

"I don't hate you anymore for not telling me about the magazine story." Kelly knew she had to tell him. "But I still wish you had told me yourself instead of my having to find out the way I had."

Cole sighed and nodded. "I've wished that many times myself. I just couldn't seem to find the right time to tell you. I was afraid you'd kick me out the front door without listening to the entire story."

Kelly instinctively knew it was up to her to make the first move. She slowly stood up and looked down at Cole.

"I want to kiss you good night." Her voice broke. "But I'm afraid that if I do, I'll want much more."

Cole reached out and gripped her hand. A tender kiss was placed in the middle of her palm.

"Good night, Mrs. Connors." His formal tone was at odds with the lambent flames burning in his dark eyes.

Afraid to speak, Kelly whirled away and ran up the stairs.

Cole remained in the den, drinking the better part of a bottle of whiskey to numb his senses before attempting to go to bed. The lure of the honey-blond witch upstairs was running strong in his veins and he knew the worst thing he could do right now was give in to his instincts.

A hung-over Cole served Kelly, Kyle, and Kevin breakfast the next morning. She noticed his bloodshot eyes and guessed the reason behind them.

"Mom." Kyle spoke up as his mother prepared to leave for her office.

"Yes, love?" She smiled fondly at him.

He drew in a deep breath before blurting out his question. "Will we ever have to go with our dad again?" He looked at her, hoping the reply would be in the negative.

"Did he—was he ever mean to you and Kevin?" Kelly asked tautly. "Did he hit you while you stayed with Grandma and Grandpa?"

"Naw, he was too busy with Tricia." Kyle scoffed.

"Tricia?" She was prepared to quiz further, but her amiable son readily provided all the answers.

"He met her at the beach. She lost her bathing suit top in the ocean and Dad helped her find it," Kevin told her. "It sure took a long time to find it and it was pretty big too!"

Cole began coughing as his coffee went down his throat the wrong way and Kelly silently counted to ten.

"I am going to work now," she said faintly, positive that murdering Dave would be a clear case of justifiable homicide. "If I'm going to have a nervous breakdown, I'd prefer having it on Mr. Baxter's time." She kissed each of her sons. "Boys, if you have any questions, feel free to ask Cole," she recommended generously.

"Thanks," Cole retorted dryly.

She blew him a saucy kiss. "Anytime."

Kelly wasn't surprised to find a stack of mail waiting for her at her office. She was just grateful that Rachel had handled a majority of the problems that had cropped up over the past few days.

"Everything all right now?" Rachel followed her boss into her office.

"Yes, thank God." Kelly gave her a brief recap of the events in Carmel. "The boys are still arguing over whether it had been a bear or a wolf that had tried to eat them. I'm putting my money on an inquisitive chipmunk." She smiled, just relieved her sons were safe.

"Darren called twice," the secretary told her. "He's been pretty anxious to talk to you."

Kelly easily knew the reason for the phone calls.

"Close the door, please." She waited until Rachel closed the office door and came back to sit down. "T's and Rags isn't renewing their contract when it expires."

Rachel drew in a sharp breath. "Brother Sheldon isn't going to like that one bit. I'm surprised Darren's doing this to you since you've been working together from the beginning and you've done so much for the business. That's certainly gratitude for you," she stated grimly.

"They've expanded so much they're beginning to think they would be better off with an in-house advertising and marketing department," Kelly explained, not looking upset at all over this turn of events. "They also want me to head it." She felt secure in telling Rachel, since she knew her words wouldn't go any further.

The secretary appeared in deep thought. "You'd be a fool not to take it. After all, I'm sure you'll have more liberal working conditions and you certainly wouldn't have a male chauvinist for a boss. Just a hairy ape," she muttered, thinking of Darren's scruffy beard.

Kelly smiled at the older woman's sharp observation. "The money offered wasn't too bad either," she pointed out.

"Then I only have one piece of advice for you."

"What's that?"

"You better take me with you!"

Kelly leaned back in her chair and laughed. "Why, Rachel, I'm surprised at you," she chided, looking properly shocked. "And here you're the boss's sister. Where's your family loyalty?"

"That and a dime will get you a local phone call," Rachel gibed.

Kelly picked up her letter opener and tapped the edge

against her fingers. "Are you serious, Rachel?" All the amusement was now out of her voice.

"Is Darren part chimpanzee?"

Kelly shook her head. "And you're offering to work for him?"

"No, I'm offering to work for you," she corrected. "You would be the one I'd take orders from. It's hard to break nasty habits."

A devilish smile curved Kelly's lips. "Hmm, Darren certainly wouldn't expect a package deal." She giggled.

Rachel leaned forward in her chair. "I mean it, Kelly," she said seriously. "If you're taking that job, you're going to need a secretary. Who better than someone who knows all your quirks, plus what lies to tell when and to whom."

Kelly grimaced. "It's amazing how you only use a few words to totally blacken my character."

"Yes, but I'd always choose the most colorful words," Rachel finished smugly, rising from her chair. "Now that I've maligned your character, I guess I'll do some work. Just remember—if you call Darren, tell him that you and I come as a team."

Kelly shook her head. "What makes you so sure I'll accept his job offer? For the both of us, that is."

The secretary looked at her over the top of her half-glasses. "Because you're not that stupid to turn down such a good opportunity," she stated bluntly. "Not to mention that deep down you know that you won't get that promotion Sheldon will dangle in front of you the way someone dangles a carrot in front of an old horse to keep him moving. Sheldon knows you're an excellent account executive, but that doesn't mean he'll promote you. He doesn't believe in women holding executive positions in his agency. T's and Rags is a young company and knows only too well that women are just as capable as men in professional matters." With that, she left her boss.

Kelly settled back in her chair, her arms resting along the sides. Smiling broadly, she reached for the telephone and punched out a number.

"Darren Gates, please. Kelly Connors calling." She spoke crisply to the unseen voice who cheerfully had greeted her with "Good morning, T's and Rags." She tapped rose-colored fingernails on the chair arm.

"Kelly, sweetheart!" Darren's voice boomed in her ear. "Where have you been the past few days? I was lucky that Rachel deigned to tell me that you were out of town."

"A family emergency," she explained tersely. "I'd be interested in meeting with your partners if you're still looking for an advertising director."

There was no hesitation in his reply. "How about meeting for lunch tomorrow. It's a Friday and there should be no reason why we all can't get away."

"Fine with me."

"One o'clock at Chamber's Garden?"

"I'll be there. Oh, and Darren," Kelly cooed into the receiver, making sure mirth didn't creep into her voice, "Rachel insists that we come as a package plan."

His groan was clearly audible. "You're a wicked woman, Kelly Connors. Oh, well, I guess we have to take the good with the bad. We'll see you tomorrow then. And, please, don't wear a suit. There's no need to impress or intimidate us the way you do with some of those stuffy clients you deal with."

"It's a deal," she agreed with a laugh and hung up the phone. She pushed the button for the intercom. "Rachel, would you put down that I have a luncheon engagement with Darren tomorrow at one."

"Now you're being smart." Rachel grunted. "Just don't blow it."

"Thanks for the vote of confidence," Kelly rejoined sardonically. "Don't worry, I won't embarrass you."

230

"I'm sure you won't."

Kelly shook her head as she hung the phone up. Now she could tackle her work, since her decision had been made.

Her day flew by as she weeded through her mail and the stacks of advertising copy littering her desk.

Kelly left the office promptly at five and drove home in record time.

She parked her car in the garage and ran into the house. She stopped short at the sight of the two large suitcases, typewriter case, and two boxes sitting in the middle of the den. She hurried into the kitchen where she found an unsmiling Cole chopping vegetables for a salad.

"I found a place not far from here," he announced woodenly. "I figured I'd move my stuff over there tonight after I washed the dinner dishes."

"Why did Cole leave us?" Later that evening Kyle followed his mother as she wandered aimlessly through the house. "Isn't he going to take care of us anymore?"

"Yes, he is. He'll be here in time to fix breakfast," Kelly replied absently. She halted and spun around. "Kyle, why are you following me?"

"'Cause you won't stay in the den with us. If Cole is gonna be here tomorrow, why did he take his clothes with him tonight? Doesn't he like his room anymore?" the small boy beseeched. "Doesn't he like us anymore?"

Kelly dropped to her knees and hugged Kyle tightly. "Baby, Cole loves you very much," she vowed. "There's just reasons for him needing to stay somewhere else at night. But he'll be here every morning and stay with you until I get home in the evening," she reassured him.

Kyle couldn't help but look skeptical at her reassurances. He and his brother had experienced too many upheavals during their few years of life. It looked as if this

231

new problem with Cole was just another housekeeper's excuse for eventually leaving for good.

"You and Kevin better get your pajamas on," Kelly suggested. "It's past your bedtime."

"Not tired," Kyle protested stubbornly.

Kelly suppressed a heavy sigh. "I'm sure you will be by the time you get undressed and into bed. I don't want any arguments, Kyle. You and your brother better be in bed in fifteen minutes. And don't forget to brush your teeth."

Instead, it took Kelly almost a hectic half hour to get them into bed. Needing some relaxation time, she poured herself a glass of wine and carried it upstairs in anticipation of a long and leisurely bath.

An hour later, after polishing her nails and taking a warm bath, Kelly smoothed scented body lotion over her skin and slipped into a sapphire blue teddy. With a book in hand she settled herself in bed intending to read until she grew sleepy.

Kelly was just about to turn her light off when the phone rang. She frowned, wondering who would call so late in the evening.

"Hello?" She spoke cautiously, just in case there was a heavy breather on the other end of the line.

"Hi, sexy." It may have been a heavy breather, but this was a welcome one.

"Hi, yourself," Kelly said softly.

"I couldn't resist calling you to say good night." Cole's voice grew husky with need. "I guess this is better than nothing."

"True," she agreed, not sounding too convincing. Then she remembered her good news. "I didn't get a chance to tell you earlier but Darren had offered me a job and I called him today to discuss it."

"As what?" he asked suspiciously.

Kelly laughed. "It's all perfectly legitimate. T's and

232

Rags has expanded so much over the past few years that they now feel the need for an in-house advertising department and the owners have offered me the job of running it. I'm meeting with the partners for lunch tomorrow."

"That's great, babe," Cole congratulated her. "I don't think you have anything to worry about. You're a shoo-in for the job." He was silent for a moment while his mind reverted back to a more interesting topic. "Are you in bed?"

"Yes."

Cole groaned. "I may throw myself out the window for asking this, but what are you wearing?"

Kelly's voice lowered to a seductive purr. "Remember that blue teddy that you discovered you could strip off me in five seconds?"

"Would you hang on a minute? I've got to open the window, jump, and then take a cold shower."

"Aren't you afraid you'll break something if you jump?" Kelly asked, laughing at Cole's fervent words.

"Are you kidding? I'm only on the first floor."

Kelly continued laughing. "Good night, Cole," she murmured.

"Sleep tight," Cole advised, hoping the opposite would be true. "I only wish I were there with you."

Kelly silently and wholeheartedly agreed, but she didn't dare say it aloud. She replaced the telephone receiver, turned off her light, and stared at the phone in the dark for quite a while. She felt as if it were her only link with Cole until she saw him in the morning.

CHAPTER THIRTEEN

Kelly was doomed not to sleep well that night, and it wasn't due to erotic dreams woven around Cole. The knowledge that Cole wasn't in the house already made her slumber restless. When she finally drifted off to sleep, Kevin's cries awakened her with a vengeance. His nightmare couldn't be easily ignored and it was some time before Kelly could coax him back to sleep. She had barely reached her bed when Kyle cried out for her with the complaint that his stomach hurt. A dose of Pepto-Bismol and a mother's soothing touch had him asleep an hour later.

This time it was a bleary-eyed Kelly who was able to finally stumble into her bed. She would have slept through her alarm except for an excited Alfie running into her room and jumping on her bed.

"Alfie!" Kelly shrieked, snapping upward and pushing the large dog off the bed. There was no doubting how he got into the house. "Kevin! Kyle!"

The boys, still dressed in their pajamas, appeared in the doorway.

"Why is Alfie in the house?" Kelly demanded.

"My nightmare wouldn't go away so I let him come to bed with me," Kevin admitted plaintively.

"My stomach still hurts," Kyle complained.

"You'll feel better once you eat breakfast." Kelly jumped out of bed and grabbed a robe.

"No, I won't!" Kyle wailed, following her into the bathroom.

Kelly drew a deep a breath. She spun around, felt his forehead, and discovered that his skin felt warm to the touch.

"Oh, no," she moaned under her breath. Could he be coming down with something, she thought guiltily. "Honey, I've got to get dressed."

"No, stay home with me!" he pleaded, wrapping his arms around her legs.

"Kyle, I can't," Kelly explained patiently, pleading for his understanding. "Don't worry, Cole will be here with you."

"I want you!" Kyle demanded sullenly.

"Kyle, please let me get dressed," she begged, gently pushing him out of the room. "I'll come in to see you in a few minutes."

Kelly hurriedly dressed in designer jeans and a flame-colored silk shirt.

"Why me?" she asked herself, stroking on a smoky blue eyeshadow and fumbling for her eyebrow pencil.

When she went downstairs she found out that Cole had already arrived and had placed a golden waffle before Kevin. Kyle sat in his chair, staring morosely at a glass of milk.

"Are you sure you don't want a waffle?" Cole asked him.

"Not hungry," he muttered, sticking his lower lip out in a pout.

Cole looked quizzically at Kelly, who merely rolled her eyes.

"Do you know where I can go to have motherhood revoked?" Kelly asked under her breath.

"That bad, huh?" he questioned sympathetically.

"I'm afraid I'm leaving you with two tired and cranky boys, one of whom woke up in the middle of the night with a stomachache."

"I don't feel good," Kyle complained loudly, as if to verify her statement.

"Kyle, why don't you go up to bed and I'll bring you some juice," Cole suggested.

"I want Mommy to stay home with me." Tears began streaming down his flushed cheeks.

"Kyle, I can't." Kelly felt helpless. "I've told you how angry Mr. Baxter gets when I take too much time off." With that, Kyle promptly began howling, Alfie joined in with a canine rendition, and Kevin loudly demanded equal time.

Cole scooped the crying Kyle up into his arms and headed for the stairs.

"You better go now while the gettin's good," he advised over his shoulder. "Don't worry, I'll hold down the fort."

Kelly dropped a kiss on the top of Kevin's head and escaped.

Naturally her morning didn't improve. She called home twice to find out that Kyle had a temperature and Cole had an idea that while he may not feel entirely his usual energetic self, his complaints could be more mental than physical.

"He's mainly looking for attention," Cole explained. "And the other is probably a twenty-four-hour virus."

Kelly could easily guess the reason behind Kyle's illness. He was upset over what he felt was Cole's desertion and the virus was intensifying his feelings.

"I'll be home early," she decided.

"Kelly, you know you can't give in to Kyle's whims," Cole warned.

"No, but I can't let him suffer alone," she argued.

"He's far from being alone," he pointed out tightly. "You know that if it was anything serious I'd call you immediately."

"Yes, I know." Kelly rubbed her forehead with her fingertips. "I'm sorry if I sound snappish, Cole. Put it down to lack of sleep and nerves."

"I know," he consoled. "You just take it easy or you'll end up sick too."

"I'm just so nervous about this meeting today."

"Maybe it's because you're wearing jeans that look as if they had been spray-painted on." A note of jealousy crept into his voice. "Are you sure you can sit down in those things?"

"I'm doing just that right now," she replied lightly. "Careful, Cole, or those gorgeous blue eyes of yours will turn a brilliant green."

"Damn right," he growled.

Kelly began to withdraw from the possessive note in his voice. During moments such as this she wondered if she wasn't getting herself too deep into a situation she might not be able to handle.

"I guess I better run." She only hoped that she didn't sound too edgy on the phone or if she did, that he'd think it was due to her luncheon appointment. "If Kyle gets worse, give me a call and I'll come straight home. Rachel knows what restaurant I'll be at." She hung up with an abruptness unfamiliar for her.

Kelly could feel a faint chill over her body. In the back of her mind she had always known that Cole was a man who didn't roam from woman to woman. There were no one-night stands where he was concerned. He would give

237

his all to his woman and would naturally expect the same from her.

Kelly hadn't been celibate since her divorce, but she had been fastidious in her choice of men. Not to mention that raising two small boys would put a cramp on any woman's social activities. Since she wouldn't bring a man home to spend the night with her, she indulged in occasional weekends spent at a quiet resort with the current man in her life. She had no wish to remarry, and she hadn't felt that her viewpoints on marriage had changed. Except she felt that Cole's outlook on permanent relationships had changed.

The possessive note in his voice a few minutes ago told her just that. She also remembered the time the waitress had referred to the boys as "his sons" and he hadn't seemed annoyed. And there was the obvious affection he bestowed on Kyle and Kevin. All the signs were there, and Kelly was running scared. That is, until her selfish half intervened.

Come on, Kelly, admit it, that little devil whispered in her ear. *He's a great lover. You've certainly never had better. He likes the boys and they like him. Why not just coast along and see what happens? Who knows, maybe once he gets back to San Francisco he might think about moving back here and the two of you could see each other more. Face it, kid, he's man with a capital M and you really don't want to give him up completely.*

"Why can't I ever have an easy decision to make," she pleaded with no one in particular.

Kelly had met Darren's two partners once before when T's and Rags had held a cocktail party the previous Christmas. Except that meeting was strictly social and this one would be all business.

When she entered the restaurant, which was known for

238

its elegant dining and abundant lush plants hanging from the skylighted ceiling, she hadn't expected to find Darren dressed in crisp slacks and a pale yellow shirt, his hair and beard freshly groomed.

"They wanted me to create good impression." He grinned, standing up when Kelly approached the table.

She quickly reacquainted herself with Wayne Sanderson and Frank Carpenter, both men in their late twenties.

"That's because we threatened him with dire consequences," Wayne interjected dryly after ordering a glass of wine for Kelly.

Kelly already knew the three men had been close friends in college and not long after graduating had begun a business of their own. The small T-shirt shop in downtown Laguna Beach had escalated into several stores and soon to their own manufacturing plant and offices on the East Coast. Now the talk was of beginning their own athletic sportswear line. Hence, the need for an in-house advertising and marketing department for the company's new growth.

"I'm sure Darren has filled you in on the particulars of the position." Frank was clearly the spokesman for the group now.

"Yes, and I'm flattered that you thought of me for the position," Kelly replied sincerely.

"That was the easy part. You've done a fine job with our account. Our sales figures are proof of that and you're always open to new ideas. We want someone who is always looking forward. We have an idea that Creative Concepts occasionally holds you back," Frank stated bluntly. "I admit your scope may be a bit limited since you'll only have us to deal with, but you will have freedom."

Kelly digested the information Frank had imparted.

"Are you absolutely sure that you have enough business

to warrant an in-house department?" she asked him. "It's a lot of work to set one up, work that I'm not afraid of, but it would be a shame to set one up, hire the additional personnel, and then realize you're falling short."

The three men nodded, obviously pleased that Kelly was considering all angles.

"Wayne has checked it out thoroughly," Frank explained. "What with our East Coast operation and the way we're growing, we can easily accommodate the new department. Now all that's left is your decision."

Kelly sampled her shrimp salad. "How much say do I have in the hiring and firing and the set-up of the department?"

"It will be your baby from start to finish," Wayne answered.

"I'd like to bring my secretary with me." She spared an impish grin at Darren.

"Genghis Khan in skirts," Darren moaned. "The woman should be outlawed."

"That woman has a computerlike mind that keeps on running when I've run out of steam," Kelly pointed out. "Rachel's an excellent secretary. I wouldn't ask for her otherwise."

"You'd certainly need a secretary and you may as well have one you'd feel comfortable with," Frank agreed.

In no time the salary was agreed upon and Kelly would begin her new position a month from that day. Lunch was interspersed with laughter and general conversation.

"I just thought of something!" Darren had walked Kelly to her car. "I'll actually be Rachel's boss. Umm!" He rubbed his hands together gleefully.

"Darren," Kelly warned. "If you do anything to frighten Rachel off, I'll never forgive you."

"Frighten *her!* Ha! She and Vincent Price would make the perfect couple."

"I'm sure Rachel would be greatly flattered by your compliment." Kelly laughed. She unlocked and opened her car door.

"I'll be waiting for the great earthquake of eighty-four when you give Baxter your resignation." Darren saluted sharply and walked off toward his car. "I have a pretty good idea that he won't be happy over your leaving."

Rachel looked up from her typing when Kelly breezed by.

"Well?" the secretary demanded.

Kelly appeared in the doorway and braced her shoulder against the doorjamb.

"Think you can handle some extra typing for me today?" Kelly asked conversationally.

"Such as?"

"Such as two letters of resignation." Kelly held out her hand, inspecting her flame-colored nails.

"I take it you mean ours?" Rachel asked casually.

"You got it." She wiggled her eyebrows. "Sound good to you?"

Rachel beamed. "It sounds just great!"

"Then why don't you call upstairs and see if Mr. Baxter can see me on Monday and I'll give him the sad news then."

Kelly obtained an appointment with Mr. Baxter for the first thing Monday morning. Then the two women left the office an hour early.

When Kelly walked into her house, she found a harassed-looking Cole coming down the stairs.

"Kevin upchucked his lunch," he told her. "I've put him to bed."

"Oh, no!"

"Don't worry." Cole hastened to reassure her. "I gave

241

both boys some children's aspirin and they fell asleep a little while ago."

"Oh, Cole, I'm sorry. I'm sure you didn't figure this as part of your job description," Kelly apologized, not missing the lines of strain around his eyes.

"Hey, they weren't any problem," he reassured her. "Just like any red-blooded male, they're a little cranky and want whatever attention they can get. All in a day's work." He grinned cockily.

Kelly then thought of the buff-colored envelope lying in her satchel. She slowly zipped it open and withdrew the envelope.

"This is yours," she muttered, pushing it toward him.

Cole frowned as he took the envelope. "What is this?"

Kelly swallowed. "Your salary." Since Cole was paid on a monthly basis, this was the first time she had paid him since their relationship had altered.

For a moment Cole's eyes darkened with anger and his jaw tightened with that same temper. Then before it could blow, it disappeared and his sense of humor took over.

"I wonder if we could call this payment for the performance of household duties," he murmured, turning the envelope over in his hands. He reached into his back pocket and pulled his wallet out. He withdrew two pieces of paper from it and handed them along with the envelope back to Kelly.

"I don't understand." She looked bewildered. She recognized the salary checks she had previously given him, and had wondered when she had balanced her checkbook why he hadn't deposited them.

"I never felt right in taking the money, Kelly," he explained. "I had planned all along to give these back to you."

Kelly blushed as she accepted the checks. "If I had

known about this cheap labor, I would have hired a man long ago."

"I could prove to be even cheaper under the right circumstances," he said mysteriously.

"Meaning?"

Cole shook his head. "I don't think you're ready just yet. Everything is pretty calm now, so I guess I'll get going."

"Must you?" Kelly pleaded, desperate for Cole's company, and not in the platonic sense either.

"It's best," he said somberly. "Those spray-painted jeans of yours could give a man some very erotic ideas."

"And here I thought that a male housekeeper would be an excellent idea after all," she grumbled good-naturedly, walking into the kitchen.

Kelly's idea of spending a quiet Friday evening at home didn't reckon with two fractious boys.

When Kyle and Kevin woke from their naps, they were bearish and demanded their mother's full attention. Kelly was constantly running up and down the stairs refilling water pitchers and dispensing children's aspirin. She had even set the small portable television from her bedroom on the boys's chest of drawers.

"No wonder men behave like small children when they're sick," Kelly mumbled, pouring herself a glass of Coke. "They start out that way!"

She couldn't help but wonder what Cole was doing that evening. Was he out enjoying the first night of the weekend? Had he flown up to San Francisco? Was that why he had been so eager to leave the house that afternoon? She didn't want to think that any of those "supposes" had happened. Maybe because she didn't want to think that Cole might be spending the evening with a woman. Deep down, Kelly doubted that Cole had another woman in his life. For one thing, he didn't have enough spare time. For another, her overactive imagination and lack of sleep the previous night were to blame for her self-pitying thoughts that night.

Kelly was glad that the boys showed marked improvement by morning. She insisted they spend a quiet day indoors so as not to bring on a relapse.

"Isn't Cole comin' over today?" Kevin asked after breakfast.

"No, it's his day off," Kelly replied.

"But he's been here on Saturdays before," Kyle argued.

She shook her head. "Things are different now."

"Did you have a fight with him like you did before?" Kevin asked.

Kelly choked back a hysterical laugh. "No, he just needs some time to himself." She wondered how convincing she sounded, and judging by the boys' looks of disbelief, she didn't do a very good job of it.

"Oh." Kevin didn't understand her answer and wasn't ready to question his mother further. Mainly because he doubted that she would give him an answer he could understand.

By Sunday evening Kelly was feeling decidedly out of sorts. She hadn't heard a word from Cole all weekend and was becoming more curious as to how he had spent his days off. Naturally, she wasn't going to demean herself by asking him when she saw him on Monday.

She went to bed with a headache and woke up with the same ailment. A couple of aspirin and an extra layer of makeup didn't make her look or feel any better, but at least she tried.

"Are you all right?" Cole asked with concern when he saw Kelly's drawn features.

"Fine and dandy," she quipped sarcastically, accepting the cup of coffee he had poured for her.

244

"I fixed scrambled eggs," he offered.

"No, thanks," Kelly declined them while sipping the hot brew. She fixed Cole with a dark glare. "You rushed off so quickly on Friday that you didn't get a chance to hear how my lunch with Darren and his partners went. Since I didn't hear from you over the weekend, I didn't get to tell you that I've changed jobs."

"You took the job?" He was clearly happy for her. "Congratulations."

"Thank you." Kelly sniffed.

Cole shot a quick glance toward Kevin and Kyle, who were busy stuffing their faces with warm caramel rolls.

"Have I got a suggestion for you," he muttered out of the side of his mouth. "Why don't we go out for dinner Friday night and celebrate?"

"I can't," she replied promptly.

"Why not?"

Kelly looked at Cole as if his mind were gone. "What will we do about the boys? I have a housekeeper who refuses to work nights."

"Ever hear of getting a baby-sitter?" Cole retorted.

"What? Some pimply-faced teenager who talks on the phone to her boyfriend, if he isn't over here, that is, and eats me out of house and home? No thanks." She set her coffee cup down. The temptation was too great though. "All right," she finally relented. "I'll see if I can find someone."

He flashed her a wicked grin. "Believe me, you won't regret it," he promised.

"Remind me of that when I come home to an empty kitchen and a thousand-dollar phone bill." Kelly silently wondered if she should take more aspirin before she left the house.

Kelly's headache still hadn't abated by the time she reached her office.

"Don't forget that you have an appointment this morning with our esteemed leader," Rachel reminded her with malicious glee in her voice.

"Ugh! Definitely not the perfect cure for my headache," Kelly complained, dropping her satchel onto her desk. "I don't suppose you want to go in my place?"

"I typed your letter, isn't that enough?" Rachel was unmoving.

"Some package plan," Kelly grumbled. "You're making me do all the dirty work."

"No, I'm not. After all, I had to type your letter for you. You seem to forget that I work best behind the scenes," Rachel concluded proudly.

Kelly grimaced. "Rachel, there are days when I feel as if your one aim in life is to drive me crazy."

"I don't need to. You do a good enough job on your own," the secretary joked.

Kelly had dressed carefully in anticipation of her interview with Sheldon Baxter. Her pale apricot silk dress was cut along conservative lines, with its modest V-necked, notched collar and deep apricot suede wrap belt.

She carried the letters of resignation in a manila folder to the executive offices.

"Mrs. Connors," Lavinia greeted her with her prune-faced smile. "We can give you ten minutes."

"You're so kind." Kelly's voice dripped syrup. "Lavinia, you're certainly the power behind the throne up here."

"Yes, I know." She smiled serenely.

No humility in that woman, Kelly thought to herself as she turned the doorknob to Sheldon Baxter's office. This was going to prove to be her happiest visit to her boss.

To say that Mr. Baxter wasn't happy about the reason for Kelly's visit was an understatement.

"I wouldn't have thought that you were a devious wom-

246

an, Mrs. Connors," he said coldly, gazing at her with frozen eyes.

"I'm not, Mr. Baxter," she replied coolly. "I'm merely a woman who looks at her best chances. That is precisely what I'm doing with this new opportunity."

"Including taking your secretary with you." If looks could kill, she would have been dead. "I hope that you remember the employment contract you signed."

"I am not doing anything in violation of the terms," Kelly informed Old Stoneface.

Mr. Baxter snapped open a leatherbound binder. "Your accounts will be divided up between the other top executives," he stated frostily.

Aware she was being dismissed, Kelly spun around and walked out of the office, feeling freer than she had in a long time.

When Kelly walked past Lavinia's desk, she gave in to the mischievous imp whispering in her ear.

"Oh, by the way, Lavinia," Kelly leaned over the secretary's desk to whisper in confidential tones, "I know of a woman who performs miracles with old wigs. Perhaps you'd like her name?"

The older woman's squeak of outrage was a more than welcome sound. Kelly's saccharine smile floated over Lavinia as she turned away and sauntered toward the bank of elevators.

Kelly hummed a popular tune as she got off the elevator at her floor and made her way to her office.

"You look as if you're still in one piece," Rachel commented laconically.

Kelly winked. "Didn't even touch me." She paused for effect. "I did promise Lavinia the name of a woman who can fix troublesome wigs."

Rachel gasped, then began coughing until a properly sympathetic Kelly thumped her soundly on the back.

"Obviously you found the cure for your headache," the secretary observed once she had gotten her breath back.

"Seems so," Kelly declared jauntily.

Little did Kelly know that her headache would return full-blown that afternoon. She drove home, praying for the moment she could fall into her bed.

"Oh-oh," Cole greeted her, guessing her ailment right away. "I'd give a pretty good guess that you have what the boys had."

"No, I just have a horrible headache," she mumbled, blindly stumbling toward the stairs. "I don't want any dinner. I'm going to take some aspirin and go to bed and die quietly."

After Cole set the boys down for their dinner and sternly ordered that there be no arguments or food fights, he went upstairs to check on his new patient. What he hadn't expected was to find her stretched out on the bed looking pale and drawn. Just as he thought—her skin was warm to the touch.

"I didn't realize a headache could turn into nausea so quickly," she whispered miserably.

Cole sat carefully on the side of the bed. "How about it if I bring you something to settle your stomach?" he asked softly.

Kelly wrinkled her nose in distaste. "It probably won't stay there long enough to do any good." She carefully turned on her side, curling her legs up into the fetal position, the jade silk short kimono she had changed into stopping at her thighs.

Cole sighed inwardly, wondering if Kelly knew how sexy she looked even as sick as she was.

"I'm going to stay here tonight," he informed her. "With you feeling so bad, you shouldn't have to worry about the boys." He cautiously pulled the sheet free and covered her with it. "I'm going to get you something for your upset stomach and fix you some soup."

"Have I told you recently how wonderful you are?" Kelly smiled wanly.

"Not lately, but I know what an authority you are regarding actions speaking louder than words." He brushed a kiss across her forehead.

That evening Kelly discovered the luxury of being pampered by a man. She had tried a small portion of the soup and luckily it managed to stay down.

Cole remained upstairs with Kelly after he had put the twins to bed. He kept the conversation light and impersonal while ensuring that she drank plenty of liquids.

At ten thirty Cole dropped a kiss on the tip of Kelly's nose, turned her light off, and left the room.

The one night he's back here and I'm too sick to enjoy it, Kelly moaned to herself, pulling her covers over her head.

By morning Kelly felt more like her old self and quickly dressed for work.

"Are you sure you feel all right?" Cole questioned, not liking her still pale features.

She nodded. She was more than determined to go in to work. "I feel much better. I think it was just a reaction from the nervous anticipation of facing Mr. Baxter with my resignation. Don't worry, I'm not going to run a marathon and I'll make sure to eat a light lunch. I'm not taking any chances, just in case."

Cole shook his head, knowing Kelly's stubborn nature would override any caution about her health.

"You be careful then," he warned her. "Just remember you have three men who care about you very much."

"Yeah!" Kyle and Kevin piped up. They hadn't understood the conversation, but the part referring to them as men was enough to make them agree to anything their hero said.

Kelly's lips curved in an alluring smile. "If we didn't have such an avid audience, I'd show you just how well I feel," she murmured, maneuvering her body so that her hips thrust provocatively against Cole's. He drew in a sharp breath, experiencing the familiar tensing of his stomach muscles.

"Witch," he muttered thickly, casting a quick eye toward the boys. He didn't want to further their sex education just yet.

"Today's the day you do the laundry, isn't it?" Kelly had quickly reverted back to the siren singing of innocence long gone.

Cole was wary. Her changeable moods could prove dangerous, as he had quickly learned in the past. "Yes, why?" he asked warily.

She merely smiled while her golden-brown eyes glinted brightly. "Oh, nothing in particular. I just wanted to make sure I had the days right. I better run. I'll be home on time," she promised brightly.

Cole later found out the reason behind Kelly's question. When he went upstairs to gather up the dirty laundry, he found a sapphire blue sheer lacy teddy lying across the bed. The same one he had once stripped from Kelly's body in a matter of seconds. An action that had led to a night they both could never forget.

"She's doing it again," he chuckled. "The little seductive vixen."

CHAPTER FOURTEEN

The balance of the week passed as a sequel to Kelly's not-so-subtle seduction tactics from a few weeks ago. Except this time she had to be more discreet because of Kyle's and Kevin's presence.

Kelly's nightgown was now always laid haphazardly across her bed. When she returned home from work she usually changed into athletic shorts and a form fitting T-shirt, and no bra. Her body had quickly grown used to Cole as a lover and the almost two weeks of celibacy had been difficult for her to adjust to. Funny, she couldn't remember ever missing sex before. But then, she hadn't had Cole around the house before either.

Kelly wasn't sure her evening out with Cole was going to come about. By Friday she had exhausted all her sources for names of baby-sitters. The few names she did scare up turned out not to be available for Friday or Saturday night.

"Damn!" she swore, slamming the receiver down after another unproductive telephone call. "Whatever happened to all those adorable girls who used to enjoy baby-sitting?"

"They're out chasing the boys the minute they hit age thirteen," Rachel answered, stepping into the office.

Kelly's eyes gleamed as she turned to her secretary. "Rachel." Her voice turned to pure sugar. "Are you doing anything tonight?"

Rachel stepped back a pace. "Why?" she asked suspiciously.

"I just thought that you might like to come over to my house."

"And?" the secretary interrupted.

"And watch the boys while I go out," Kelly finished in a rush.

"I thought you had a housekeeper for those so-called emergencies." The answer quickly came to mind. "Aha!"

Kelly held her hand up. "No aha. I'm just pleading with you to watch the boys for me tonight."

"Only if they promise not to set anything on fire, especially me."

"They'll be so good you won't even know they're around," Kelly vowed, relieved that the problem had finally been resolved. "Is seven o'clock all right?"

"I'll be there."

Kelly raced home that afternoon.

"Rachel's agreed to watch the boys tonight," she told Cole. "What would you say to us going out for Mexican food?"

"Are you sure you wouldn't prefer doing something a little fancier?" Cole was surprised by her plebeian request.

Kelly nodded. "It's been a hectic week trying to get my files pulled together and a quiet evening out would be wonderful for me."

"Sure," he agreed. "What time do you want me to pick you up?"

"Around seven?"

"I'll be here."

Rachel's suspicions were verified when Cole showed up at the house as Kelly's date.

"I figured," she murmured, smiling slyly at Cole.

"Will you play Jungleland with us?" Kyle asked Rachel.

"Is it easy?" she asked.

"You only have to follow picture cards," Kevin explained, tugging on the older woman's hand.

Rachel shot Kelly and Cole a parting glance. "I won't watch the clock."

"Dirty old woman," Kelly muttered, walking outside.

"Then she must have taken lessons from you!"

Kelly planted her hands on her hips and glared at Cole. "I thought this was let's-be-nice-to-Kelly day. Why isn't it happening?" she asked in an aggrieved tone as Cole walked toward his jeep.

"We don't want you to get a swelled head."

"If I had wanted to be driven crazy, I could have stayed home with my kids," she muttered, climbing into the passenger side of the jeep.

Kelly talked animatedly during the short drive to the tiny Mexican restaurant they had dined at before with the boys and had gone to once by themselves.

"I think I'll have a tostada." Kelly studied the menu carefully. Her double margarita was putting an attractive flush in her cheeks and a saucy sparkle in her eyes. "Shall we share some nachos first?"

"Fine with me."

Kelly crunched happily on the corn chips covered with hot sauce, melted cheese, and guacamole.

"How's your article coming along?" She asked the question she had been wanting to be answered for the past week.

"It's finished."

Kelly polished off the rest of her margarita. "Finished? As in 'the end' 'thirty'?"

Cole nodded. "I finished it last night."

"I thought that you were going to let me read it?" She gazed at him through narrowed cat's eyes.

"I will." He studied the dregs in his margarita glass. "I have some polishing to do on it first."

"Had you worked on it last weekend?" she quizzed artlessly.

It didn't take much for Cole to guess the reason for Kelly's interrogation. "Actually, I ran into this lovely lady at the grocery store and—"

"That's really low, Cole," Kelly hissed, sensing that he was teasing her.

"Gave you something to think about though, didn't it?" he chuckled.

Except that Kelly had her own method of getting even. Smiling archly, she slipped her foot out of her shoe and casually lifted her leg, teasing his leg with her toes.

Cole almost leaped out of his chair at the intimate contact.

"You're awfully tense, darling," she purred. "In many ways." Her toes further caressed the inside of his thigh.

Cole's jaw worked convulsively. "Kelly, you're playing with fire," he warned on an ominous note.

"Oh, is that what they call it now?" But she removed her foot from his leg and flashed him a demure smile.

As so many times before, Cole silently marveled at the many facets of Kelly's personality. The cool, efficient businesswoman; the warm, comforting mother; the seductive temptress; and not least, the passionate, all-giving lover. Tonight she was the tease. If she was this tempting in a restaurant, what was he in store for once they were alone again!

Kelly's behavior was circumspect for the balance of the meal and she took his hand in a loose grasp as they walked through the parking lot to the jeep. Just before she climbed into her seat Cole spun her around.

"Kelly, let's go to my place," he suggested huskily, threading his fingers through her hair.

Her smile was answer enough. "I'm certainly glad I don't have to be the brazen woman and suggest it myself," she murmured.

Cole groaned and tore himself away. "If I kiss you now, I won't be able to stop. Let's just get going and hope there's no cops on the road."

They purposely didn't touch each other during the short drive to Cole's apartment. The anticipation was built so high that even the air around them was thick with frustration. It wasn't long before Cole parked in front of a small apartment building with a sign advertising furnished apartments on the lawn.

"This is where you're staying?" Kelly turned to him with shock and amusement mingled in her voice.

"Yes, why?" he asked warily.

She laughed throatily. "Oh, Cole, these apartments are not only rented out by the day or week, but by the hour too."

"How would you know that?" he demanded.

"Because they advertise in the newspaper about the special movies they offer." Kelly lowered her voice. "I'm sure you know what kind of movies I'm talking about." She smiled seductively.

Cole shook his head. "I could have made a big mistake bringing you here," he muttered, getting out of the jeep and going around to the other side to assist Kelly.

"I've always wanted to see one, Cole," she confided as

255

he unlocked the door to his room. "I'm sure they're very steamy."

"Among other things," he sighed, flipping on the light. Kelly looked around the small room with interest. It was little more than a hotel room with a double bed against one wall, a couch, and a color TV in one corner, with a small black box on top. She wandered over to the TV and flipped it on. It took her a moment to master the controls, but she soon satisfied her curiosity.

"Cole, can it really be done that way?" she asked with perverse delight.

He took one look at the screen, groaned loudly, and walked over to the TV to switch it off.

"Believe me, the last thing I need is instructions," he muttered thickly, lowering his head to hers.

"I've missed you," Kelly breathed against his lips.

"No more than me, babe," he sighed, rubbing his fingertips over the top of her collarbone. "I never realized a bed could feel so empty."

It was soon apparent that the two lovers had been deprived of each other too long.

"Empty and cold." Kelly turned her face into the hollow of his throat and breathed in the warm, musky scent of his skin. The tip of her tongue darted out to find the rapid pulse at the base.

"You're driving me crazy!" Cole groaned. His mouth hungrily devoured hers, his tongue parting her lips to delve into the warm, moist cave of her mouth.

"Oh, Kelly," he muttered roughly, impatiently pulling her shirt out of the waistband of her cotton pants to trace the lines of her bare back. "Good girl, you're not wearing a bra."

"Don't talk," she moaned, tugging at his hair to bring his mouth back to hers. She was just as eager for the taste of him. Kelly's arms circled Cole's neck tightly. She couldn't remember ever feeling the strong intensity she felt at this moment. Nothing mattered more than Cole's kissing and caressing her.

Cole unbuttoned Kelly's blouse and palmed a full breast, swollen with passion. His thumb teased the dusky nipple into a taut point. Her whimper of delight was swallowed by the driving force of his mouth.

"God, Kelly, we can't continue standing here like two teenagers petting outside the girl's front door." He tore his mouth away to gasp for air.

"Do you have someplace better in mind?" She moved her hips against him provocatively.

Cole's fingers dug gently into her hair as he pushed her face away a few inches so that he could study her. "If I'm going to make love to you, I intend doing it in a bed," he stated bluntly.

"Yes!" Kelly's eyes shone. "Please, Cole."

They hurriedly tore each other's clothes off and found their way to the bed. But something had changed in just those few moments. It wasn't long before Kelly realized that Cole was discouraging her caressing him in return and his face was taut with some unknown emotion. Each time her hand drifted to below his waist he gripped her hand tightly and brought it to his lips.

"Cole?" She spoke softly, running her fingertips over his cheek and along his jawline.

His reply was short and explicit. He turned over and closed his eyes as if he were very weary.

"Cole?" Kelly asked again, reaching out to touch him, but he jerked away as if he had been burned. She propped herself up on her elbow to enable her to see his face.

"God, Kelly, I'm sorry," he muttered hoarsely, refusing to look at her.

Her fingertips fluttered over his closed eyelids. He moved away again, rejecting her caress.

"Don't shut me out, Cole," she begged, shifting her body to lie next to him.

He rolled over onto his back and viewed her with dark eyes filled with bitterness. "Where's the ranting and raving?" he jeered. "Why not call me the tease? After all, I've got you all primed and ready and now I can't do a damn thing about it!" he ground out, angrier more at himself than at her.

Kelly grasped one of Cole's clenched fists and drew it against her. She gently pried his fingers apart and laced her own fingers through them.

"Is that what you think?" she teased him gently, knowing that the moment had to be treated very carefully. "Oh, Cole, you of all people should know that lovemaking is so much more than the physical act." She lifted his hand to her lips and nibbled each finger.

Cole eyed her askance. "This has never happened to me before," he admitted reluctantly in a low voice.

"It's been a rough time for both of us lately." She laid her head next to his on the pillow and placed their intertwined hands on his damp chest. "I'm just glad that we're here alone. There're no boys to interrupt us and that means I can even do unspeakable acts to your body." Her voice lowered to a throaty purr.

Cole couldn't help but smile. "I seem to remember you promising me that on one other occasion," he commented wryly.

"And I intend to keep my promise." She sat up, unaware of the provocative picture she made with her skin glowing gold in the dim lamplight spilling across the bed. "Turn over," she ordered briskly.

"Why?" he asked suspiciously. "Are you getting kinky in your old age?"

Kelly climbed off the bed and walked over to her purse lying on the carpet. "I won't even dignify that with an answer," she declared haughtily, rummaging through her purse. "Ah, here it is!"

Cole watched Kelly with wary eyes as she approached the bed carrying a small plastic tube.

"What are you doing?"

"You'll see." She smiled mysteriously. "Just turn over," she instructed.

Cole slowly turned over, his body tense with curiosity.

"Don't worry, you'll enjoy this," Kelly cheerfully promised.

The bed dipped slightly under Kelly's weight. She knelt close to Cole's hip and unscrewed the top. She squeezed some of the contents into her hand and warmed the lotion between her palms before applying it to his back. The warm scent of cinnamon permeated the air.

"It's body lotion," she explained, smoothing the rich lotion over the broad planes of his shoulders. "I just want you to lie here and relax." Her fingertips dug into the knotted muscles of his neck and massaged them free of tension. The same action moved down his spine as her thumbs pressed along each vertebra to the strong buttocks. She moved down quickly before her touch became too intimate. More lotion was applied to the back of his thighs and along the muscular legs. She kneaded each leg with strong pressure designed to relax. When she finished she moved back up to his shoulders and began all over again. As she continued, her movements became slower and more drugging to the senses. Within a half hour Cole was lulled into a nether world.

"It still isn't fair," he mumbled sleepily when he felt her hands caressing the sides of his chest.

"Sure it is. I'm having the enjoyment of touching you," Kelly said honestly.

Cole turned onto his back and faced Kelly with a gleaming sapphire gaze. "Then it's only fair that I have my turn." He picked up the tube lying on the bed.

Kelly stretched out on her stomach, her arms at her sides. She literally purred when his strong hands kneaded her shoulder muscles and down her back.

"Is this how they do it in a massage parlor?" she asked throatily.

"With a few added touches of my own."

Kelly's head snapped up. "You mean you've been in one of those indecent places?"

Cole grinned. "Sure, during my younger and more impulsive days."

Kelly didn't even want to picture some bleach blonde dressed in a cheap, spangled costume administering to Cole in a sleazy room.

"She was a redhead with dark roots, dressed in a white bikini. I met her when I was in Hong Kong," Cole whispered in her ear.

"I understand the weather is very steamy there. How many degrees did you raise the temperature?" she asked caustically.

"You're so easy to tease, my love."

"Rat!" she denounced and would have said more, but Cole's palm, slippery with lotion, smoothed over her buttocks, silencing her. Even more so when his fingers dipped down between her thighs. Kelly bit her lip to hold back her moan of desire.

The lotion was also stroked down her legs, tickling the arches of her feet, and back up over her calves and thighs. Time and time again, his fingers dipped between her legs. Kelly shifted her position, allowing her thighs to drift open slightly.

"I think I like you best this way," Cole remarked, allowing his hands to rest possessively over the dimpled cheeks of her buttocks.

"You're in a complimentary mood tonight," Kelly murmured, wishing she could anticipate his next move. Now he slid his hands along her sides, just barely touching the sides of her breasts.

"That's because I'm such a great guy," he said expansively.

"That's big of you," she retorted sarcastically.

"Am I?" he asked facetiously.

"Are you what?"

"Big."

Kelly uttered a shriek and turned over. With Cole straddling her legs, she couldn't move far.

"You haven't answered my question," he prompted with a broad smile.

There was no doubting Cole's intentions now.

"Come here," she invited, holding her arms out.

In one lithe movement Cole stretched out over Kelly, using one silken thrust to encase himself in her warmth.

"You feel so good," he whispered against her mouth. His hands slid under her buttocks and lifted her to receive him even more deeply.

Kelly moved under Cole, feeling the heat flow through her body.

"Wrap your legs around me," he ordered hoarsely, quickening his thrusts.

She obeyed, lifting her mouth to receive the hot penetration of his tongue. Even with their mouths fused together, whispered words of love and need passed between them. Her nails dug into his hips as the pleasure spun through the center of her body and radiated through each nerve ending. She felt as if her body were ready to explode into millions of fragments. When the dizzying sensation reached her brain, she began crying out loud for release.

"I can't take any more," she whimpered against his mouth. "No more!"

"Yes," he breathed, increasing his movements in reply. "Let it all flow, Kelly. Keep up with me. Move with me. That's it."

Following his whispered instructions, Kelly found herself experiencing more than spinning through space. She erupted at the same moment Cole did, leaving them arching and thrusting wildly to the final second. In the end, all Kelly could do was cling helplessly to Cole and allow him to carry her into the ultimate fulfillment.

Resting his weight on his elbows, Cole brushed a kiss over Kelly's damp brow.

"It was beautiful, love," he whispered. "I have never experienced anything like this until you."

Kelly smiled weakly. "I didn't know it was possible. I thought it was only something that happened in books."

Cole shifted until he lay on his side, one arm resting possessively across Kelly's waist.

"It can happen between two people who mean a great deal to each other," he informed her.

She rolled over to face him. "And here you thought it wouldn't happen again," she teased lovingly, fingering damp strands of hair lying on his forehead.

"I guess it just goes to show that a sexy lady like you can bring a dead man to life again." His eyes raked over her with lazy humor. "You are very special to me, Kelly."

"You are to me also."

Cole framed Kelly's face with his hands. "Marry me, Kelly," he entreated with an intense note in his voice.

She froze. "I haven't compromised you, Cole," she replied, striving to bring a light touch to his proposal. "You're perfectly safe with me."

"I'm serious, Kelly. You know that I love you and I know that you love me. There's no reason why we can't get married."

Kelly carefully disentangled herself from his embrace and slid off the bed. She walked over to the pile of clothing and picked up her bikini panties. She slowly pulled them on and reached for her slacks. She was completely silent as she dressed.

"Kelly?" Cole frowned, not understanding her silence.

"Please don't ruin this for us, Cole," she requested quietly, digging a hairbrush out of her purse. She walked over to the small mirror hanging over the dresser and began brushing the tangles from her hair.

"My proposing to you is ruining our relationship?" His voice rose in agitation. "Pardon me if I don't understand. I admit I'm not the most eligible bachelor in the world, but I can think of a few women who wouldn't mind hearing a proposal of marriage from me. I never thought I'd consider getting married again. And then I met you and the boys and knew you had what I needed. A home, a family, and love. There's no reason why I can't do my own writing down here as well as in San Francisco. Hell, I'm not asking you to give up your job! I've discovered that it's not so bad staying home and taking care of the boys. So what's so wrong with all that?" he demanded tersely.

Kelly took her time putting her hairbrush into her purse and snapping it shut. She turned around and leaned back, bracing her hands on the edge of the dresser.

"When I divorced Dave I vowed I wouldn't marry again," she said in a low voice with no emotion surfacing. "I've met many men since my divorce and slept with a few." Cole winced at her blunt words. "But it didn't take much for me to realize that I can't offer a man what he really needs."

"And what is it that you think I need so badly that you can't give me?" Cole challenged.

"A full-time wife . . . children. I love my job, Cole. Just

as much as you love yours," Kelly replied. "I've worked hard to get where I am today and I just can't go back to being a housewife. I'd grow to resent the house, the boys, and even you."

Cole got off the bed and retrieved his slacks. "I don't recall asking you to give up your job. And the boys are certainly family enough for me. I don't feel a need to prove my masculinity by fathering a child," he bit out. "I don't work out of an office, Kelly. My apartment has a fully equipped office and I see no reason why the downstairs bedroom couldn't be outfitted with my word processor, desk, and file cabinets."

Kelly bit her bottom lip in vexation. "It appears that you've got it all planned."

"I thought I had." He walked over to her and placed his hands on her shoulders. "You've said you love me. Is that true or just empty words spoken during lovemaking?" he speculated.

Kelly shook her head. "I'm just not cut out for marriage anymore, Cole," she whispered. "I have one bad marriage behind me. I don't care to have another."

Cole released her and walked away as if afraid he might be tempted to strangle her. He combed his fingers through his hair. "Thanks for the vote of confidence." He laughed harshly. "You're not the only one with a bad marriage in your past, honey. But I'm not letting it color my future. I want more than an affair with you, Kelly. I want to wake up with you every morning, to be there when you come home from the office, and to kiss you good night before we go to sleep. I want to see Kyle and Kevin grow up and hand you my handkerchief when you begin crying at their weddings. There may be times when I may have to travel to work up an article, but I'd do it as little as possible. Is it so wrong to want that?"

Kelly shook her head. "Of course not," she murmured. "I just don't think I'd be such a good bet for you, Cole. As for the boys, well, taking care of them for a few months and having them around for years to come is two different things. You might regret letting yourself in for a full-blown family and then regret being married to me. Plus I've been sour on the subject of marriage for so long that I don't think I can change now."

"You mean you don't *want* to change," he rapped out, pulling his shirt on with jerky movements. "Then I guess you don't love me as much as you say you do."

"Of course I do," she assured him in a small voice. "I just don't think I can make that final step."

Cole's deep sapphire eyes were openly derisive. "Then I guess there's only one thing to do," he snapped. "The first day of September is on Friday. That will be my last day."

"So soon?" Kelly asked, dismayed.

"I promised to stay until September and that is exactly what I will be doing," he bit out.

He shrugged. "There's no reason for me to stay." His reply was like a slap in the face. "If you're ready, I'll drive you home now."

Kelly turned back to pick up her purse. She caught a glimpse of her reflection in the mirror. Where were the healthy flushed cheeks and slightly swollen lips that had alluded to their lovemaking? Instead, there were only her pale, pinched features and trembling lips to reveal the torn state of her emotions. Why couldn't he understand her reluctance to commit herself?

Cole drove as if the very devil were after him. When they reached Kelly's house, he waited silently until she got out of the jeep before roaring off without a backward glance. Kelly stood on the porch watching him drive

265

away, a squeal of tires and the smell of burning rubber in the air.

"I don't want to lose you, Cole," she pleaded to the rapidly disappearing taillights. "Can't you please understand?" Her shoulders slumped in defeat, she turned around to unlock the front door. The evening that had started out so beautifully now tasted like ashes.

CHAPTER FIFTEEN

The weekend never seemed so long. Kelly moped around the house, feeling as if she had lost her best friend.

"Do you hurt, Mom?" Kevin asked his mother. Sensing all wasn't well, he was ready to offer his comfort. "Can me and Kyle make it better?"

She smiled wanly and pulled him into her arms. "That's very sweet of you, baby," she whispered. "I feel better just knowing you love me."

"I love you, Mom," he assured her, bewildered by her show of apathy. "Me and Kyle love you a lot. Cole loves you too."

Kelly's eyes filled with hot tears. She couldn't remember crying as much as she had the past two days.

Rachel had eyed her curiously when she had come into the house Friday night but was tactful enough not to ask any questions. After Rachel had left, Kelly had gone to bed and had cried herself to sleep. She only wished she had known exactly why she had cried. After all, she told Cole the truth, hadn't she? She didn't want marriage again. So why was she so upset?

Kyle and Kevin had realized that Kelly was sad about something and tried their hardest to cheer her up.

Saturday night, when Kelly realized that she was eating her fourth Ding-Dong in a row, she knew she was in trouble.

"Damn it, I'm not going to gain fifty pounds because of him," she snarled, tossing the remains down the garbage disposal.

In desperation she took the boys to Knotts Berry Farm Sunday afternoon. She followed them around on all the rides and even allowed them to stuff themselves with junk food. When she finally took them home, they were tired and irritable from their long day. Kelly put them to bed and poured herself a glass of wine to sip while she tried to relax in a hot bath.

An hour later she rummaged in her dresser drawer for a nightgown. A strangled sob hung in the air. The topmost garment was the infamous sapphire blue teddy.

The moment Cole entered the house Monday morning, Kelly was out the door.

When he later went upstairs to straighten up the bedrooms, he found scraps of bright blue silk on the carpet.

"Oh, Kelly," he sighed, kneeling down to pick up the remnants. "You're hurting just as much as I am, aren't you?"

Kelly was glad that she didn't have to concentrate too hard on her work. She was also glad she would have two free weeks before beginning her new position. Perhaps she'd take the boys up to Carmel. Time with no-nonsense Josh and Inez might help her put her life back into its perspective. If only their house wouldn't carry memories of Cole.

She picked up the phone at the sound of the buzzer intruding into her thoughts. "Yes, Rachel?"

"Mr. Babcock would like to know if you have time to see him?"

"Of course." She pasted on her best smile. She stood up when Michael entered the office. "Michael, how good it is to see you," she greeted him warmly.

"If it's so good, why am I handed over to another account executive?" he asked her coldly.

"I was going to call you this week, Michael," Kelly replied. "The letter I sent you was a formality inspired by Mr. Baxter."

"What agency are you moving to?"

Kelly shook her head. "I'm not to going to another agency. I'm going to work for T's and Rags as their advertising director."

Michael sat down, yet even in his agitation he remembered to pull up his slacks to prevent wrinkles.

"If you had wanted to leave here, you could have come to work for me," he told her somberly.

"It wasn't that, Michael," she explained. "Darren offered me the job and I finally decided it was time for me to move on. Craig is an excellent idea man. You'll enjoy working with him."

"Yes, but he doesn't boast your measurements."

"Behave yourself, Michael," she chided.

He sobered. "If this change is such a wonderful opportunity, why aren't you looking happier?"

"Oh, it's just one of those days." Her lame excuse sounded false to both of them.

"The man you left with at the party? Is he the one who took the sparkle out of your eyes?" he asked, his sharp glare dissecting each inch of her saddened features.

"Just too much work," she lied flippantly. "I'll have two weeks before I begin at T's and Rags. I haven't had a vacation in well over a year and the rest will do me good."

Michael studied Kelly with a keen eye. "Remember one thing, Kelly. I like to think of myself as your friend. Even if you need someone only to talk to, I want you to remember that I'm here and I want you to feel free to call me anytime."

She knew his offer was sincere and his concern for her well-being touched her. "I'll remember and thank you for being my friend."

"These are the last of the files." Rachel entered the office after Michael had left, promising to take Kelly to lunch later in the week. The secretary dumped an armload of folders on Kelly's desk. "I didn't realize that leaving here would make you look as if you were attending your own funeral. Are you sure you quit instead of getting fired?" she asked dryly. "Funny, I always thought people were cheerful when they had what they wanted in life."

"Maybe I haven't achieved that goal yet," Kelly murmured, then stirred. "You may as well advertise for a housekeeper. I'll need a new one before I begin at T's and Rags."

Rachel expelled a silent "oh." "You're not really going to let that hunk get away, are you?" she challenged. "Kelly, he's the best thing that's ever happened to you. Don't throw away something as beautiful as what you've obviously shared with him."

Kelly started crying. Rachel sat down and quietly waited for Kelly to compose herself.

"Damn," Kelly muttered, blowing her nose into a Kleenex. "I probably resemble a raccoon now. Whoever said this mascara is waterproof never gave it the true test. I didn't even cry this much when I kicked Dave out."

"Think you can talk about it now?" Rachel prompted sympathetically.

Kelly wasn't sure if she ever would be able to talk about Cole, but she knew she had to at some time. And no matter how caustic Rachel might be at times, she also had a sensible head on her shoulders. Kelly took a deep breath and told Rachel the entire story about Cole researching a magazine article and how she and the boys were the basis for his story. She didn't state that she and Cole were lovers, but she didn't need to. Rachel saw the knowledge in Kelly's face and heard it in her voice when she mentioned Cole's name.

"I want to hear the *real* reason why you won't marry him," Rachel demanded once she'd heard the entire tale.

Kelly turned away. "You did."

"Don't lie to me, Kelly Connors. I know better."

Kelly ran her fingernail over her bottom lip. "Pure and simple, I'm scared," she admitted softly.

"Of Cole or of yourself?" Rachel asked.

Kelly laughed harshly. "You really know how to cut to the bone, don't you? Actually, I'm scared of both. When you've had one unfaithful husband, you're always worrying that your second one will commit the same sin. Dave's infidelity left me feeling angry and disillusioned. It was almost two years after my divorce before I would agree to go out with a man. And longer than that before I could allow one to touch me as a lover. Yes, I love Cole. Yes, I want him to stay here with me; but no, I just can't take that final step. I don't know if I can allow one man to have so much control over my life," she stated simply.

"From what you've told me, it sounds as if Cole is asking to share your life, not take it over," the secretary commented. "Would that be so bad? To find a man who obviously loves you and your children. Someone who's willing to take on a ready-made family. Someone who just

271

might want a home and family. I'd say he's disposed to offer a great deal to you. If I were you, I'd not only accept, but I'd also want to contribute to a special marriage like that. Think about it." She stood up. "Your boys won't be living with you forever. Then what will you do?" Leaving Kelly to mull over her advice, Rachel left the office.

Kelly crumpled in her chair. "The most irritating factor about that woman is that she's always right," she muttered wryly.

When Kelly arrived home Cole had dinner ready and served the meal with a strange disquiet about him. Even Kyle and Kevin were more subdued than usual.

Just before Cole left the house he stopped in the den and held out a manila envelope to Kelly. She looked up quizzically.

"It's my article," he explained quietly. "As promised, you have the first read. If you feel there's anything there pointing to you directly, just make a note and I'll correct it." He said no more and silently left the house.

Kelly laid the envelope on the lamp table next to the couch and the sight haunted her as she passed the evening watching television with the boys. Once they were in bed she curled up on the couch and picked up the envelope. She stared blankly at the neatly typed pages before she began reading. And the more she read, the unhappier she became.

IS IT REALLY JUST THE WOMAN'S PLACE IN THE HOME? For some time now I've wondered about the sudden influx of house husbands in today's modern society. In order to research this new role reversal, I worked as a housekeeper for several months in a single-parent household. I not only gained a new respect for the housewives in this world, but also discovered that many men could be missing out on an important part of their children's growth. My employer was divorced with two small children whom I looked after on a full-time basis. I found out that I enjoyed learning their games and teaching them skills that would come in handy over the years. I made many mistakes but I gained a lot of self-confidence in myself as a man. There is nothing feminine in performing housework. If anything, there is quite a bit of physical labor involved. No wonder why the wife is sometimes tired when her husband comes home from the office!

Kelly continued reading, heedless of the tears streaming down her cheeks. There was no mention in the article as to whether Cole's employer had been male or female, the sex of the children, or even the locale of Cole's research. But that wasn't what hit her so strongly. It was the writing, the way he let her know in small ways how much he loved her. If only she weren't so afraid! If only she could put aside her fears! If only . . .

The next morning Kelly handed the envelope back to Cole.

"It's a wonderful article, Cole," she said sincerely. "If they give out awards for magazine articles, you certainly deserve one."

"Thank you." He inclined his head. For one brief instant their eyes clashed and held, his, full of sapphire fires, reminding her of all they had shared and what they could still have together, hers with the same fear she had been harboring for years. In the end, Kelly's eyes dropped. She swiftly left the house.

The balance of the week passed quietly. Kelly and Cole saw each other only for a few moments in the mornings and through dinner in the evenings. Kyle and Kevin had already been informed of Cole's leavetaking at the end of the week and they were loudly vocal in their pleas for him to stay.

By Friday Kelly was jittery and unable to perform even the simplest task. She had snagged four pairs of panty hose before she finally gave up and wore pants to hide the tear in her last pair repaired with clear nail polish.

Ironically, Mr. Baxter took Kelly to lunch as if to make amends for his previous boorish behavior. She was silently grateful that just this once he didn't choose his favorite health food haunt but picked a small French restaurant not too far from the office.

"We will miss you, Mrs. Connors," he stumbled over his words. "And I want to let you know that if this position doesn't work out for you, you would certainly be welcome to return to Creative Concepts."

"Why, thank you, Mr. Baxter." She was surprised and pleased by his offer. At least she hadn't burned all her bridges.

"Of course, you would be starting from the bottom, since I wouldn't be able to revert your old accounts to you. But I'm sure you would be back to your level of competence in no time," he concluded pompously.

So much for graceful gestures!

Rachel had already announced that she was taking a two-week ocean cruise during her vacation.

"Who knows, maybe I'll meet some nice man who knows a good thing when he sees it," the secretary quipped as she finished cleaning out her desk.

"I'll see you in two weeks then," Kelly said as Rachel left the office.

Several of her coworkers wanted to take her out for a

274

farewell drink and after calling Cole and asking if he wouldn't mind staying a little later, she accepted their invitation. She only wished she could get drunk. At least it would dull the ache in her body.

By the time Kelly arrived home Kyle and Kevin had been fed their dinner and put to bed. Cole was seated in the den watching a news show.

"Have a nice time?" he asked politely, watching her collapse in a chair and kick her low-heeled shoes off.

"My meetings with Mr. Baxter have been more exciting than the last few hours I've spent socializing," she grimaced. "I guess I'm just not into the drinking scene. Spending Friday nights in a bar and rehashing the entire work week isn't my idea of fun."

"I left you a plate of food warming in the oven," Cole informed her.

"Thank you." Kelly's eyes were openly hungry as she stared at him. "I want to thank you for, well, for not getting annoyed with Kyle and Kevin when they probably followed you around the house with their endless questions and for helping them polish their swimming technique, and well, just for being here," she said in a low voice.

"It wasn't difficult to do," he returned harshly. "I enjoy the boys."

Kelly wished she could swallow the lump in her throat. "Will you be leaving tomorrow?" she whispered.

Cole nodded. "There's no reason for me to stay. Or is there?" he challenged.

Kelly tried to speak, but nothing would come out. Why couldn't she say what he wanted to hear? Why couldn't she grab at some happiness?

Cole watched her for a moment, then, with a muffled curse, pushed himself out of his chair. "I promised the

275

boys to stop by the house in the morning before I leave. I hope you don't mind?" he questioned in a formal voice.

Kelly shook her head. "Why—why don't you come around nine and I'll fix breakfast?" she offered softly.

Cole threw his head back and stared at the ceiling with a frustrated expression on his face. "Is this another form of punishment, Kelly?" he gritted. "No thanks. I'll be here around ten, and I don't expect to be fed." He grabbed a book that had been lying on the couch and stormed out of the house. The vibrations of the door slamming behind him continued long after he had gone.

"Why can't I be some cold-hearted bitch who feels nothing from all this?" Kelly moaned, burying her face against the back of the chair. She stayed there a long time before she roused herself to get her dinner from the kitchen.

Kelly slept very little that night. The hours were spent wandering about the house. She looked into the bedroom Cole had slept in during his stay and remembered the few times they had shared the comfortable double bed. She walked outside and sat in one of the chairs near the pool. Alfie, having worked his way out of his kennel, came to her and pushed his nose into her hand. He whimpered and butted his head against her leg.

"You know what, boy," Kelly whispered to him, "I think it's time that I began growing up. All these years were just part of the learning experience for what was to happen now. I only wish I knew that I can come through it. And not for the boys' sake as much as for my own."

When the sky lightened to pale gray then to a rosy-orange shade, she finally got up from her chair and went back into the house.

Cole arrived promptly at ten in the morning. The minute the jeep's engine had been heard, Kyle and Kevin were running to the front door and flinging it open.

"Cole! Cole!" Each boy grabbed a leg, almost tripping him in the process.

"Hey, guys!" he laughed. "I was here just last night."

"Yes, but now you're going away," Kevin said mournfully. "What will we do without you?"

Cole looked up and saw Kelly standing in the doorway. He could see the lack of sleep etched on her features and knew his shadowed eyes reflected the same condition. He had sat in a chair in the small living room all night, watching the sky change from dark to light. If only he could wave a magic wand and take away her fear. But he knew that was all up to her.

"I forgot to give you the house key back," he said quietly, managing to extricate himself from the twins' hold.

"Thank you," she murmured, accepting the metal object that was warm from resting in his jeans pocket.

Cole's jaw clenched at the tight hold Kelly was keeping on her emotions. "Good-bye, Kelly." He almost snarled. "I hope you'll be happy with your life. But before I leave, I want you to remember this." He swept her into his arms and captured her mouth with a kiss that possessed every nerve ending in her body.

Kelly could only hang on for dear life as Cole's tongue thrust into her mouth and traded her taste for his own. She doubted she would ever forget the taste of his mouth, the unique musky scent of his skin, and the feel of his body against hers. Before she could surrender to the strong tide washing over her, Cole had released her. Without another word he walked out the door and left her standing numbly in the hallway. The boys followed him outside with tearful pleas to remain.

277

The sound of the jeep backing down the driveway and roaring up the street snapped her out of her trance.

Do you really want him to go and never see him again? she asked herself. *Do you always want to think about what you could have had instead of living that dream?*

"No!" she shouted.

Kyle and Kevin ran into the house.

"Is something wrong, Mom?" they asked in unison.

"Yes." Kelly took several deep breaths. "Come on, we're bringing Cole home!" she announced gleefully, laughing when she heard their exuberant cheers.

Cole drove slowly down the street, all the while glancing in the rearview mirror.

"She won't let me leave," he muttered to himself. "Naw, there's no way she could after that kiss I gave her. There was surrender in every bone of her body. She still wants me." He kept glancing up in the mirror, but there was no green Cutlass barreling down the road. Cole hastily changed gears. He had to be careful. If he went any slower, he'd stall the jeep. "She'll be after me before I reach the freeway," he concluded confidently.

Meanwhile Kelly was turning the house upside down.

"Did you look in the den?" she yelled at the boys as she ransacked her bedroom.

"Your purse isn't there, Mom," Kevin called back.

"Then look on the table by the front door," Kelly shouted, cursing under her breath. She remembered dropping her car keys in her purse the night before. She just couldn't remember where she left her purse after that. "Also check your room. Right now, anything is possible!" She had to find it! Pretty soon it would be next to impossible to find Cole when he reached the freeway.

"Mom," Kyle called from the backyard, where Kelly had sent him to search, "I found your purse."

Kelly ran to the screen door and shrieked. Kyle held up a torn leather strap and a few jagged pieces of leather. A repentant Alfie sat next to Kyle.

"Did you find my keys?" she asked her son.

He shook his head.

Kelly took a deep breath and racked her brain. They could be anywhere in the backyard, and for all she knew, even in the pool, thanks to Alfie deciding to make a meal out of a one-hundred-and-fifty-dollar purse. She'd kill him later.

"There's only one thing to do. Come on." She called for Kevin and ran out the back door into the garage. The two boys, followed by Alfie, followed her to the car. "Get in," she ordered briskly, sliding her hand under the front left fender and finding the spare key she kept there for emergencies.

"Alfie too?" Kevin asked even as the sheepdog scrambled into the backseat.

"I don't care if we take the entire neighborhood, just get in the car." She opened the driver's door and activated the garage door opener.

"You can't drive without your license, Mom," Kyle pointed out.

"As long as we don't meet any policemen, I can," she said grimly, switching on the ignition. "Fasten your seat belts, this could turn into a pretty hectic ride."

"Are you gonna marry Cole, Mom?" Kyle asked.

"You're damn right I am," she muttered, putting the car in gear. "And he's not going to back out of his proposal now. He's right. Why should I worry about things that won't even happen with us? I'll concentrate on the good times instead."

Kelly kept one eye on the rearview mirror and exceeded

the speed limit by a good twenty miles as she sped through the housing tract. She was only glad there was little traffic that morning.

By this time Cole reached the ramp for the freeway heading north.

"Where the hell is she?" he muttered, still glancing in the rearview mirror. So far all he had seen was a Volkswagen and a battered Honda. Deep down he still felt Kelly would follow him, although there was a very tiny voice asking if perhaps she just hadn't loved him enough to overcome all her fears.

The speed limit may have been fifty-five miles, but Cole tried to keep it to a safe forty and remained in the far right lane. He knew he wouldn't be able to keep it up for long. He only hoped that he wasn't going to be wrong where Kelly was concerned. A few miles down the road he glanced up and saw the familiar green Cutlass roaring onto the freeway. Cole hastily averted his gaze and punched the accelerator to bring the jeep up to the speed limit. After all, he couldn't allow her to think he was just waiting for her.

"There's Cole's jeep, Mom!" Kyle announced, pointing ahead. "Go faster."

"I'll do more than that." She leaned on the horn.

"Mom, you can't honk the horn on the freeway. They'll give you a ticket!" Kevin cried out.

"Who told you that nonsense?" she asked him.

"Timmy Barnes."

"Well, Timmy is wrong." Kelly continued honking her horn which got Alfie barking and the boys opening the window and yelling Cole's name.

For a moment Kelly could visualize the scene as something out of a bad movie. She watched her speedometer creep up to 60, 65, 70 as she vainly tried to catch up with

Cole. She only prayed that the highway patrol decided to roam another freeway that morning. Finally she drew abreast of the jeep.

Cole glanced over, surprise showing in his eyes.

"Pull over!" Kelly shouted through the open window at the same time ordering the boys to shut up so that she could hear herself think.

"Why?" he yelled back.

"Because I love you and want to marry you as soon as we can," she called belligerently.

Cole slowed the jeep and pulled it over to the side of the freeway. Kelly cut across the lane and stopped her car a short distance ahead of Cole. She flung her door open and climbed out of the car. She ran back to Cole, who was getting out of the jeep.

"You're right, I am a coward," she babbled, now crying because she was afraid that she might have lost him after all. "Please, Cole, be there with me. Help me fight my fears. Love me, yell at me, fight with me. Just be there when I need you. Because I do need you. I love and need you more than anything. Even my job with T's and Rags isn't as important to me as you are. I'll quit if you want me to. I'll move to San Francisco. Just don't go away without me." She buried her face against his neck.

"Actually, I'd rather do as I suggested before," he replied. "I'll work out of our home and you keep your job. If you quit, it's because you don't want to work anymore, not because you think I want you to stop working. I make enough with my writing to keep us comfortably. You'd never have to worry." He rained kisses over her face.

"Oh, I love you so much," she cried, flinging her arms around his neck.

"Then let's go back to the house and get rid of one of these cars and plan a quick trip to Las Vegas," Cole suggested. "How does San Francisco sound for a honeymoon?"

"Delicious." Kelly returned each kiss with a love nip of her own. They remained locked in each other's arms oblivious to the catcalls and jeers from the passing cars.

"Excuse me, ma'am, but is this man bothering you?"

They turned to find a highway patrol officer approaching them.

"I certainly hope so, officer." Kelly smiled brightly. "This gentleman just agreed to marry me. Isn't that wonderful?"

"Don't let him put you in jail, Mom!" Kyle and Kevin called frantically from the car. "It's not your fault you don't have your license."

The officer looked at Kelly curiously. "You're driving without a license?"

"The dog ate my purse," she explained. "As it was, I had to use my spare car key to even get here."

"So that's what took you so long," Cole muttered.

Kelly looked aghast. "You mean you expected me to follow you?" she ranted. "Talk about the arrogant male!"

"I just knew you wouldn't let me go that easily," he said smugly.

Kelly's sense of humor soon overrode her temper. "I'll get even for that," she promised softly.

"I certainly hope so."

The officer coughed loudly. "Do you think you folks could finalize your wedding plans somewhere else besides here?" he asked wearily. And here he thought he had seen it all!

Kelly flashed him a sunny smile. "Of course, officer," she assured him. "I honestly do have a driver's license. It's just a question as to whether it's in the dog kennel or at the bottom of the swimming pool."

"Lady, I don't care if it's lying in the dog's stomach. Just go on home," he advised.

"Great idea." Cole dropped a kiss on Kelly's lips. "One last thing, darling," he whispered. "When we're in San Francisco, let's see if we can find a bright blue teddy. I'd like to shave a couple seconds off my previous record."

"There should be no problem. After all, you'll have plenty of time to practice on our honeymoon."

"If I give you enough time to put it on in the first place," he grinned wickedly. "But don't worry, I may let you wear it fifty years from now."

CANDLELIGHT
Ecstasy Supreme

CANDLELIGHT Ecstasy Supreme

☐ 21 **BREAKING THE RULES,** Donna Kimel Vitek 10834-9-28

☐ 22 **ALL IN GOOD TIME,** Samantha Scott 10099-2-28

☐ 23 **SHADY BUSINESS,** Barbara Andrews 17797-9-10

☐ 24 **SOMEWHERE IN THE STARS,** Jo Calloway 18157-7-20

☐ 25 **AGAINST ALL ODDS,** Eileen Bryan. 10069-0-16

☐ 26 **SUSPICION AND SEDUCTION,** Shirley Hart 18464-9-10

☐ 27 **PRIVATE SCREENINGS,** Lori Herter. 17111-3-19

☐ 28 **FASCINATION,** Jackie Black 12442-5-10

$2.50 each

At your local bookstore or use this handy coupon for ordering:

DELL BOOKS
P.O. BOX 1000, PINE BROOK, N.J. 07058-1000   B265C

Please send me the books I have checked above. I am enclosing $ _____ (please add 75c per copy to cover postage and handling). Send check or money order—no cash or C.O.D.'s. Please allow up to 8 weeks for shipment.

Name _____

Address _____

City _____ State/Zip _____